'I will not sl[...]
in the same [room as you, my lord!]

De Sable threw a few casual words over his shoulder as Gilbert Helias led him away. 'Gather your belongings together, girl, and have them moved into my room. The woman Bessie will see you settled.'

Eloise was beside herself. 'I will not, my lord! To be your mere chattel is one thing, but to enter into a sinful existence is quite another!'

De Sable's eyes glittered suddenly as she faced up to him. 'I own you now, girl. You will do as I say, at all times.' Suddenly the harshness left his expression and another indefinable look crossed his features. 'Old Bessie and Edgar have shared the same room with me on many of my travels. They don't consider themselves to be in moral danger, lady.'

Born in Somerset, Polly Forrester has been writing for as long as she can remember.

Her working career began with twelve years as a humble office clerk. Escaping to combine her love of history and the countryside in a new career as a writer, her work is used by several national publications.

She now lives in the depths of rural Gloucestershire with a cat, a dog and a flock of very eccentric poultry.

KNIGHT'S PAWN

Polly Forrester

First published in Great Britain 1990
by Mills & Boon Limited

© Polly Forrester 1990

Australian copyright 1990
Philippine copyright 1990
This edition 1990

ISBN 0 263 76913 5

Masquerade is a trademark published by
Mills & Boon Limited, Eton House,
18–24 Paradise Road, Richmond, Surrey, TW9 1SR.

Set in Times Roman 10 on 11 pt.
04-9008-78011 C

Made and printed in Great Britain

CHAPTER ONE

THE cuckoos had arrived early in Gloucestershire that year. Now all the spring shouting had worn out their voices, and only hoarse notes filled the summer-warmed green wood.

Eloise paused in her work, but not to enjoy the birdsong. The sleeves of her gown would keep wriggling down, and were already soaked and dark with splashes of water. The bucket tipped each time she manhandled it on to the lip of the well, slopping water over her and the beaten earth of the castle courtyard.

She pushed her sleeves up once more, then let the bucket down to fill in the dark, chilly depths. When the Lord Gilbert Helias went out hunting it was impossible to tell when he would return, but he always expected fresh water and clean linen to be ready before he and his guests dined. It was the least that Eloise could do to ensure that those items were provided. The Lord Gilbert treated her kindly enough. If ever her work became especially wearisome Eloise thought of the debt of gratitude her poor dead father had owed the Lord Gilbert, and laboured on.

Other members of Gilbert's staff busied about the courtyard, fetching wood to stoke up the forge, shepherding geese and ducks out to the river or ferrying saddles to and fro. All stopped to congratulate Eloise on the music she had played for the banquet the evening before.

The staff were always shyly eager to please her with their conversations. Even though she considered herself their equal and nothing more, Eloise knew that because

of her past the staff looked on her with a certain amount
of awe. She reflected that after four years in England
her position was still uncertain: would the staff ever come
to accept her properly?

High above on the roof a look-out warned of an im-
pending arrival. Dry with age and unexpected warmth
early that summer day, the great oaken gates of the castle
courtyard groaned noisily as they were swung open on
their creaking leather hinges.

Everyone paused to see who was coming, but it was
nothing exciting. Only a member of Lord Gilbert's
hunting party, riding an exhausted horse and leading a
lame one. He was angrily berating an unfortunate groom.

Eloise poured water into Lord Gilbert's silver ewer.
She felt sorry for the groom, but glad that she always
took care not to warrant such public disgrace. Working
in the Helias household gave her bed and board, and
she would do nothing to jeopardise the arrangement.
Musician and general hand might be a lowly position,
but it was better to be alive and poor than a mere stat-
istic of the bloody civil war that had raged through her
native Normandy.

Eloise was lucky—she had a quick mind and a cheerful
disposition. Rare qualities in a servant, and Gilbert
Helias was not one to miss an opportunity like that.
Musical skills secured her position still further—Gilbert
was a man who enjoyed the finer things in life.

The courtyard gates thundered shut. Eloise paid little
attention, busy placing Lord Gilbert's ewer on the ground
to make room for the full bucket she was about to wind
up from the well. As she turned back to the winch handle
she heard the tirade of abuse from the horseman end in
a resounding blow to the stable lad.

His cry startled the horses, which backed and reared
as they passed Eloise. One blundered sideways into her
collection of buckets and pails and in the confusion Lord

Gilbert's silver ewer was kicked tumbling beneath their hoofs.

'Deus! What now?' The rider was struggling to maintain his seat and control of both horses, the slither of their hoofs on the wet ground frightening them even more. The two sets of fancy embroidered reins cut roughly into the rider's ungloved fingers, infuriating him still further.

'Stupid—blasted—animals! Stand still!'

Eloise stepped forward, disapproving of his tantrum. 'Your temper upsets them, my lord. Control yourself first, and they will follow.'

'Shut up! If that stupid boy had brought out a fit horse, I'd still be up with Gilbert. Instead, I have to come all the way back to change horses because of one servant's stupidity, then I'm delayed and half killed because of the carelessness of another.'

'I was about my duties, my lord, and you disrupted them. The Lord Gilbert's property has been damaged.' She picked up the ewer, now sadly dented. 'And I shall most probably be punished. All because you lost your temper.'

As the rider whipped around at her retort, the hood of his cloak slipped away and she recognised him. He was Richard De Sable, a visitor from the Continent who had arrived a few days earlier. Eloise neither knew nor cared whether he was one of the Helias 'favourites'—all she knew was that the kitchen girls were all hopelessly in love with De Sable's fair, athletic good looks. That he had taken his ease with his feet on the table during last night's feast had immediately stung Eloise to silent anger, not worship.

De Sable had been staring at her and he now dismounted, leaving the quietened animals to the lad.

'You're the little musician that entertained us all so capably last night!' Laughing, he ruffled her hair, causing the dark curls to dance in the July breeze. She ducked away from his rough caress but he held her fast, forcing her to look up at him.

'Norman dark hair with Saxon grey eyes. Unusual! One of us playing fast and loose with your mother, then!'

Eloise kept her fury at bay. She was in enough trouble with the Lord Gilbert already, ruining his ewer, without assaulting one of his guests.

'I am from purest Norman stock, my lord, fallen upon hard times.'

She returned his stare fearlessly, seeing casual fancy fade in his cornflower-blue eyes. No upper-class playboy would use her like a common jade, and De Sable had to be made to realise that.

He released her, his mouth twisted in a knowing grin showing even white teeth. 'So. Gilbert amuses himself with charity work, does he? Taking in the fallen and forlorn. I'd suspect his motives if I were you, lady.'

'I receive fair recompense for a fair day's work. It is a shame that the Lord Gilbert does not receive such kind acknowledgement at the hands of his guests, my lord.'

De Sable's face tightened with displeasure. 'A still tongue in a wise head, lady. You would do well to re-member that.'

'And it ill becomes those who spend time in dissolute living to lecture those who would work for their daily bread. If you would excuse me, my lord, I must carry this water into the hall ready for dinner and think of some way to explain to my lord the ruination of his ewer.'

Eloise turned away quickly and picked up a pail in each hand. She had not gone two steps when he de-manded her attention with a sharp summons. Expecting more trouble, Eloise stopped and put down the buckets. In a moment he was at her side, the dented pitcher in his hands.

'Don't bother with the pails. Take this. The farrier may be able to beat out the worst of the damage.'

He thrust the ewer into her hands and made to pick up the pair of buckets.

'What on earth are you doing, my lord?'

'Helping you,' he snapped, plainly uncomfortable.

'I can't possibly let you carry the water—it isn't right...'

'Do as I say. Get the pitcher fixed before Gilbert gets back.'

His eyes flashed frost and fire, but then took on a curious guarded light. 'When a man spends his time in dissolute living, doing nothing but whipping peasants and eating babies all day, it sometimes does him good to get a taste of reality.'

He cast an imperious look of scorn over the staff who watched him, giggling, from the yard. Taking the buckets he set off towards the hall, but, instead of doing his bidding, Eloise trotted along beside him anxiously.

'I can manage, my lord. Please don't strain yourself. I know how tiring it gets, especially when there are fifteen or twenty more trips to do...'

'Deus—you're joking! You don't expect me to do that many?'

'*I* have to.'

'Old Gilbert must exert some strange hypnotic force over women, that's all I can say.'

'Perhaps you will think twice in your own household before insisting on a copious supply of fresh water to waste, my lord,' Eloise said slyly.

'Typical. Do a woman a favour and she throws it back in your face.'

De Sable showed no signs of amusement in the remark and Eloise considered herself rebuked, although it was difficult to avoid bursting out that good money was hard to come by, and a job was a job.

'What awful pass have you come to that makes a pretty girl like you have to work like a pack pony? I'm damned if I'd let any child I was unfortunate enough to father

skivvy like a slave. And when you have such talent.'
Grinning, he waited for her to open the door of the great
hall. 'For musical accomplishment,' he added artfully.

The breeze flickered at the hem of his fine woollen
riding cloak, lifting it away to reveal a colourfully
fashionable shirt and breeches. All brand-new, Eloise
observed, scornfully conscious of her own dull, serviceable working clothes.

'Come along, lady. I want to get in, because you're
going to entertain me with a little music of my own
choosing.'

Eloise laughed, incredulous. 'You surely cannot expect
me to accept a request to be alone with you, my lord.
Would you really expect any decent girl to accept an
invitation like that? I think not. Especially in view of
the work I still have to do.'

She glanced at the row of buckets waiting to be carried
up to the hall, but when she looked back to De Sable
he had laid his right hand menacingly on the hilt of the
sword at his waist.

'It wasn't a request, it was an order,' he said quietly,
pushing the door open with his boot and inclining his
head for her to enter. 'And I am unused to my orders
being disobeyed.'

Eloise tried to back towards the step, but he moved
quickly to bar her escape. Trapped by the look in his
eyes, she could neither move nor cry out.

'Now, we can do this the easy way, or the hard way.
Which is it to be, lady?'

He spoke quietly and evenly, but, when she did not
scoot into the hall like a frightened coney, he barked out
an order that made her jump violently.

'Edgar! Get out here and persuade the lady that I am
in great need of her company.'

A small aide ran up, sword drawn and eyes mocking.
'It'll be the worse for you, miss, wilfulness.'

Eloise knew when she was beaten. With a scathing glare at De Sable, she walked into the empty hall with as much dignity as she could muster. De Sable followed, with an order to Edgar that he was to ferry the buckets to the foot of the hall steps outside. Edgar was also to ensure that De Sable was not disturbed, Eloise heard with growing concern.

Edgar would surely prevent any escape from the hall. Eloise was trapped. She could do nothing but wait for De Sable to approach. He looked into her face, doubtless trying to read her thoughts, and with a conscious effort Eloise kept her usually busy mind a blank.

'You look frighteningly honest, lady.' His eyes were wary, but his voice still cold and distant. 'I believe that if I had any sense I should fear you as much as you obviously fear me.' Suddenly he turned on his heel, cloak furling like a banner. 'Play "Weeps Still The Green Willow?".'

Eloise was overjoyed. 'Then you are a true Norman, my lord——'

'No!' he snapped viciously with surprising speed.

'It is just that my father used to say that, wherever he was, a Norman soldier could never resist that song...'

'You talk much and entertain little. Normandy and her people are fit only for ridicule now, and she——' he seemed to have to search hard for something sufficiently cutting to say '—is peopled only by rogues and the servants of rogues.'

Eloise bridled at the savagery of his attack, fuming as she went to lift her psaltery from its hook. 'Willow' had been a favourite tune at home, in happy times, even with its melancholy message.

She put her heart and soul into the performance to spite him. Silvery notes from the psaltery streamed up to the high-vaulted roof, mingled with the sweet cadences of her singing and fluttered to earth like the apple blossom and poplar leaves of the song. With the last

brush of her fingers across the strings and the dying fall
of the echo fell the breathless hush that always greeted
the tale of longing ache for homeland.

'You played three wrong notes in each verse,' he said
curtly, after a pause.

Eloise raised her head to realise for the first time that
he had not been watching her, but instead sat on the
great high table, swinging his boot against its leg and
studying the wall-hanging.

'Apologies, my lord. I played only from memory,
never having performed it myself before. Such
nationalism is frowned on here, I am afraid.'

'Nationalism?' He turned to her with a wry smile.
'That is an important word for such a pretty head.'

'I would not expect a lion of society such as yourself
to be familiar with the meaning of the word, my lord,'
Eloise said in a low voice.

De Sable was not in the least perturbed by the ice in
her voice, but continued brightly. 'I am a citizen of the
whole world!' He laughed and flung his arms wide in
an expansive gesture. 'I have no feelings of nationalism,
or the like. I go where I will, and speak with whom I
choose.'

'It is said that much the same applies to your sleeping
arrangements, my lord.' Eloise smiled sardonically.

De Sable stood up quickly and strode towards her, his
face tight with anger. Before he had time to chastise her,
there was a furious tapping at the door and Edgar the
serving-man peeped in, cowering.

'Beg pardon, my lord, but look-out reports that the
party's coming back. Due in a few minutes.'

'Bring that water in, then. And be quick about it. It
wouldn't do to get my lady into trouble, would it?' De
Sable spoke in clipped tones, but his ice-blue eyes never
once left Eloise's face. She returned his stare calmly.

'Of course, my lord, one cannot expect a gentleman
to speak with civility to mere staff.'

'Fine feathers can be singed playing with fire, my little nightingale. Don't goad me too far.' His strong, handsome features were set in quiet fury.

'I merely speak as I find, my lord.' Eloise put her psaltery back into its cover, determined not to be threatened by his attitude.

'Why? What can you possibly know about me, or understand in the space of a few minutes? Those who know me never comment adversely upon my behaviour. Only those who are misguided can be stung to hasty judgements.'

'That's true, miss.' Edgar stumbled into the hall under the weight of two buckets. 'Best not to cast stones unknowing, as it were.'

Eloise stood up and replaced her psaltery upon its hook. 'Don't worry. I doubt that our paths need cross again during your visit, my lord,' she finished icily.

'You do surprise me, little nightingale. I would have thought a lady of your "refined" tastes,' De Sable grinned mockingly, 'would play a central part in social life here. How can one of such delicate sensibilities be relegated to the rough and tumble of serving life? What are you, little nightingale? A poor relation, thrown upon the generosity of a rich guardian? A runaway with a guilty secret?'

'I have no guilt, my lord. My lord Gilbert was good enough to take me in, although he was under no obligation to help a destitute girl.'

'You? Destitute? I'll warrant you're from good family. What happened? You didn't run away, did you?'

He gasped with pretended glee at the thought of unearthing a scandal, but Eloise had better manners.

'My father was indeed a great landowner, my lord. However, that is in the past. My present position is that I am left an orphan, alone in a foreign country. I must do what I can to keep myself.'

De Sable put his hands behind his back and strolled back and forth before Eloise. All trace of any anger had dissolved and now he was openly mocking her. 'It seems so unfair that I should spend a life in idle pleasure, while past sins have relegated you to a life of dull, wretched servitude.'

'It was not my sins, my lord——' Eloise was staggered, but a glance at Edgar's face warned her not to continue.

'I have the best of everything—I can pick and choose what I do and when. A meal here, a day spent hunting there. I was born to it, you see—a child of the leisured classes. As you should be too, little nightingale. What have you done that you and your family were cast out from the fold?'

Eloise kept her temper only with difficulty. 'You should find something useful to do, not waste your life in taunting those less fortunate than yourself, my lord.'

'So that some lucky woman can snap me up, make me her husband to provide free board and lodging?' he spluttered with mirth.

'You would understand what real responsibility, perhaps even real independence, was then.'

De Sable ruffled her hair patronisingly. 'And I would settle down, have a flock of children, and gout, and die before I was forty? Poor little innocent. There's more to life than that!'

'What you do is your own affair,' Eloise started hotly. 'All I know is that if I were in your position I'd use my travels and talents to learn and better myself...' Her own foolish dreams were surfacing now, she thought bitterly, and fell silent.

'Ah! The little nightingale has dreams beyond the confines of its safe little cage!'

De Sable stopped and bent down to look her full in the face. Shrinking under his gaze, Eloise lowered her head, but at once he lifted her chin sharply with strong,

cool fingers. He was so close that she could see that the
pale honey gold of his skin owed its refinement to recent
sun. Where the collar of his shirt had worked away with
his movements the skin revealed was fine and pale. Blond
lights in his hair accentuated the Mediterranean blue of
his eyes and the dark of his thick lashes.

'Eyes grey as steel or a dove's wing, as the mood takes
her. What an eloquent feature, lady!'

Eloise tried to give him a steely glare, but it was
hopeless. He was looking too deeply into her soul,
searching, questioning.

'You are very beautiful, little one. Ah, but then I dare
say that you are used to hearing such words.'

She was, although she had learnt not to trust them.
In the England of King William Rufus, it was not pretty
girls that were in fashion. The procession of young men
Gilbert Helias surrounded himself with often trapped
her in corners with soft-mouthed flattery, it was true,
but they were not to be encouraged. Lord Gilbert was
a jealous man. At least Eloise could be thankful that
the Lord Gilbert was unlikely to press unwanted attentions upon her.

In truth, Eloise knew little of her looks. Her only
looking-glass had been left behind in the flight from
Normandy. For all she knew, De Sable too was making
fun of her.

'Such modesty is rare in a beauty, and I should know.'
He stood up abruptly and gave a short laugh. 'Deus—
some decent clothes, a more worldly air about you—I
wouldn't be surprised if you could play the part of a
duchess, and play it well. Everyone loves nobility. Especially if it is talented...' His voice had become soft
and thoughtful. 'Ah, but then a Norman maid would
be too retiring for what I have in mind. Your blushes
are too pretty by far for such a wicked world!' He patted
her cheek.

A clatter of returning horsemen was heard in the yard and Edgar toiled faster to bring in the final buckets. Eloise hurried to place filled ewers on the trestle-tables while De Sable went to the doorway.

Eloise was confused. She had expected the worst from De Sable's reputation, but he had not taken advantage. Instead, he had ridiculed her and patronised her, turn and turn about.

Her thoughts were disturbed by De Sable's shout of laughter from the doorway. As she looked up, he strolled aside to let two of the men of the Helias household bring in a third, much battered and bloodied.

At once Eloise took control, pushing an old hound out of the warmest position beside the fire to make room for the patient.

'It's always you, Ralph. Are you sure you really can ride? You seem to have far more accidents out in the field than the rest of the men put together.'

Ralph submitted to her attentions meekly. Casting aside his mud-soaked cloak, she ran her hands expertly over his arms and legs but found nothing more serious than cuts and bruises.

She applied a cooling salve of honey to Ralph's cuts before binding them, then dabbed butter on his bruises to bring them out.

'I saw how he was riding out there. He seemed too hesitant to me. Nervous riders make most mistakes,' De Sable said, with amusement at Ralph's discomfort.

Eloise frowned at him meaningfully. 'A little more caution in others might not come amiss.'

Any retort by De Sable was silenced as Lord Gilbert and his entourage hurried in. Unfortunately the first thing Gilbert laid eyes upon was the damaged ewer, and he raked the rapidly filling hall with an accusing glare.

'Who did this? More expense! Well, I'll not foot the bill this time!'

Eloise spoke quietly into the guilty silence. 'My lord—it was my fault—I was careless...'

She looked across at De Sable and saw him smiling, arms folded.

'It isn't good enough. I don't buy myself nice things to have some ham-fisted, idiot girl ruin them,' Gilbert grizzled crossly. He unhooked the silver brooch at his shoulder, letting his cloak slip off into the arms of a waiting page.

Having contemplated her reply over a goblet of wine, he rounded on Eloise again, suspiciously. 'Not covering up for someone else's clumsiness again, Eloise?'

She ran her hands down the front of the plain brownness of her gown and wished that she weren't always so accommodating. 'No, my lord. It was entirely my own doing.'

'In that case, then, you will see that it is mended, and no dinner for you until it is put right. If the smith considers it irreparable then the cost will be deducted from your pay.'

Gilbert eased his vast bulk down on to a bench and Eloise moved to take up the ewer. Before she reached the door, however, De Sable had moved up to Gilbert and stood before him sternly.

'The girl did not tell you the truth, my lord. It was my fault. I caused the damage.'

Gilbert grunted, unimpressed.

'Let me pay for the damage, my lord.'

'The girl should learn. Only fools cover up for others. Thinks because her folk were landed gentry back in Normandy that she has to defend all and sundry. Well, it won't work this time. She's done it once too often.'

De Sable grinned at the company now assembled in the great hall and winked at Eloise, who looked away quickly. Turning his attention back to Gilbert, De Sable poured every ounce of his considerable charm into a plea that Eloise be released from her charge.

Gilbert thawed slightly, his heavy brows raised as he watched a hen search haltingly for scraps beneath the table.

De Sable reasoned that the matter was really only a very little thing, and wasn't it best passed over quickly so that dinner would be delayed no longer? In reply Gilbert was adamant: Eloise should learn that misguidedly covering up for others would never do her any good.

With a regretful sigh, De Sable turned and addressed the company. 'So it would seem that this isn't the first time that this young—Eloise, is it?—has concealed the truth from you, my lord.'

'Indeed. Although I feel she is not really wicked, merely over-solicitous to others.'

De Sable grinned slyly. 'Then perhaps you are better rid of her, my lord Gilbert.'

A ripple of concern flickered through the crowd, but turned to laughter at De Sable's next words.

'I'll take her off your hands, if you like!'

Eloise leapt forward in fury, but he anticipated her.

'She seems to have a few skills already, in music and physic. The woman who cooks and cares for me is getting a little long in the tooth. It's time a younger servant was trained to take her place.'

'Well...' Gilbert flicked a flea from his breeches with pale, podgy fingers. 'It is true I only keep her here through charity. From a good family, you see, Richard. Escaped the civil war in Normandy, but only she and her father survived the Channel crossing. No sooner did I agree to employ the father than he goes and dies...' Gilbert trailed off regretfully.

'So you really are an orphan, then, little one? Better and better. No family ties to keep her here. Take my money and be rid of a hungry mouth, Lord Gilbert!'

Faltering, Gilbert seemed to realise that he was faced with a superior argument. He resigned himself to the inevitable. Now all he could do was hope to get a good price. 'She's quiet. And talented. You're unlikely to ever come across one so gently bred again, Richard. And with the servant situation as it is, you'll be lucky to find one at all...'

De Sable was listening to Gilbert, but grinning wolfishly at Eloise. She had yet to learn that his expressions were all deception. Behind that handsome, careless exterior, a cunning mind was already running on apace.

Eloise could only stand and worry. Would Gilbert let her go? It was madness—a man with a reputation like De Sable's—but Eloise was powerless. All she could do was stand by while they discussed her like an item of merchandise.

'She is of a good family, mind, Lord Richard,' Gilbert said in a low voice. 'Be very careful. It wouldn't do for you to court scandal...'

'Indeed not. I shall acquit myself with honour at all times. How much compensation shall you require for her, my lord, bearing in mind that you can't have expected more than another year's good work from her before nature led her and a village lad astray?'

Laughter at this stung her eyes and Eloise stepped forward. 'Don't judge others by your own low standards, my lord.'

De Sable watched her thoughtfully, then spoke in a voice softened by mockery. 'Mettlesome already, my lord. You might have had trouble there. Five shillings only, then, I'm afraid. Including the damage to your ewer. It might have been more, but if she is going to prove intractable...'

Gilbert's small eyes gleamed. 'Ten shillings.'

De Sable sucked his teeth and looked Eloise up and down, hard. 'Hmm. That's a fairly hefty sum, my lord. Seven and sixpence. That's my final offer.'

With a slow, crafty smile Gilbert extended his hand. De Sable took a small drawstring-bag of soft leather from his waist and counted coins into the plump white hand.

'Now. Dinner, my lord Richard. Sit beside me and I can tell you of the last hour's sport that you so sadly missed...'

De Sable threw a few casual words over his shoulder as Gilbert Helias led him away. 'Gather your belongings together, girl, and have them moved into my room. The woman Bessie will see you settled.'

Eloise was beside herself. 'I will not, my lord! To be your mere chattel is one thing, but to enter into a sinful existence is quite another!'

Gilbert frowned, obviously seeing De Sable's warning about Eloise's being mettlesome begin to come true.

'I will not sleep in the same room as you, my lord.'

De Sable's eyes glittered suddenly as she faced up to him. 'I own you now, girl. You will do as I say, at all times.' Suddenly the harshness left his expression and another indefinable look crossed his features. 'Old Bessie and Edgar have shared the same room with me on many of my travels. They don't consider themselves to be in moral danger, lady.'

Eloise looked at him, but he did not seem to think she warranted further attention and was already deep in conversation with Lord Gilbert. She told herself she was foolish to have thought the tone of his last remark almost kindly.

With a slight bow to her new lord, she turned and went quickly to prepare for her new life.

CHAPTER TWO

ELOISE took her dinner in the kitchens along with the rest of the staff. Although the meal was tasty and satisfying, she had too much to think about to enjoy it. Even the rare white bread seemed as ashes in her mouth. Everyone was delighted at what they saw as her good fortune. Eloise thanked them all, but in her heart she wondered whether her new life would be a blessing or a curse.

Their lordships were still dining in noisy disarray when Eloise walked through to fetch her few belongings. She had very little to call her own: a sleeping-rug, a wooden bowl, mug and spoon, a small bone-handled knife and a few bits of much-mended clothing.

Small personal possessions, a comb, thimble and small sewing-set she kept in a purse at her waist. The other items were rolled into the sheepskin rug and carried to De Sable's quarters. There she stowed the rolled rug safely out of the way in a corner.

By the time De Sable returned to his room Eloise had swept it and made the bed, pulling the furs and cushions into some sort of order.

'I shouldn't bother with that.' A heavy perfume of wine and woodsmoke hung upon him from the hall, but he seemed sober enough.

'Oh, but I must, my lord. It's one less job for your Bessie to do.'

He yawned and stretched, extending long, lithe arms towards the low ceiling. Then with nonchalant ease he released the belt that held the sword at his waist and, setting it aside, kicked off his boots.

'I'm going back to bed for an hour. See? All your good work wasted.' He flung himself down upon the bed and laughed at her dubious expression. 'You're still afraid of me, aren't you, little nightingale?'

'I find your manner somewhat carefree, my lord.'

'Oh, come on. We can't all spend our time in selfless devotion to others.' There was a sarcastic tinge to his voice which irritated Eloise.

'Of course not, my lord. You must be quite weary from enjoying yourself. I shall leave you to sleep it off.'

He sat up abruptly and at once Eloise realised that she might have gone too far with her new master.

'I mean, I will leave you in peace, my lord,' she added hurriedly, hoping to pacify him.

He leaned forward, his face stern and forbidding. 'One day that busy tongue will get you into trouble, lady— Eloise, isn't it? Since you are working for me now I feel entitled to ask your full name. Eloise what?'

'Eloise Emeron, my lord.' She twisted the silken belt about her waist between nervous fingers.

'A pretty name, for a pretty child.'

He gave a slow, taunting smile, and Eloise was immediately on her guard.

'As my lord Gilbert said, I am of good family,' she said nervously, taking a small step backwards.

'Of course.' He continued to smile and Eloise realised it was the same half-mocking expression that he had used when going to her assistance out in the yard.

She reminded herself that he had got her out of a difficult situation with Lord Gilbert, and thought that perhaps some form of thanks might be in order. It was difficult to think of something to say with him lounging in front of her. He was so off-putting. Eloise was relieved when the door to the room was opened and Edgar appeared.

'Perhaps you can keep our new young friend amused, Edgar, and stop her from disturbing me.'

Eloise baulked at his tone. 'You need only have asked for my silence, instead of engaging me in conversation, my lord.'

De Sable gave his serving-man a wink. 'The little one has a sharp tongue, Edgar. Like a lion cub, she respects no man's position—mind yourself!'

He could never take anything seriously. Eloise determined to dislike him for that if nothing else. A life of ease must have addled his brain.

'The little one thinks I should travel to broaden my experiences, Edgar. Whether I should be splitting infidel heads on Crusade in the Holy Land or studying political intrigue under King William Rufus she does not say. Ah, what I could do if I had more education and less animal passion for the good things in life...'

Eloise put in, 'You have more education than you will admit, my lord. I saw you bow your head to say grace before dinner—no, not for long, I admit, but a betrayal of a very good education, I would say. And you studied the text above the wall-hanging earlier on in a way that no illiterate person would...'

His eyes narrowed, cutting off any further comment. Suspicion flicked across his face too readily for him to mask it altogether.

Edgar laughed. 'Bless you, miss, call a man cultured because he can look at a pretty picture? An ape might eat figs, but it don't make him a man of taste!'

Eloise was not convinced. 'Even so, I suppose my new lord is widely travelled? Perhaps you have gained some little education abroad painlessly, without noticing?'

De Sable lay back, hands behind his head, and studied the hangings about the bed. 'Never been further afield than Paris. And I was Brittany born and bred,' he added with a sigh.

Eloise was suddenly spellbound, forgetting all her reservations about De Sable. 'Paris? Oh, I'd love to go to Paris. Did you see the King of France?'

'Indeed. And a very fat, lazy and stupid fellow he is.'

'Oh, how can you say such things? He is a great patron of the arts—it is said that musicians are offered fortunes in his employ.'

'Put all thoughts of that road to riches out of your head, little Eloise. That is behind your desire to see Paris, is it not?'

'Yes, my lord,' she answered, eyes shining.

'Well, talented though you may be, my little nightingale, if you manage to make a fortune from your art, I'll let you purchase me a fine education with it. How's that?'

Eloise bit her lower lip in consternation. 'I think it cruel of you to laugh at me. Everyone needs hopes and dreams, a little colour in their life. Paris is mine.'

Realising he would get no rest, De Sable sat up and looked at her with a concentrated scrutiny. 'Out in the big, wide world that you seem to know precious little about, Eloise, musicians are spoken of in the same breath as actors, gleemen and...'

Here Edgar cleared his throat warningly and De Sable grinned at him.

'Wicked, naughty girls who are no better than they should be.'

'I shall be different. People will realise that I am of a good family and treat me accordingly,' Eloise burst out hotly.

'When was the last time you heard of a musician with a pedigree? Nobody's interested in who they are as individuals. They're all lumped together as a generally bad lot.'

Eloise had to agree with him, but fury and disappointment kept her silent. Entertainers of one sort or another had been frequent visitors at her home in the old days, but it was true that they had been shown kindness rather than respect.

'Well?'

She had been studying the fresh rushes covering the floor in an attempt to avoid his scrutiny, but he was plainly demanding an answer.

'I shall make a success of my life!' she snapped adamantly.

After a pause De Sable shrugged and got up off the bed. 'Suit yourself. But I've just paid out good cash for you and I intend to get value for my money.' He laughed at her expression and added, 'You aren't sure of my motives yet, are you? I meant that I am going to make you work. Try to run away to Paris or anywhere else before I give you leave, little one, and retribution will be swift.'

Eloise nodded meekly, knowing the penalty for a runaway servant. De Sable had her trapped far more securely than Gilbert had held her with past kindness. This was the harsh economics of the real world.

Pulling on his boots and refastening his belt, De Sable swung his cloak about his shoulders and moved to the door. 'I'm tired of talking. I'm off to the stable, Edgar, to see what a mess they've made patching up my horses. I'll take the girl with me.' He tipped his head towards the girl. 'Come on, then, little one. You can start paying your way. See if your human nursing works as well on animals. And you can carry their tack and saddle back for me afterwards, as well.'

Eloise followed him out through the hall where Gilbert snored fatly beside the fire. The courtyard outside was noisy with its scratching fowls and arguing dogs. The few servants not out working in the fields tugged forelocks or removed hats at De Sable's passing, but he barely acknowledged them.

'I'm surprised that you ignore everyone, my lord. A sociable person such as yourself.' Eloise lifted her skirts a fraction to avoid dragging them in the damp earth beside the well.

'I'm too busy to bother with other people's servants. It looks as though I'm to experience quite enough problems with my own.'

He threw his cloak aside as they entered the sweet, clean perfection of the stable block. Horses were a visible sign of wealth and status, frequently living in better, more luxurious conditions than their owners. Deep, fresh straw was laid thickly in each stall and sweet meadow-hay spilled from each manger.

'It looks as though your horses have better manners than you, my lord,' Eloise risked cheekily, as the first animal in the rank stood aside to let her move to its head.

'Perhaps that is because it has learnt from experience that correct behaviour leads to kindly treatment. Servants and animals alike, I am ruthless when crossed, but fair when humoured. You would do well to remember that, Eloise.'

'I hope that I never have need to cross you, my lord.'

Eloise intended it as a warning, and one glance at De Sable should have assured her that it had been understood. Instead a wry smile crept across his face.

'Now, beholden to me as you are for everything, don't you think that attitude might be a little ungrateful, Eloise? Nice girls should be kind to their generous benefactors.'

He stroked his freshly shaved chin in thoughtful amusement. Eloise was careful to put the horse between her and De Sable before answering. Tucking her gown around her protectively she bent to examine the lame foot.

'Only a stone bruise, my lord. There is no treatment other than a lotion of steeped rocket leaves.'

'Why are you so nervous, Eloise? Something in your murky past made you wary?'

Eloise was grateful for the high neck of her working-gown. She knew De Sable was staring at her and could imagine why. He would have treated her differently if they had still been equal in status, she was sure.

'I—I was educated in a convent, my lord.'

'And I dare say they filled your head with all sorts of biased rubbish about men and their evilness.' He leaned against the wall and smoothed down the pale creamy fabric of his breeches. 'What misdeed got you thrown from the convent's protection? Eating? Sleeping? Enjoying yourself?'

'My family and I were lucky to escape from Normandy with our lives. The convent was sacked, but fortunately my parents had taken me away the day before.'

De Sable stopped leaning against the wall and now went forward to look at her over the horse's withers. A look of concern shadowed his face. 'What happened? Who was the cause of the trouble?'

'You jest at my expense, my lord! Even in Brittany they must know that civil war is never far below the surface in dear Duke Robert's liberal duchy.'

Her bitterness shocked him, she noticed with queer pleasure. His expression faltered, then hardened once more.

'Trouble was never widespread, though. You must have been unfortunate.'

'We were not the only ones, my lord. Many others have worse tales to tell. Still more will never tell tales again,' Eloise finished a little sadly, and stood to turn her face from him.

'If what you say is true, Eloise, then I have sorely misjudged the situation there. I never before heard such a tale. High spirits among the nobility, yes. But then they were sadly disappointed that the Conqueror saw fit to divide his empire by giving England to William Rufus and Normandy to Robert. Those left behind in Normandy after the invasion of '66 thought to see Robert his father's sole heir, so that they could expand in the new country.'

'Please don't expect me to weep tears of blood for them, my lord. One way and another, their acquisitiveness and the Duke's feebleness have cost me my entire family.'

'But rumour has it that the Duke's four years on Crusade have changed him. I have heard tell that he has been a great warrior against the Infidel and is coming back now with new resolve and a beautiful new wife. And he ever was a kind and happy man.'

'A pity his unruly subjects are not similarly inclined.'

De Sable patted his horse and picked a wisp of straw from its mane. 'That you should suffer all that and yet still have retained dignity...'

'It was either that or go under, my lord,' Eloise said quietly.

'Things will have changed, you'll see. One day you'll be able to go back home, and everything will be all right.'

'My home in Normandy was destroyed by looters. There is no place for me there any longer. Now, if you will excuse me, my lord, I will return to the hall if you have no further tasks for me here.'

He gave her a queer look, but said nothing. Eloise picked up the saddle and harness removed from De Sable's horse and stepped quickly out into the yard. On the way back to the room they met fat, jolly Bessie who had coaxed a few bottles of wine from the castle stores. She was determined to enjoy herself and, once settled in De Sable's room, poured out generous measures for herself and Edgar. Eloise refused the wine politely.

'You should have something to wet your whistle,' Edgar said solicitously.

'I drink wine only with meals, sir.'

De Sable laughed. 'You must get extremely thirsty, then, little one. No one lives long drinking English water, that's for sure!'

The straw mattress crunched beneath him as he sat down to clean and check the saddlery.

'There is always milk, my lord. It is refreshing enough after the cream has been skimmed off.'

'I'm surprised circumstances haven't turned you to drink long ago.'

Lost in thoughts of the past, Eloise did not acknowledge his remark. Her grey eyes clouded, her pale face even more serious.

'No,' De Sable continued, quietly, 'I suppose you've seen what strong drink can do.'

'But please don't feel you have to resist on my account, my lord. I realise how difficult abstinence must be for you.' She looked meaningfully at the richly decorated goblet he held out for Edgar to fill with dark purple wine.

'Be fair, Eloise. I've told you before about judging others by your own standards. I like a drink, and shall continue to do so whether my newest recruit scorns me for it or not.'

Bessie and Edgar laughed, and De Sable returned to dismantling the leather harness he was cleaning.

The room was small, merely an alcove partitioned off from the rest of the hall and reserved for special guests. Eloise had never seen inside it before, De Sable being the first guest in the four years she had been with the Lord Gilbert's household.

While the others enjoyed their drink Eloise looked about her, only half listening to their tales of past travels and those still to come.

For security reasons there was no window, the room being on the ground floor. Light was provide by fat white candles, something Eloise had not seen outside of a church since leaving Brionne. The poor, like she was now, had to make do with rushes dipped in rancid dripping to light them.

Ventilation was provided by the ill-fitting door. While the atmosphere was heavy with candle-smoke and the scent of dried herbs that Eloise had scattered on the floor, it was much more pleasant than the smells of wet dog and long-unwashed bodies out in the great hall.

Eloise was relieved to note that De Sable and his companions were all clean, both in clothes and bodies. She supposed it was because they were almost professional house guests. No one they visited wanted to seem mean, so they were always indulged with washing facilities.

The sound of great excitement and a bell ringing came from outside. All four in the little room stopped and listened.

'Fire alarm,' Eloise said, without much concern. 'It's always the same with these "temporary" wooden castles. The sooner they're replaced with proper stone ones, the better.'

De Sable threw aside the rein he was oiling and sighed deeply. 'I suppose you'd better get out there and see if you can be any help, Edgar.'

The servant disappeared and, for want of anything better to do, Bessie started explaining the routine of De Sable's small retinue. He had been travelling the length and breadth of the country for many weeks, 'visiting'. The purpose of this was not explained, but at present they were on their way to Bristol. From there they would turn east, travel down to Southampton and then cross the Channel for Brittany, and home.

De Sable himself made no comment. Soon Edgar returned and bundled himself into the room.

'It's the kitchen block, my lord. Well alight now, and looks to be no way of saving it.'

As he spoke, there was a dull, crackling crash from outside.

'That would seem to be the roof gone. Let's hope sparks don't jump across to here. The wood's all tinder-dry.'

'It seems as though our stay here is to be cut short, then.' De Sable laid aside his cleaning for the final time and stood up unhurriedly. 'Gilbert won't want to be bothered with guests when he has no kitchen to feed them. Edgar, you and I will go and move the horses out to save them undue distress. The girls can pack up here.'

He strode out with Edgar at his heels. Bessie, the wrong side of fifty, giggled at his compliment but soon set Eloise to work. Packing had been reduced to a fine art through long practice. Within minutes the essentials of their life were stowed in oak travelling-chests, leaving the room bare and lonely again.

'Don't rightly know about that,' Bessie said, looking at the multitude of leather strips and straps laid out on the bed. 'I don't like to shovel it in regardless in case some little bit gets lost.'

Eloise had the answer. 'Hold out your arm, Bessie,' she said, with a quick smile. Suspending one anonymous-looking loop of leather from Bessie's wrist, she set to work. With deft fingers she reassembled a bridle out of the jumble of pieces. By the time De Sable returned, Eloise was buckling the reins together.

He looked irritable, and his expression darkened when he saw the bridle. 'I hadn't finished cleaning that.'

'You could hardly have moved off with it in pieces, my lord. It would not have got you very far.'

'It is a spare one,' he retorted sharply.

Eloise glared at him openly. It was all very well for him to look preoccupied—he might be put out at the disturbance, but there was no need to vent his temper on her. Eloise was coming to the conclusion that De Sable was reasonable enough when humoured, but a child when crossed.

'We move off directly, to save the Lord Gilbert any embarrassment by needing hospitality. He has other things to worry about.'

He passed a hand across his face and Eloise realised he looked exhausted. Suddenly he sensed her scrutiny and looked directly at her. All trace of weariness was gone, and in its place was grim determination.

'They're bringing the ox cart around to the front.'

De Sable lifted one end of a travelling-chest while Edgar took the other. Eloise threw on her cloak, then helped Bessie with hers, and they all went out into the hall.

As the men loaded the cart, Eloise fetched her psaltery from its hook beside the hearth. She paused, bending to pet the old, half-blind hound that basked at the fireside. It stretched up slowly to sniff at her, sending puffs of ash across the dusty floor with each thump of its tail.

Whether she still possessed the ability to be happy after all she had experienced, Eloise did not know. She had not been unhappy in this place, though. Perhaps that was all she had a right to expect.

'Hurry up.' De Sable's voice was tight, his eyes harsh.

With a final look back, Eloise crossed the hall and went out into the sunlight.

Everyone had gathered to see her off. Their good wishes delayed the journey for some minutes and De Sable made no secret of his irritability. Finally Eloise took her place beside Bessie, who was driving the cart, and they moved off through the courtyard.

The oxen were slow and it took a long time for the castle to disappear from sight. When Eloise finally turned round from waving, she realised that she had never been so far from the castle since she had arrived there.

'This will be a whole new experience for you, then,' De Sable said shortly, when she said as much.

'Where are we going, my lord? What's the next stop?'

'The Lefèvre estate, about twenty miles south of here. With good weather and good luck we should reach there by tomorrow afternoon.'

'Hope you don't mind a night under the stars, pigeon!' Bessie laughed amiably. 'It's a good job there looks to be no rain about!'

They moved on for several hours, until the novelty of her new life had been bounced and buffeted out of Eloise by the rough country cart. She ached from a dozen bruises by the time dusk crept from the wayside trees and bats flickered around them. De Sable brought them to a halt in a great open glade, with the sound of running water not far distant. This would be as safe a place as any in which to remain overnight.

Bessie and Eloise filled buckets from the nearby river while the men hobbled the animals and released them to graze for the night. The buckets of water would prevent them trying to stray towards the river.

Once the cart had been made secure, the sleeping-rugs were laid out beneath it and kindling gathered. As night closed in they ate bread and cheese around a blazing camp fire to the sound of wood owls in the trees nearby. After they had eaten, Eloise entertained with a merry song about a runaway pig, then a sad tune of a girl forsaken by her lover.

She laughed at De Sable's preoccupied expression as the last few mournful notes died away. 'You seem especially thoughtful, my lord. Shall I sing "Willow" to match your melancholy mood?'

'No,' he said sharply, then gave her a sidelong glance. 'Thank you. Not tonight.'

Edgar stood and asked permission to retire, which De Sable granted. Eloise was more tired than she would admit after the strain of journeying, but still had a little wine left to finish. While Bessie nodded sleepily in the firelight, she sipped her wine slowly and observed De Sable as he stirred idly at the fire with a stick.

He wore his hair long, almost to collar length, as was the fashion in England. One unruly lock fell forward across his brow, sun-streaks lightened in the firelight. Even though he was in a crouching position, the trained athleticism of his body was evident. There was not an ounce of excess flesh on his tall frame, despite stories

that she had heard of his excesses. He chose his clothes
with obvious care, and an equally obvious disregard for
expense. Eloise had noticed previously that his riding
boots were of the finest polished leather. Now that the
evening chill had arrived, he put on gloves of the same
supple material and pulled up the hood of his soft
woollen cloak.

'A penny for your thoughts, little nightingale.' He
looked across at her, as though guessing them already.

'I was—that is—nothing...' Eloise finished lamely.

'That won't do. You were looking at me, young Eloise.
What was going through your mind?'

His comment had given her a little time to think. 'I
was reflecting that my lord De Sable dresses with greater
care than my lord Gilbert ever did.'

'That jumped-up, treacherous popinjay?'

'He was a generous host to you, my lord.'

'That doesn't make him any more honourable. And
why so formal? Call me Richard—I call you Eloise,' he
finished softly.

'No, my lord. It wouldn't do.'

'Why not? The others won't mind. They'll think what
they like, however high and mighty your morals might
be.'

'No, my lord,' she said firmly. Bessie muttered in her
sleep. 'I've managed to reach the advanced age of sev-
enteen without being ensnared. I don't intend to fall
victim now.'

'I see. So you think that the one and only reason for
all this—travelling, stopping in this particular place, even
Bessie dropping off to sleep when she did—you think
I've arranged it all with the express purpose of seducing
you?' He gave a dry, humourless laugh.

'After some of the things I have seen in Brionne I
would not trust a man further than I could see him
thrown.'

'And I wouldn't trust a man who couldn't arrange rather more palatial surroundings for an assignation,' De Sable retorted. He stood up, throwing the stick into the fire with sudden savagery. 'Get to bed. It's late.'

The next morning, summer birdsong woke them before it was really light. Faint shadows still hung about the trees and trails of mist floated with gossamer softness over the grass.

Eloise ran down to the river to fetch fresh water for the horses. After filling the buckets, she looked longingly at the icy water licking against the banks. It had been a long time since Eloise had done any swimming, and she wondered if she could remember how.

In a moment she had cast off her clothes and slippers. Scooping her hair into an unruly coil, she pinned it up and slipped silently into the water.

A moorhen barked from rushes on the far shore, but all else was peaceful. Her body ached with the bone-gnawing cold, but the water still held her up. In a few slow, strong strokes she reached a pebbly spit in the centre of the river and paused, her feet on the shingly bottom but water lapping around her shoulders. She was without soap, but cleansed herself as best she could before turning back to the shore.

De Sable crouched on the bank beside her clothes. How long he had been there Eloise had no idea. As she swam back she tried desperately to think what she had done—whether he could have seen anything.

'You stupid girl. You could have been drowned, and you have most probably caught your death of cold.' He spoke calmly, but his expression was fierce. Eloise crouched nervously in the shallows, mindful of his anger but unwilling to emerge while he remained.

He stood up and dropped a towel on to the bank within her reach. 'You have delayed us for long enough. You will dry yourself and be quick about it.' He turned around and stood impassively, arms folded.

'You won't look, my lord?'

'At least credit me with some decency,' De Sable spat fiercely.

Eloise crept from the water and dried herself vigorously, keeping both eyes firmly on De Sable. He never moved.

'You must have seen me earlier, to have brought a towel,' she snapped, hurt with embarrassment.

'There was quite enough notification from all the splashing that was going on.'

Eloise pulled her thin linen pettitcoat over her head and sat down to pull on her stockings. Her cold, damp fingers fumbled over tying the garters, and De Sable snorted impatiently.

'Don't look, my lord!' Wriggling into her all-concealing work-dress, Eloise smoothed out the full, heavy skirt before refolding the towel. Handing it back to him with a nudge, she bent to pick up the buckets. 'You shouldn't have been spying on me.'

'Oh, now there's a thing. You would have been glad enough of my help if you had got into difficulty.'

'Well, I didn't.' Eloise immediately regretted the retort, for he had been right. De Sable seemed to have taken no offence. He grinned at her.

'I would say you must have got out of the wrong side of the bed, Eloise, but that can hardly be true, can it?'

She put the buckets down and tried to flex life back into her frozen fingers.

'Look, you're shivering still. Loose your hair. It will keep your neck warm, and here's my cloak. Put it around your shoulders.'

'I'm all right!' Eloise struggled with the pins holding her hair as he encircled her with the light, warm cloak. The hairpins wedged themselves in tighter despite her best efforts to release them, and De Sable laughed at her struggles.

'Let me. Turn around.'

Obediently she faced the river while he released her dark tumble of curls with gentle fingers. He was standing very close behind her, so close that she could hear his soft breath in the encircling silence. The moorhen barked again. All the world was still. Only the river murmured, lapping against its banks, and it was as though they were the first to ever disturb this lonely spot.

With the last uncoiling of her hair, De Sable's arm slipped unhurriedly about her waist.

She was trapped.

CHAPTER THREE

ELOISE froze with fear. Mistaking her terror for complicity, he drew her backwards and held her tight to him. Only when he buried his face in her neck did she find the will to resist.

'No, my lord.' She purposely kept her voice level, although fear was clutching at her in earnest now.

He muttered something between the rough kisses that threatened to coax her into submission. Held fast, Eloise wrenched away from his caresses and desperately found enough voice to cry out. No one came. No help could be expected from Bessie or Edgar, then. They were probably only too aware of what was going on.

Supple as an eel, she tried to twist in his grasp, but he held her firm. There was no way in which she could match his strength. In a last effort she lashed out at his face with her nails, but he trapped both her wrists in one of his hands and held them tightly.

'Naughty girl.' He withdrew, grinning wolfishly. 'There's a surprise. I never expected you to play rough...'

His voice died as he saw that the fear in her eyes was not only due to his treatment. Without letting her go to inflict damage, he turned, spare hand to the hilt of his sword.

Two horsemen stood at the top of the bank watching them, as De Sable had watched Eloise. Both were dressed in full armour and smirked with enjoyment at the free show.

One of the two touched his helmet briefly, still grinning. 'Beg pardon, my lord. Folks over there said you might be able to help us with a few enquiries we're making hereabouts.'

De Sable stayed where he was, but let go his sword and put his hand instead to Eloise's throat. In the guise of giving her another kiss he whispered fiercely so that only she could hear, 'Speak and we're all dead.'

He laughed at the newcomers, but brief pressure on her neck frightened Eloise into silence.

'Course I'll help, if I can, gentlemen. Although I'm surprised my staff recommended me as a source of information!'

The soldiers exchanged a knowing glance. Eloise felt De Sable's fingers clench in her hair.

'No need to worry yourself unduly, my lord. It's just that we've reason to believe there might be a few undesirables roaming the countryside. With news of Duke Robert of Normandy supposedly on his way back from the Holy Land, King William Rufus can't be too careful now, can he?'

The soldier spoke carefully, as though to one slow in the wits. De Sable concentrated earnestly upon the speaker's face, then frowned. If the soldiers considered him witless then he was certainly not going to show them otherwise.

'Surely the King does not fear his own brother, gentlemen?'

The soldiers laughed indulgently. 'Politics is a terrible thing, my lord. You're well out of it. The Duke needed money to fund his Crusade. He got it from King William in return for the King's having the benefit of Normandy for the duration of the Duke's absence, see?'

The second soldier joined in, laughing. 'But the King don't intend giving Normandy back to Duke Robert now he's returning, that's the top and bottom of it!'

De Sable looked from one to the other, shaking his head slowly in disbelief. The first soldier continued.

'Seems Duke Robert's sent spies on ahead, trying to whip up support for the Duke's claim. Not content with making a mess of Normandy once, seems he's set his heart on getting it back and bagging England now, too!'

De Sable continued to look doubtful at the soldier's words, but twined his fingers tightly in Eloise's curls with no such indecision. 'Well, we've been doing quite a bit of travelling over the past few weeks,' he said at last. 'My parents got pretty sick of me hanging about the place back in Brittany. They sent me over here to visit a few relatives—ah, now wait a minute...'

He kept a firm grip on Eloise, but cast his eyes heavenward as though in deep thought.

'A few days ago we stopped for shelter at a place on the London road. There were some pretty rough types there, I can tell you.' He laughed, and the soldiers joined in. 'I'm sure some of them must have been spies. Swarthy, dirty and crawling with vermin too, I shouldn't wonder.' He gave a shiver of distaste.

The soldiers smirked at each other and asked for directions to this den of iniquity. De Sable seemed not to notice the sarcastic irony in their manner and went out of his way to be helpful.

With a flourish, the soldiers saluted and wheeled their horses about to set off in the direction that De Sable had indicated. Eloise braced herself for another on-slaught, but De Sable merely loosed his hold on her slowly as he watched the soldiers go out of sight.

'There's nowhere for you to run,' he said before letting go completely. 'You might as well stay with us, however despicable you may find me.'

Picking up the buckets, he set off at a rapid pace. He looked back once, and only then did Eloise make a move to follow him. She had seen something in his eyes, and knew it to be the nearest that he would come to an apology.

She fancied that Bessie and Edgar looked at her shiftily as she reached the cart. Let them, she thought mutinously. Her conscience was clear.

'Everything was all right, then, boss?' Edgar said quietly as De Sable offered water to the horses.

'You knew what they were after, didn't you, my lord?' Eloise asked. 'Before they said anything, you knew to shut me up. How? Are you in league with the Duke? Is that it?'

De Sable patted her patronisingly. 'Isn't she adorable when she's angry?' Laughing, he sprang lightly on to his horse, eager to be on the move again. 'You'd have too much sense to ally yourself with your sworn enemies, now, wouldn't you, my little nightingale?'

Eloise said nothing, but was uneasy. He had changed too abruptly from insistent lover to harmless fool. Why did she suddenly find it difficult to look at him directly? His evident amusement embarrassed her even more. She spent the rest of the journey pointedly looking in the opposite direction to him, even when he moved his horse to ride alongside her as she sat in the cart.

The forest track was wide and grassy. They made good progress over the close-cropped turf while shadowy forms of deer watched them warily from pools of shade. While Bessie steered the cart, Edgar rode beside the oxen, exchanging a few words with De Sable but more often continuing in companionable silence.

With the sun playing hide and seek among the topmost leaves of the forest trees, they stopped for dinner. Eloise took care to keep a good distance from De Sable at all times, although he seemed to pay no heed to her now. Eventually Bessie busied herself cleaning the cutlery with damp earth, and Edgar went to check the horses. Only then did De Sable approach Eloise.

'If you continue to pester me, my lord, I shall have no alternative but to obtain sanctuary at the next church.'

De Sable held up both hands in a gesture of peace. 'Hold hard a minute. You don't know what I'm going to say.' He smiled slowly, winningly, and Eloise felt herself torn between common sense and an unfamiliar feeling of barely recognised desire.

She turned away sharply and continued to put the mugs and plates away in the cart. The man was plainly a monster, who preyed on innocent women.

'I only wanted to say——'

'Sorry?' she interrupted sharply. 'It's a bit late now.'

'No. Eloise—look, I'm very grateful that you kept quiet this morning. If they had heard your Norman accent, had thought you anything more than a serving-girl—well, it could have gone very badly for us. You heard them say how the land lies for native Normans found in England at the moment. They're treated as spies, no questions asked.'

Eloise was drawn to look at him, despite herself. He had not shaved that morning and she remembered the roughness of his skin against her bare neck. She had almost yielded then, at the warm, sensual caress. Now, in the harsh midday light, she despised her momentary weakness and faced him bravely.

'I must work for you, because you are my lord. But don't expect me to like you.'

'Ah, then you have yet to learn that it is possible to love a person without liking them, in the same way that one can like without necessarily having to love.' He smiled at her, blue eyes teasing.

'I don't know what you mean.' Eloise busied herself briskly with the plates. It was untrue. In her brief life she had held innocent, unspoken infatuations for un-suitable rogues. She had also found much pure friendship with thoroughly likeable boys.

'Fibber,' he said craftily. 'I think you know exactly what I mean.'

Eloise felt warmth rising from her breasts to bloom as blushes. De Sable gave another slow, irresistible smile.

'I don't mean to embarrass you, little one.'

A light breeze cooled her cheeks and, seeing she was not to be tempted, De Sable leaned back against the wooden side of the cart.

'So much boring grass, so many boring trees.' He sighed, looking around.

'I suppose your tastes are too "sophisticated" to enjoy pure peace and quiet, my lord,' Eloise said slowly.

He toyed idly with the brooch at his left shoulder. A fine silver and gold lacework, it caught up the luxuriance of his riding cloak so that the cloth fell in cascades almost to his right ankle. The brooch, let alone the larger matching belt buckle at his waist, must have been worth a small fortune, Eloise thought.

'If you spent a little less money on pleasures and expended a little more thought on others, you might get more enjoyment from life, my lord.'

'What could I do? Ask Bessie and Edgar—they'll tell you I can't put two thoughts together.'

'You aren't nearly as witless as you make out, my lord. It may fool others, but it doesn't fool me.'

He put back his head and laughed. 'Deus, but you sound just like my mother! Always "could do better"!'

'I'm sure you could, if you could bring yourself to try,' Eloise persisted. 'For instance, I haven't seen any books among your luggage. I'm sure you'd be able to afford one, and you could turn to it in moments such as this, to save you from yourself.' She stepped away from him pointedly.

'Books? They're all religion. Sermons and sin. In my lifetime I've already had too much of one and not enough of the other.'

'They aren't all religion nowadays. Not at all. We had one at home—*The Song of Roland*—that would have suited you down to the ground. Bloodthirsty, plenty of men knocking the wits out of each other and, most important of all as far as you're concerned, my lord,' she smiled at him mischievously, 'plenty of pictures.'

'Oh, no, I can't be bothered with all that. It would ruin my image.'

Eloise was beginning to lose patience with him. 'I suppose when one drops out of a dame's ABC class it must be difficult to appreciate the finer things in life.'

In an instant he was on the defensive. 'How dare you? I'll have you know——' Then he stopped and laughed carelessly. 'I have learned all I need from the university of life.'

She looked at him closely, but there was no flaw in his devil-may-care exterior.

'I don't entirely trust you, my lord. It may suit you to play the fool on occasion, but there must be more to you than meets the eye.'

'What a wise little nightingale!' He tweaked her chin mischievously before walking away. 'I don't entirely trust me, either!'

They reached the Lefèvre estate in the late afternoon. After a scout had intercepted them to find out their business, they were led into a large courtyard similar to the one at Gilbert's residence.

Eloise was torn between shyness and curiosity at a familiar scene peopled by strangers. Their horses and oxen were led away to a stable exactly like the one she knew. A girl drew water from a well, exactly as she had been used to doing. The difference was that now Eloise was the guest, and others could be expected to do the donkey work.

Things were not as different as she had liked to imagine. The luggage was taken to a guest room much like that at Gilbert's. Then De Sable disappeared with his affable host, and Edgar went to look around the stables. It was left to Eloise to draw a basin of water from the well, one of the tasks she thought she had left behind her.

When she returned to the great hall, Bessie already had the fire stoked and a clean sheet laid out on the dusty floor. Two flat irons stood warming at the fireside, pushed hard up against the glowing coals. Together Bessie and Eloise went through the clothes De Sable had chosen to wear at dinner that night. For some time they inspected each garment minutely, mending, sponging, and pressing, pausing only to wipe the soot from each flat iron before they were used.

While they were still busy, De Sable strolled in to watch, armed with a goblet of wine. He draped himself casually over the only chair that the room possessed, one of his long legs swinging casually over the arm.

'Mind you teach her properly, Bessie. I'm not one of these Norman louts that come to the dinner table tattered, torn and threadbare!'

Eloise looked up and saw him watching her, an impish grin playing over his features. Seeing her disapproving look, he took a long, slow drink, watching her over the rim of the goblet with merry eyes.

'You should not drink so much, my lord,' she said curtly.

'Ah, I'm drinking your share, little nightingale.' He regarded the goblet, turning it this way and that so that the firelight danced over its chased surface. 'If everyone refused wine, we should soon be drowning in a sea of it. I do my meagre best to keep the level down.'

'I say again: you are not half as witless as you would have us believe, my lord.' Eloise nipped at a stray thread and cast it into the fire. Why did De Sable continue to play the fool and waste his life when his sort were born with all the advantages? If he chose, De Sable could make something of his life. Instead he chose to fritter his time wastefully. That was what really irritated Eloise.

He laughed at her words and rearranged himself in the chair. In doing so he automatically put one hand to his sword, shifting it into a more comfortable position at his side. 'You jump, Eloise. Think I'd cut your tongue out for such cheek?'

'Not at all, my lord. It is simply that I do not like swords, and wish that you were not so attached to yours.'

'This is 1100, Eloise. Everybody wears swords, unless they want a short life, and a none too merry one.'

'Men wear swords, and they are the troublemakers, it seems to me,' Eloise snapped self-righteously. She would have said more, but a muffled ringing sound from out in the yard stopped her.

Bessie got to her feet stiffly and hobbled to the door. 'Only a yard full of beggars,' she said sullenly, 'thinking they got the right to prise good folk from their money.'

Eloise had never learned to harden her heart and, always a fool to herself, went to look out of the door for herself. 'Oh, they've got a baby with them—oh, the poor little mite...'

'Probably stolen.' De Sable was cynical. 'When it dies for lack of mother's milk, they'll throw it away and steal another.'

'How can you say such a wicked thing? You don't know that. It isn't their fault they've got no money. Two poor blind men—led along by a cripple and her baby— and you'd see them as rogues?'

'How can you say they haven't been blinded for treachery, or lust?' He joined her at the doorway. 'And that woman—for all you know she was lamed for running away from her master.'

There was no answering him. Eloise knew the penalties for law-breaking, like everyone else. Even if she hadn't been brought up along strict moral lines, the common mutilations were deterrent enough for her. Men and women with tongues cut out for perjury, hands removed as a matter of course for theft...

'Whatever the reason, I think it's dreadful. Poverty might have driven them to dreadful deeds, and now they're in a worse state than they were before. Perhaps their only crime was to want food when they were hungry.'

'Then they should have taken care not to have been caught in the act.'

De Sable took another drink and wandered back to the fire. There was something about his manner that made Eloise turn back to her work, too. As she rejoined Bessie at the pile of clothes, however, there was a sudden noisy disturbance in the yard outside.

Always alert, De Sable went unhurriedly to the door, one hand on the hilt of his sword. 'Our host, Lefèvre. He's taken exception to beggars littering his immaculate courtyard.' De Sable shook his head regretfully, but before he could say more Eloise was once more at his side.

While the residents looked on, convulsed with mirth, Lefèvre flailed at the beggars with a stick. The woman had already gone sprawling in the dust, child screaming, and the two blind men cowered in confusion under the rain of blows.

Without pausing to think, Eloise flung herself out into the yard and straight at Lefèvre. As he raised his arm to strike again, she grabbed at the stick, clutching at his wrist.

Lefèvre dropped the weapon more in sheer surprise than anything else. 'What's this? Begone, girl, or you'll get a taste of the same!'

Lefèvre was a large, heavily built man with a coarse, loutish face. Clothes were heaped upon him, rather than worn, and the layers of sludge-coloured twill gave off a sour, stale smell. He shook her off like a tiresome puppy and picked up the stick to strike again.

'Shouldn't waste your energy if I were you, my lord.' De Sable strolled easily out into the sunshine, smiling.

'I thought perhaps you and I might go out for a ride. It seems silly to waste such a day as this, when there is so little fine weather in England.'

With a grin Lefèvre threw his stick at the nearest beggar and dusted his hands off noisily. 'Good idea. This rabble will have got the message by now. Garn! Clear off!'

He aimed a kick ineffectually at the beggars as they scrambled about, trying to regroup themselves. Then he laughed and nudged De Sable confidentially. 'Use the stick on your girl. Looks as if she needs a bit of discipline!'

De Sable shrugged, already more concerned with the whereabouts of his horse. 'She's young. There is a lot that she must learn.'

'And you'll have some sport in the teaching of her, eh?'

Lefèvre leered at Eloise and clapped his arm around De Sable. Eloise felt sick to her stomach, but could not speak even if she could have found the words.

'What?' De Sable's attention was dragged back by Lefèvre's coarse laugh.

'Reckon you'll have no need of an early call tomorrow morn. Can't see that you'll get much sleep, eh?'

De Sable gave him a twisted smile, and looked at Eloise. She shrank under his scrutiny.

'Eloise, go back to your work this instant.' He spoke sharply, belying the grin he'd given Lefèvre. Her head hung in shame, Eloise made her way through the dispersing crowd of residents and back to the hall door. Only when she heard their tread on the steps behind her did she realise that De Sable and Lefèvre were following her. She pushed at the weather-warped wooden door and tried not to dash into Bessie's arms for safety.

Lefèvre was persistent. 'No wonder there's not an ounce of spare flesh on you, boy. The little vixen keeps you fit, I'll be bound!'

'I prefer my sport a little less refined, my lord,' De Sable said with a sarcastic lilt in his voice. Eloise could not look at them, but sensed that they were only waiting for their horses to be made ready. The torture of their presence would soon be over.

'But a change is as good as a rest, eh, lad?'

'Pardon my interruption, my lord Lefèvre.' Eloise had gone beyond embarrassment now, and steeled herself to glare at Lefèvre. He turned, somewhat bemused that a servant should find a voice. 'I am my own woman. No man makes sport with me.'

He frowned, beetle-black brows knitted as he peered at her. 'Quiet! Good God, De Sable. What do these women think they are nowadays?'

'Honest and hard-working, my lord, but not figures of fun or toys for your pleasure.' Eloise continued to survey him icily, with assurance bred of knowing that she was in the right.

Lefèvre spluttered with laughter. 'Honest! In a dress like that! I tell you, De Sable, they ask for it, her and her type. Ask for it, they do.'

He continued to sneer and Eloise returned hotly to her mending. She had been barely able to keep herself, and there had been no money left over for the luxury of new clothes. In the past few years her body had developed while the shape of her dresses had not. They were a little tight now, she had to admit, but it took a mind like Lefèvre's to read anything other than poverty into that. Eyes prickling with tears, Eloise tried to concentrate and keep her mind from his evil words.

The fine-rolled seam on the shirt De Sable was to wear had come unpicked around the cuff. The needles Bessie had given her would have been of more use sewing sacks, not delicate linen, and Eloise reached into the purse at her waist for the small sewing-set she kept.

Lefèvre had continued to mutter with De Sable, but his eye was attracted by the swift flash of firelight on metal. Seeing the richly embroidered needle-case and tiny jewelled scissors, he sneered openly, assuring De Sable that somebody was providing her with nice things, even if he didn't care to.

Eloise gritted her teeth and carried on with her work. If Lefèvre's words didn't give De Sable ideas that she had no intention of fulfilling... She stopped abruptly. Ever since he had kissed her there had been a nagging little devil sitting on her shoulder. Every idle moment it whispered, 'What if...?' and 'Just suppose...' in her ear.

She looked up, unable to help herself, and found that De Sable was watching her. He said nothing to Lefèvre, letting the older man prattle on. Did De Sable know what was going through her mind? He looked as though he did, and for shame Eloise blushed and looked back to her work.

There was a cry from the look-out, high upon the roof, and mercifully Lefèvre stopped talking.

It seemed that his wife and daughter were returning from a visit to neighbours and, guilty at his indiscretions, Lefèvre immediately became the formal host again. Taking his leave of De Sable, he hurried out to meet his family, much to Eloise's relief.

Hearing De Sable's footsteps, she expected him to have followed his host. Instead he came to her and, bending down, cupped his hand beneath her chin and so lifted her face.

His gaze was cool and steady, different from the mocking passion she thought Lefèvre might have ignited.

'You're certainly able to give as good as you get, young lady,' De Sable said thoughtfully, then started to laugh as he put one finger to her lips with a touch as light as thistledown. 'But it might be as well if you were to keep a still tongue in a wise head, as I have said before. Nobody will ever trust you with any secrets if they think confidences might pop out by accident in a fit of your righteous indignation!'

'Discretion has got nothing to do with it. I would never betray a confidence, my lord, although I hope you do not intend to stop me defending my honour. It seems that I am the only person willing to do so,' she finished triumphantly.

De Sable stood up to leave, brushing imaginary dust from his breeches after kneeling on the grimy floor. 'I think perhaps you should continue your work. I must look my best for dinner this evening. As Lefèvre has a daughter, then he will probably want me to propose to her.'

The words were light enough, and his expression merry, but as De Sable strode away Eloise fancied there was something else. There had been a seriousness, a depth in his expression that she had not noticed before. Eloise might think that perhaps he was not the feckless idiot he liked to portray, but perhaps she had only scratched the surface. Perhaps there was a great deal more to Richard De Sable than even she had imagined.

Exactly how much more there was to her new master Eloise had still to discover. A little was revealed later that afternoon. Eloise was heating a large pan of water over the hall fire, ready to top up the half-barrel of cold water she had painstakingly filled in De Sable's room. He would bathe and shave before the evening's festivities, he had decided. Eloise thought ruefully that he must have found Lefèvre's daughter worth cultivating, and hoped he drowned in the stupid bath.

The hall door opened, and without undue interest Eloise watched a girl enter. She was younger than Eloise, probably only ten or eleven, but tall and large-framed. Her ungainliness was not all down to youth, either. The girl was lame, and walked with a loose-limbed generosity.

'Are you Eloise?' The girl squinted with a happy smile. 'Come on. Richard says I'm to find you something!'

Though plain and unfortunate, the girl was well dressed, and had to be Lefèvre's fabled daughter. She set off at a surprising pace and, by the time Eloise had pulled the pan of water from the fire, the girl had already negotiated the stairs and was scampering along the upper landing to her room. Eloise had to run to catch up. When she reached the girl's room, there were already dresses and cloaks and slippers scattered everywhere in joyous disarray.

'Richard thinks some of my clothes might fit you. You're to sing tonight, aren't you? Then you must have a new dress.' Words tumbled out of the girl in a torrent as she sat on the floor amid the fine silks and furs. 'Daddy buys me treats every time he goes into town, you see. I suppose I shall have to make the most of it,' she added wistfully. At once Eloise crouched down beside her.

'You're very lucky to have such lovely things. You should be grateful,' she said softly. At once the girl looked up at her, but there was no self-pity in her voice as she spoke.

'Mummy says that if the new baby that's coming is a boy, then I shall have to go off to a convent. They'll have a proper heir then, you see. Because all my baby brothers have always died, I'm their only hope at the moment. If Mummy goes on being silly, and losing our babies, then they will have to find someone for me. That's why they buy me such lovely things, you see. Hedging their bets.'

Eloise was horrified, and had to stop herself from hugging the child. 'Is that what they say to you?' Anything could be expected from the odious Lefèvre.

'Oh, no. But I hear them talking, at night, when they think I'm asleep. ''What shall we do with Alisaun?

What's to be done?''' She picked up a battered doll and cradled it to her thoughtfully.

'I wish I could marry Richard,' she said, as Eloise picked up the gorgeous clothes and folded them neatly on to the bed. 'I've been riding next to him all afternoon, you see. He's lovely.'

'I think perhaps he might be a little old for you, Alisaun,' Eloise said, too tactful to tell the girl what she really thought of De Sable.

Alisaun shook her head gravely. 'He's only twenty-eight, I asked him. Daddy says if I marry it'll have to be old Hardinge, our neighbour. He's nearly seventy. And blind, which I suppose is the important part when it comes to me.'

Dear God, thought Eloise, That it comes to this. Even children are wise beyond their years. An idea began to form slowly in her mind, developing as the two girls sorted through the clothes.

Alisaun chose a kirtle of finest velvet for Eloise, the sapphire colour of a summer night. High-necked and with long sleeves caught tightly at the wrist, the gown fell in generous folds to a hem measuring some five yards around.

It would cost an ordinary man several lifetimes to save enough for his daughter to dress like this, Eloise thought, as Alisaun helped her into an overdress of silvered brocade. This was cut low both back and front to show off the velvet kirtle beneath, and the three-quarter-length sleeves were tight to the elbow then blossomed into elegant points that nearly brushed the floor. The two girls were close in height, despite the difference in their ages, but meagre living had reduced Eloise to a shadow of Alisaun's robust figure. A belt of silken silver drew in the fullness at her waist, and Alisaun rummaged through an overflowing jewellery box for a suitable circlet.

With a flutter of filmy gauze secured over her curls by the circlet, Eloise stood back to let Alisaun give her verdict. The girl laughed in rapturous approval.

'But why don't you come and see for yourself?'

She took Eloise by the hand and led her to a far corner of the room. Here, cradled on a wooden stand, was a large sheet of polished metal. It gave an almost full-length reflection, and Eloise gasped.

The metal surface was crazed with the million tiny scratches of a burnisher's art, but even so the misty, rippling reflection showed only poise and grace as it looked back at Eloise.

'Nanny says that if I look in the mirror for too long, one day I shall see the Devil himself looking back!'

Alisaun laughed, circling Eloise as she watched the moving images slither across the smooth metal surface. The thoughtful concentration with which Eloise regarded the reflections was not entirely due to the novelty of seeing herself in the borrowed finery.

'Alisaun,' she said at last. 'What will you be wearing to the banquet this evening?'

'Oh, I shan't be going. It will be bread and milk and prayers at seven, like always.'

'Perhaps I might be able to change that for you, just for tonight. Just for this one special occasion. You never know, Alisaun.'

CHAPTER FOUR

ELOISE marvelled at the speed with which De Sable and Lefèvre had gone from host and guest to firmest of friends. She had been too busy during the day to pay much attention, but, just before she had gone to the guest room to change for dinner, she had an opportunity to watch them together. The two men had come into the hall. Standing at the warmth of the fire, they continued their murmured conversation, despite the increasing flurries of activity around them.

The night's banquet was destined to be a very grand affair. Two oxen had been slaughtered in honour of the occasion. Without time to allow the many, many hours required to cook the animals whole, the carcasses were hacked into rough chunks. These were roasted through the whole afternoon on iron cart wheels hung over a huge bonfire in the courtyard.

The late afternoon was chilly for July. Already the shades of evening were drawing in and the hall was beginning to busy with people. As Eloise combed her hair into careful coils, she competed for Bessie's attention with the thunder of jostled tables and benches from out in the hall.

'My lords De Sable and Lefèvre seem as thick as thieves, Bessie. It doesn't seem natural.'

'Ah, don't you worry yourself, young 'un,' Edgar said, having entered the guest room cheerfully. 'Old Lefèvre's all right. One of the best, eh, Mother?'

He winked archly at Bessie and Eloise felt the pang of unmellowed aquaintance. She was not part of their little confidences, yet.

'Boss wants to see you sharpish, miss. Better nip along straightways.'

He stepped aside and held the curtain door back for her to leave. Thanking him, Eloise went out in her finery to join De Sable. He was standing at the hearth, still deep in conversation, but as she drew near Lefèvre grinned and muttered something that made him turn around.

For an instant his eyes might have registered surprise, or even pleasure. Whatever his emotion, he kept it from affecting the rest of his countenance. Eloise considered extending her hand to him graciously as he gave a short, almost mocking bow. Remembering his behaviour at other times, she resisted the temptation to join him in the game.

'You wished to see me, my lord?'

'Indeed. My lord Lefèvre informs me that you have taken over the running of his household. That is not what I employ you for.' His glance at Lefèvre was quick and bright as a robin's.

Eloise bridled uncomfortably, knowing that she was in the wrong. The most that she could hope for was to talk her way out of the situation. 'Not at all, my lords. I merely offered the suggestion that Lady Lefèvre would be advised to rest after her journey this afternoon.' She looked from De Sable to Lefèvre, who leered at her over-encouragingly. 'I know how eager my lord Lefèvre is that his wife should produce a healthy baby. Besides, your daughter is of an age when she should come to accept more responsibility. I thought it would be for the best if she——'

'You thought?' Lefèvre threw back a mouthful of wine and laughed. 'Not even master in my own house now, then, Richard!'

'The girl has some skill with physic, my lord,' De Sable said amiably, accepting a refill from Lefèvre's ever-handy wine jug.

'Perhaps she can conjure me a healthy son, instead of another weakling or half-made girl!'

Eloise studied the floorboards fiercely. The tone of Lefèvre's voice made it clear that it was not physic that he had in mind. Lefèvre would have to be treated with care—he might have no scruples in his desire for a male heir. Securing a succession might hold more importance for him than the name or rank of the boy's mother.

Lefèvre's voice dropped to a whisper. 'Looks all right in that outfit, Richard. Paying her in kind, are you, lad?'

De Sable smiled and shrugged. 'Your daughter kindly lent it, my lord.'

'By the... Well, I'll warrant my little cripple will never look as fine in it!'

Eloise felt herself start to blush, but did not want either Lefèvre or De Sable to have the satisfaction of seeing her do so. 'If I may be excused, my lords. Dinner is to be served directly in the kitchen block. I would not want to miss it——'

'Oh, don't be so ridiculous, girl. Eat with my servants, dressed like that? Your lord says you're to eat in here with the rest of us, though goodness knows what that means the world is coming to...'

Eloise looked at De Sable enquiringly as Lefèvre muttered on.

'There are to be other entertainments, while we eat. I thought you would like to enjoy them, little nightingale, before you sing for us.'

'Thank you, my lord.' She bobbed in a brief curtsy. 'But don't feel duty-bound to entertain the poor staff.'

She met his gaze with a look of flint. If De Sable thought that he was going to get anything out of being nice towards her he was going to be sadly mistaken!

Lefèvre's staff worked as a well-practised team and soon the tables and benches were set out. The household began to arrive and take their places: first, Lefèvre's ancient

mother, who had been old before Duke William had
conquered England, then his argumentative shrew of a
sister, who was to spend the whole evening criticising
her poor unfortunate mouse of a husband. He was a
frail, greyish figure who said nothing more than 'Yes,
dear' all evening. Several of Lefèvre's half-brothers
strolled in, drank, fought, then fell noisily asleep before
the dinner ended. Old Madame Lefèvre mashed bread
and gravy sops between toothless gums and watched them
all with black button-eyes. Not much gets past her, Eloise
thought privately.

The star of the whole banquet was undoubtedly
Alisaun. Masquers sang and danced, tumblers leapt and
cavorted, but no one sparkled as she did. From her place
at the very lowliest end of the table, well below the salt,
Eloise could see everything. Alisaun was resplendent in
red brocade and took her place at the head of the table
beside her father. The whole company had risen as she'd
entered, and, if there were any smiles or whispered com-
ments, they were not about her ungainliness or misfortune. Alisaun was going to seize this opportunity to
shine, and was perfecting the manners of a duchess.

She bade the company sit with a regal wave of her
hand. Eloise watched the accomplished way Alisaun
beckoned the water carrier. The younger girl kept up
restrained conversation with her neighbour De Sable
while washing her hands and drying them on the towel
provided. Alisaun must have watched her mother carry
out the same act, and remembered.

Eloise thought what a fine wife she would make De
Sable. Sensible and level-headed, even while so young,
she would force him to grow up. Lefèvre obviously
thought so too, from the way he kept leaning across
Alisaun to bellow cheerfully at De Sable, reducing
Alisaun to coy embarrassment.

This was no ordinary meal. There was no thick broth
to kill the appetite and so economise upon more ex-

pensive delicacies. As soon as the water carrier had visited each person and given them the opportunity to wash and dry their hands, real food began to arrive.

First the great quarters of ox were laid in a place of honour along the length of the table. With all speed these were joined by a split and roasted goat and a flock of fried chickens. Bread and wine were brought, but to Eloise's surprise there was none of the frantic grappling for food that went on at all the other meals she had attended in England. Instead, Lefèvre rose and addressed the expectant crowd.

'Now, I don't intend letting good food get cold, but I know you'll want to begin these celebrations in the proper manner.' There was a ripple of agreement. 'Seeing as how we've got one of our brave boys here today, home from the righteous struggle, it's only right that he should say a few words.'

The righteous struggle? That was what they called the Crusade, still raging in the Holy Land. Eloise was astonished. He had never said . . .

De Sable stood, nodding happy acknowledgement to the cheers that greeted him. Eloise automatically bowed her head as he began to say grace over the meal, but her thoughts were racing back and forth. She didn't think that Brittany had sent many to the Crusade. Barely a handful. The Lord Alain Fergant had gone, of course, but then he would do anything for money. Look at the way he had fallen in with the Duke of Normandy.

Eloise looked up as the prayer ended, only then realising that De Sable's Latin had been faultless. Her suspicions had been correct. He was immeasurably more clever than he let on. She scowled at him along the length of the table, but in reply De Sable merely winked cheerfully.

The meal was civilised, a rare treat in England. There was no flailing of knives over the roasts, or snatching at the wine. Although every guest at the table but Eloise

seemed to have a title, she was not overawed. She had
been brought up among well-mannered folk, and grand
visitors had been frequent at her father's house.

The meats were blackened outside, but the larger cuts
were only warm and pink near the bones. Along with
everyone else Eloise accepted her share of both cremated
and raw. Unlike the others, however, she ate little and
drank less. It would not do to make a fool of herself or
her master in such distinguished company.

When the meats had been consumed, Lefèvre stood
once more and clapped his hands for silence. 'And now—
a little treat in honour of our guest...'

A servant stepped forward to present Lefèvre with a
silver salver. On this lay two small creatures, roasted a
rich golden brown. With a flourish, Lefèvre began to
carve.

'What in the world is it?' a gentleman beside Eloise
said, in clipped English tones. 'Some Saracen delicacy?'

His lady-friend sitting opposite him, plump, perfumed and perspiring, giggled. 'Little Moorish babies,
perhaps. Oh! I couldn't!'

Several more ladies began to twitter nervously at this,
and Eloise decided the situation needed saving.

'It looks a little like rabbit to me. I do hope so, don't
you, my lord?'

The man beside her looked blank, then muttered to
cover his confusion. 'Rabbit? Oh, yes... of course.'

'My father owned a bury,' Eloise said wistfully, half
forgetting where she was. 'You could clap your hands
and the greenery would move, there were so many
rabbits.'

All those within earshot had fallen silent, but with the
approach of servants bringing slices of meat a new curiosity grew.

'Doesn't look as though we are to receive over-large
portions, my lady.' Her neighbour smiled indulgently.

'Indeed no, my lord. Though common where I come from, I believe rabbits are a rarity in England. My lord Lefèvre is a generous host to provide such a delicacy.'

'My lord Gamberon won't have to get a taste for them, then.'

Her companion laughed as he accepted a parchment-thin slice of yellowish meat. Cutting the meagre portion in half, he speared one piece on the tip of his knife and shovelled it into his mouth. 'Where do you come from, my lady? I warrant your features have a certain familiarity about them!'

His woman-friend shot Eloise a meaningful glare before simpering at her wayward lord.

'Brionne, my lord,' Eloise said carefully, then, 'Normandy.'

The company laughed, jewellery jingling and flashing in the firelight as they all sampled the rabbit.

'Oh, dear. In that case my lord Gamberon will doubtless already have sampled the stuff. Likely, then, that we shall get no peace until the greenwoods of England are filled with rabbits, swinging from branch to branch!'

Eloise wondered whether it was worth explaining about the habits of rabbits, but decided to keep quiet. Let someone else face ridicule and disbelief.

The rabbit tasted truly dreadful. Badly smoke-dried, then salted, it must have been imported, and some while ago to judge by the texture. Many were impressed, though, or pretended to be. All agreed that Lefèvre was an exceptionally generous host.

There was fruit to follow. Small crimson apples, the earliest of the year, were sharp and refreshing after the rich meal. Servants arrived quickly and quietly to remove the leavings, while the diners sat about and threw apple cores to the dogs rummaging beneath the tables.

Wine flowed freely as the entertainers were summoned to perform once more. Tumblers bounded around

their audience, jugglers tossed flaming brands into the
air. Gasps of amazement greeted these antics, the fear
of fire in a wooden building never far from the surface.
Eloise waited for her summons, but De Sable seemed
far too interested in talking and laughing with Alisaun
to give her any thought. Eloise felt a tiny pang of resentment. Her intention had been to interest De Sable
in a prospective bride, and so relieve her of his attentions. It seemed to be working admirably, so why did
Eloise suddenly feel so left out? When at last the
summons came from Lefèvre, she rose and went to the
centre of the hall without a further glance at De Sable.

At Lefèvre's direction, Eloise played a country dance,
although at first only three hardy souls braved indi-
gestion by stepping a measure. A movement at the head
of the table caught Eloise's eye, and she saw De Sable
rising to lead Alisaun into the dance.

The tune finished just before De Sable and Alisaun
reached the floor. With a sweet smile, De Sable strolled
over to Eloise and winked archly.

'Another dance? Make it an easy one, mind, I'm a
little out of practice.'

'Could my lord not find Saracen maids enough to in-
dulge his leisure time in dance?'

He backed away, still grinning. 'You need to be turned
upside-down and given a good talking to—but not right
at this moment. That,' he finished slowly, 'can come
later.'

Eloise played a slow, stately tune and gradually seats
emptied and the floor filled with lines of graceful women
and self-conscious men. As the evening progressed and
more wine flowed, the atmosphere became light-hearted,
and livelier dances were called for. Eloise forgot her
strange envy of Alisaun, and took comfort in her music.
Soon everyone was breathless and laughing. The evening
had slipped away so quickly that the dwindling rush-
lights around the hall were hardly noticed.

Only Lefèvre had sat through all the dances. Finally, when Alisaun called excitedly for her father to join in, he stood up slowly and raised his hand for peace.

'Enough jollity. The evening is drawing to a close, friends. Perhaps it is time for a last song, girl.' He nodded to Eloise gravely. 'Something fitting for this great occasion.'

'Very well, my lord. What is your wish?'

'"Weeps Still The Green Willow?"'

Lefèvre spoke in a tone that was not to be questioned, but Eloise hesitated. It was not an English song, yet Lefèvre's wife and many of his guests were English. It seemed insensitive in the extreme to suggest a song from the enemy camp, as it were.

'Well, girl? What's the matter? Don't you know it?'

Eloise squirmed frantically. 'Yes, but——'

'Get on with it, then. This is a special occasion!'

De Sable stood beside Alisaun, apparently deep in conversation. Suddenly he looked up, eyes flashing, and with a sharp nod of the head gave Eloise an unmistakable direction to proceed.

Confused, Eloise began to sing. At first her voice was hesitant, but within a moment the full, sad beauty of the words worked their magic. Only with the last lines did Eloise think to look at the effect the song was having upon the previously carefree party.

> Sings still the salt breeze as it sighs from the sea?
> Weeps still willow green?
> Yea, it weeps there for me...

They were very quiet, and still. As the last few notes drifted into silence, so movement and slight sounds started to ripple through the crowd. A collection was in progress—purses were rifled, coins amassed and thrown into a large pouch as it circulated through the throng. With little persuasion the ladies began to cast rings, brooches and richly jewelled hair-ornaments into the bag.

It was amazing. Far from needing any prompting, everyone seemed woefully eager to outdo each other in generosity. What did it mean?

Eloise had a horrible suspicion that she knew the answer to that.

Bessie had retired early to her sleeping-mat, leaving Eloise to prepare spiced wine as a nightcap for De Sable. He and Lefèvre were sitting beside the embers of the fire, while, silent as shadows, servants moved about clearing away the party debris.

Eloise had pounded sweet spice in the kitchen, then stirred it into a flagon of wine before carrying the pot to the fireside and lodging it amid the glow.

'Shall I fetch a goblet that you might share the wine, my lord Lefèvre? Perhaps you have something to celebrate.'

De Sable turned and grinned at her words, but his expression became guarded when he saw the look on her face. He looked back at Lefèvre. 'Truth is, my lord, I'm asleep on my feet already, and will have no need for inducements to sleep. You may have the wine that Eloise has prepared, if I can have leave to go to my bed.'

Lefèvre laughed his agreement and De Sable rose. Eloise made to hurry past him, but he caught her lightly by the arm.

'We are headed for the same destination, my fine young lady. May I make so bold as to offer you my arm?'

If only I had thought to change back into my working-clothes, Eloise thought with a sinking heart. De Sable's voice was low and sweet, but Eloise sensed that he would only be trying to make fun of her. She looked pointedly at his hand resting upon her arm. At length he released her with a light laugh, and followed her towards the guest room.

'It is a very long time since I experienced the company of a true lady.'

Eloise began to hurry along the quiet, darkened corridor, convinced that he was laughing at her, but De Sable caught her up.

'Perhaps I should ensure that you are always dressed as finely. I knew that you were talented, but tonight you were—inspired. You played and sang delightfully, little nightingale.'

'For you and your lady Alisaun, my lord.'

De Sable looked at her curiously, then shook his head. 'Not mine. Lefèvre offered her, but I refused.'

Eloise stopped and scowled at him. 'I hope you were tactful, my lord.'

'The very heart and soul of discretion, lady. I impressed upon him the dangers of choosing such an unstable chap as his son-in-law.' He gave an ironic little bow. 'Some of your grace and good manners must be rubbing off on me, little *maman*. And me such a poor, ignorant oaf, too.'

'That is not true, my lord,' Eloise said hotly, determined that he should not consider her fair game for his deceits. 'Your behaviour this evening at the banquet merely confirmed what I have known all along.'

'Oh?' He thrust his arm across the guest-room door, barring her way. 'And what have you known all along? Come now, tell all...'

His voice was soft and light, but in the dim torch-glow of the hallway Eloise could see that his face was tense and determined.

'That you are not the fool that you choose to play. Even if you did choose to travel with the Lord Alain Fergant.'

He watched her closely for an instant, then laughed. With the lightest of touches his hand dropped from the door-frame to her shoulder.

'Ah, but I was young and even more foolish then, if that were possible! A lot can happen in four years on Crusade, little one!' He laughed, his voice becoming more

confiding as though he was speaking to her as an equal.
With gentle hands, he rearranged the film of gauze upon
her hair. 'A man can be shown for what he really is.
The lord Alain Fergant is not to be trusted, even I was
quick to learn that. Whereas my dear Lord
Gamberon——'

He stopped suddenly. For a long time there was silence
between them, rustlings of mice in the rushes covering
the floor the only sound.

'Go on, my lord. The people at dinner were speaking
of the Lord Gamberon. I have never heard of him
before.'

De Sable hesitated for the briefest instant, but loyalty
overcame him. 'He is the dearest, kindest lord a
gentleman could wish for. Generous to each and all
without fear or favour. When we freed the Holy City
and marched in victorious, it was he who was first offered the greatest honour of all, the crown of Jerusalem,
but in his selfless humility he refused...'

'Like Duke Robert of Normandy?'

Quiet fell with the steel of her voice, so that Eloise
heard De Sable swallow in the darkness. For once she
had rendered him speechless.

'The collection, my lord. This evening. Was it to fund
the Duke—your "Lord Gamberon"—when he comes to
overthrow King William?'

Her tone was brisk and formal, but, if Eloise was in-
wardly impressed at her own calm, then she was equally
amazed at De Sable. All trace of the social butterfly had
gone and he pulled her roughly from the doorway into
a darkened corner.

'You cannot know the truth of the situation. Things
are not always as they seem, Eloise. The right can become
obscured...muddied. Not a word of what you might
think you know to Edgar. Not one word, understand?'
he hissed, shaking her to drive home the point. 'He is
a loyal and trusted servant. He would kill, no questions

asked, rather than have me exposed to any risks. And this whole castle is dedicated to the cause. You are in more danger here than I.'

'But you will be moving on. What then? I'll be too dangerous a companion for you. What is my fate to be? A slit throat and a flooded ditch at midnight?'

His hands tightened convulsively on her shoulders. Eloise prayed that he could not feel her trembling.

'You have made your views on the Duke perfectly clear. Fortunately neither Bessie nor Edgar can be aware, or you would not have lasted this long. I am not asking you to join us, or even to modify your judgements. All I am asking is that you do as I say. Keep silent. That way, you may be allowed to live.'

'Duke Robert was such a hopeless, feeble ruler of his hideous hordes that I have lost everything—home, family, friends, even my proper place in society. What makes you think I would want to go on living if I thought I could strike back at the root cause of all my misfortunes?'

De Sable's grip on her shoulders loosened and very slowly he moved away from her. 'Because...' His voice dropped to a whisper. 'Because you hold the lives of others, too, in your hands.'

Eloise had wrapped herself tightly in her sleeping-mat, but sleep would not come. What could she do? Running away was impossible. She could not hope to travel very far on foot, even if there had been anywhere for her to go. Now that the fancy dress had been taken back to Alisaun, she was back to her old servant's clothes. Anybody who met her on the road would be eager to collect a bounty for returning a fugitive. Who could guess what De Sable's punishment would be then?

There was no alternative. She would pretend to go along with the deception, but inform upon De Sable and his party to the first authority that they met. There were flaws in this plan, too. It was her word against theirs, for a start—three against one. The accusation would be thrown out, and then she would have to face Edgar in some dark, lonely place. Even if her story was believed, what good would it do her? Her master executed as a traitor, she would be cast out to wander, with no means of supporting herself. That way led to beggary and starvation. Eloise had tasted quite enough of that in her short life.

Perhaps there might be a way... An idea swam into her exhausted, tangled mind. If she could develop what skills she had while in De Sable's employ, then she might be able to earn enough when he was gone...

Sleep closed over her. Even then there were still tiny doubts flittering through her head. The last thing to cross her mind was the firm insistence of De Sable's hands upon her shoulders, and the memory of those forbidden kisses...

Eloise woke with a start. It was still very dark, but the room was full of movement. As Bessie lit candles, Eloise could see that Edgar and De Sable were already up and about. As she struggled to rise from sleep, De Sable approached and crouched beside her.

'It's still early. I'm off with the hunt. Go back to sleep.'

His voice was harsh, unlike the finger he placed lightly against her lips. Edgar did not notice the movement, being too busy gathering together saddle and bridle for his lord.

Eloise sank back, watchful but silent. When De Sable left the room, she did not join Edgar and Bessie in wishing him a good day. Edgar started to tease her gently, imagining that the girl had been affected by jealousy at the thought of De Sable spending the day with Alisaun. Bessie cut him short with a few choice words and they all settled down for the luxury of an extra hour's sleep.

Once more Eloise drifted between dream and reality when sleep would not come. Why was she loath to denounce De Sable right away? The country that had taken her in deserved to be saved from such traitors. Again the memory of his strong arms around her suffused her thoughts. She shuddered, waking properly in the dim light. How could she even think of sullying herself with such a dangerous man?

The whole idea was repulsive. Eloise frowned. If common sense said De Sable was so repellent and worthless, why did she keep torturing herself with thoughts of him?

It was barely an hour later that the look-out disturbed the staff's breakfast with a shout. Once more it was De Sable returning early from the hunting field, but this time he had a gentle companion. As the sound of hoofs drew nearer outside, De Sable was heard calling frantically. Edgar left his bread and milk with a sigh, but was soon back.

'Better get weaving, Eloise. The Lord Richard wants your company out there, not mine.'

Eloise finished her meal unhurriedly and folded her napkin before replacing it upon the table. Only then did she stand up and go to see what De Sable wanted.

He stood alone in the yard, holding both the bridle of his own horse and that of the palfrey that Alisaun had been riding. As Eloise approached he looked up, but the lines of care etched in his face did nothing to reassure Eloise.

'Alisaun? Has something happened to her?'

'What?' For a moment bewilderment had blotted out everything else. Then he smiled ruefully. 'No, no. The lady was a little overtired after the banquet last night, not having slept well. She wished to return, but was eager that I should not ride unaccompanied.'

With a nod he gestured to where Alisaun was trundling out through the hall to meet them, arms full of rich green velvet.

'Here we are, Richard. You'll have to hurry, Eloise. If the field get too much of a start on you, then you'll never catch up.'

'But—I can't! I can't go out riding... What will everybody think? A servant on horseback?'

'Good or ill, people always have to think about something. It might as well be you.'

De Sable swung himself into the saddle and turned his horse away, as Eloise cast aside her work-dress and pulled on the velvet riding-habit. With Alisaun's help, the change was managed with little loss of dignity. Swirling the matching cape about her shoulders, Eloise jumped on to Alisaun's horse and tried to make her arguments sound convincing.

It was no good. Embarrassed as she might feel, imagining accusations of a mere servant aping her betters, Eloise couldn't deny the thrill of once more entering the life that had been denied her. To wear beautiful clothes, even if they were a little on the large side; to ride, even if it was only on this one occasion...

Alisaun waved them off as De Sable and Eloise started their horses towards the gate at a trot. As soon as they reached the grassy ride outside the confines of the castle, De Sable spurred on into a gallop.

'Not scared?'

'Of course not. You needn't think you have to spoil your day's hunting worrying about me.'

'Not any more. That's why I came back.'

He made his horse put on a quick spurt so that Eloise had to hurry to catch him up. Around a gentle curve in the ride, out of sight of the castle, he slowed, then eased to a halt.

When Eloise stopped she made sure to keep her horse well clear of De Sable. If he tried anything, she reasoned, then she could soon get back to the castle and safety. He made no move to approach her. Instead he merely studied the surroundings carefully. Apart from a few threadbare gorse bushes, there was nothing to overhear their conversation.

'Now, look. I have to admit that taking you on as I did was partly for selfish reasons. I thought that, being Norman by birth, you'd be only too keen to persuade others to join the fight.'

He hesitated, seeing her horrified disapproval.

'A pretty girl, and one so talented. A novelty, and as such you have very persuasive powers. With your help, last night was a great success.'

'I would never have aided your cause had I been as certain then of your objectives, my lord.'

De Sable sighed heavily, his face weary and careworn. 'I took a risk on you, but it seems that I was wrong. It was my fault, and now I am saddled with the responsibility of saving you from yourself. Damn fool that I am,' he muttered to himself.

'Yes,' Eloise said curtly. 'And as I have no love for your precious cause, my lord, there is but one course left open to you. Abandon me at the nearest convent. The Church has no love for King William Rufus, I believe, but then neither is it likely to side with an invader. I shall be safe there, albeit at some expense to you. Your party can then travel about its evil business without cause to worry unduly.'

'If that is your wish.' De Sable tightened the girth of his horse, but did not look at her.

'It is. Although I must warn you, my lord, should any man question me directly about your motives while we are still travelling together, I shall not hesitate to tell the truth as I see it.'

'Indeed,' De Sable said shortly, then rode his horse forward once more. 'The party were heading for a covert not far ahead, lady. We should hurry if we are to catch them for the draw.'

CHAPTER FIVE

ELOISE could appreciate why Alisaun had not been over-
eager to remain with the hunting party. This was not a
sporting occasion, but merely a chance to be seen. While
the men stood about, testing the wind, discussing tactics
and generally showing off their knowledge, their
womenfolk sat on the sidelines. They were pinched up
with cold in their fashionably flimsy attire. Each would
have been grateful for a warm cloak, but they all pre-
ferred to suffer for the sake of fashion. Butterfly-bright
linen and gauzes did little for pale blue complexions.

One by one the women turned to look as Eloise drew
near with De Sable. She returned their stares with a smile
and polite greeting. At least the women were gracious
enough to return the compliment, whatever they might
say among themselves.

'I suppose you will wish to go closer and watch the
sport, my lord. I shall go and stand with the ladies.'

De Sable was watching two hounds quartering the
tussocky grassland and did not answer her immediately.
At last he looked across at the knot of shivering women
and shrugged. 'I prefer to have you within earshot, little
nightingale. That way there is less strain upon my nerves.'

Eloise too watched the dogs, and did not look at him
as she said slowly, 'If you suffer with your nerves, my
lord, espionage would seem to be a rather foolish choice
of career.'

He gave a hollow laugh. 'No one in their right minds would choose to do this work. But as for nerves—remember, little nightingale, you are in far greater danger here than I am. The faithful will not harm me, and as for the other sort—I take good care to find how the land lies before inviting others to join the cause.'

The dogs put up a hare. As the lithe brown form streaked away, so the hunting party erupted in noisy encouragement, clapping and shouting. There was little need to spur the dogs on. One pair easily outpaced the rest, following each jinking swerve of the hare as it zigzagged frantically to escape. Both dogs were evenly matched for speed, but one had quicker wits. Learning to anticipate, it lurched to one side a split second before the hare thought of the same manoeuvre. In an instant it was over. The winning dog had thrown up his head, limp hare drooping from his jaws, and was trotting back before his opponent had managed to pull up.

The victory was short-lived. All the other hounds immediately pounced on the winner and a free-for-all ensued. While a rolling, tumbling jumble of tails, legs and snapping jaws writhed over the grass, servants were urged to act.

Eloise could not take her eyes off De Sable as he watched the fight. While the women squeaked and their husbands urged luckless servants into breaking up the fray, De Sable was silent and grave. In profile his strong features were handsome and clearly defined, but there was a faraway look in his eyes. Weightier matters concerned him far more in that instant than any smart social occasion.

'Why don't you face facts, my lord? There is no more hope of the Duke of Normandy controlling England than there was for that poor hare. Your "Lord Gamberon" will be nothing more than a helpless puppet, as he was in Normandy.'

'He is a good man,' De Sable said quietly. 'Too soft-hearted to see that he had been led astray by evil men. With good friends, and now a clever wife in the dear Lady Sibyl to support and guide him...'

'And who is to say when support and guidance become leading strings, however "good" the friends, however "dear" the wife? Look at this crowd.' She gestured at the refined, well-bred hunting party. 'They'll give you promises, money and good wishes now, but when the fat's in the fire only the overpoweringly ambitious will stand the heat.'

De Sable looked at her sadly, and spoke as though to one weak in the wits. 'England is tired of cruelty and vice. There must be change.'

'King William Rufus might be repulsive and un-natural, but he has right on his side, my lord. The Conqueror gave England to him. He is the chosen one, not Duke Robert. As King, William Rufus is ruthless, cruel and repressive—he has to be. Even I can see that. Being nice isn't a qualification for kingship, my lord. It is a positive disadvantage.'

The party began to gather itself together to move for another draw. Ever eager to play the chivalrous hero, De Sable exchanged pleasantries as the ladies drew near. Before Eloise knew what was happening he had been engulfed by the crowd and engaged in animated con-versation with a flashy redhead.

'Tell me, my dear...everyone is simply bursting with curiosity...' A middle-aged woman trapped into bright

red linen had ridden close, and pawed at Eloise confidingly. 'Is it true what they say about young Richard?'

Eloise inclined her head graciously. 'I dare say, my
lady. I would believe anything of a man who brought
his servant out riding, wouldn't you?'

The woman giggled nervously, but her eyes could not
have conveyed more horror if Eloise had actually struck
her a blow. For her part Eloise was equally horrified. It
had not occurred to her that she had been taken for anything other than a servant.

'Please, do not let me offend you, my lady. I did not
realise——'

'No . . . no, it was I who did not realise . . .'

The woman faded back to her friends, but they were
close enough for Eloise to hear the muttered
exclamations.

'A servant? Riding with us?'

'And she was at the dinner table last night, too!'

'Well, if that is what the new empire will be like . . .'

Let them talk, Eloise thought. They'll wait a long time
for their new empire if I have anything to do with it.
They might as well fill in the time with idle gossip.

There was much sport to be found on the open
downland. Several hares were bolted, although the first
kill of the day was the only one. Later the dogs stalked
a small group of bustard, but were too tired to prove
much of a threat to the birds. The party decided to break
for dinner, and give the dogs a chance for rest.

The ladies dismounted and found shelter from the cool
breeze in a shallow depression. De Sable was a great
favourite, the women fluttering and cooing around him
under the kindly smiles of their husbands. As he was
the only member of the party who had been on the

Crusade, it was only fair that he should be indulged as the hero he obviously was.

Eloise sat a little distance from the ladies. She had offered to help the servants as they unloaded the pack ponies' panniers, but Lefèvre's staff wouldn't hear of it. Once more Eloise was faced with the old problem: she was not considered suitable company for the fine ladies, but neither was she accepted by the staff as one of their own.

Lefèvre's staff had the meal served in moments. Dinner consisted of soft cheese with oaten biscuits, followed by almond cakes and wine. Eloise enjoyed the meal almost as much as she enjoyed the thought that there would be no washing-up to be done. Mellowed by good food and wine, she found it pleasant to sit in the breezy sunshine and look out across the down. After a little while Lefèvre came to sit beside her, which spoiled the moment.

'Letting the day-shift take over now?' He laughed, nodding in the direction of De Sable and his covey of admirers. Eloise looked directly into Lefèvre's wine-dulled eyes and frowned slightly, as though puzzled by his words.

'Perhaps you could provide me with a little entertainment?' There was an ugly emphasis in his words, but Eloise refused to be goaded.

'Gladly, my lord, but I fear that my psaltery is left back at your castle.'

Lefèvre wiped his mouth upon his sleeve. Innocence such as this was rarely met with in servants. He would have to think about it.

Without giving him time to gather his drink-scattered wits, Eloise put aside her cup and platter and began to rise.

'I can sing unaccompanied if my lord wishes,' she said courteously. 'Some small thing of my own devising.'

Lefèvre muttered indistinctly, then waved a hand for her to proceed. It was little enough encouragement, but Eloise was full enough of her own ideas not to care. It would be good to perform some of her own work, for a change. Then she could judge her chances of making a living for when she had denounced De Sable.

She stood up and brushed the creases out of her gown. Clasping her hands before her, she began to sing.

Soon all idle chatter stopped. The sad, sweet song caused all to turn and watch, even though the performance had been intended for Lefèvre. When she had finished, Eloise was surprised to feel herself warm with embarrassment at the applause. Normally she took praise in her stride, but today was special. Today she had been composer as well as performer. Perhaps this one little triumph meant that supporting herself was not such an idle fancy.

Even De Sable had been impressed. Eloise had seen him and the flashy redhead pause in their mutual admiration of each other and clap good-naturedly.

It was much later in the afternoon before De Sable managed to tear himself away from his female admirers. Eloise had followed the hunt miserably. Any conversation she had tried to begin among the ladies had been viewed with suspicion. Only the gentlemen seemed keen to converse with 'De Sable's servant', and Eloise had more common sense than to encourage them.

'You ride well,' De Sable said as he moved his horse up beside hers. 'For a servant.'

Eloise looked at him sharply, then saw that he was grinning. 'I wish I hadn't come.'

'Rubbish. A day in the fresh air, no work to do, fêted by all the gentlemen...'

The low rays of the setting sun touched his hair with gold and burnished the glittering metalwork on his gauntlets and buckles. There was no one in the company that could match him in either looks or personality. And he knows it, thought Eloise savagely.

'It would be but a simple matter to obtain your correct station in life, Eloise. Merely be nice to those who can be of use to you.'

'And so consort with traitors? No, my lord. Some of us have our pride.'

They rode on in silence, trying to avoid the hounds lolloping around their horses' legs. Afternoon was slipping away into evening, and conversation among the company was nearly exhausted. As the group approached Lefèvre's land once more, the scratchy rasping of corncrakes drifted over the grassland.

'Summer's here,' De Sable observed quietly.

'And soon a new song will be heard in the land,' Lefèvre added smugly.

De Sable looked to his host, but, seeing Eloise shiver, removed his cloak and in one swift movement cast it around her shoulders. Eloise protested, conscious of the sullen silence that had fallen upon the women riding behind. It was no use. She rode the last mile with the warm male scent of De Sable wrapped about her with the cloak.

Trying her best to feel mutinous, Eloise wished for the time when she could denounce him and his over-chivalrous ways. With horror she found that anger at De Sable was becoming difficult to sustain. It was easy enough to dislike him for his views, but then he would laugh in that certain way, or show some little kindness to a lady...

Eloise shook herself sternly. It must all be part of the plot. Traitors were supposed to win people over. That was their job. Well, De Sable needn't think that he was going to succeed with her. Oh, no.

Dinner was a more relaxed affair than the previous evening. Eloise took her meal with the other servants in the kitchen, and felt better for it. At first Lefèvre's staff were wary of her, but by the time she had helped prepare the meal and done her fair share of fetching and carrying they were won over.

After a few songs around the kitchen fire, De Sable's staff were allowed to retire. Eloise had been nervously formal towards Bessie and Edgar since receiving De Sable's warning. They in turn had become cool towards her. The atmosphere was decidedly difficult as all three walked back to the guest room.

Passing through a spirited game of blind man's buff in the great hall, Edgar went to see if De Sable was in need of anything before they retired. Bessie continued to the guest room with Eloise.

Once inside it was plain that there was something on Bessie's mind. She refused to look at Eloise directly, glancing at her guiltily instead. After an age of edging around polite conversation, Eloise could stand it no more.

'What is it that you want to say, Bessie?'

The older woman hesitated, rubbing her hands nervously in her apron. 'It's just that ... well, with us being all you got as family, you might say, child, Edgar and me thought as how you'd better be told——'

Eloise decided to bide her time. She was in no hurry to test Bessie and Edgar's fanaticism. 'Told? What?'

Bessie exclaimed sharply, then poured a cup of wine for both of them. Eloise refused politely, so Bessie drank both.

'Now, don't get me wrong, child. Edgar and me, why, we do love the master like he was our own. Only... well, the fact is, he's not safe around the young ladies, child.'

Eloise sighed with relief. 'Is that all?'

'Don't let him turn your head.' Bessie was on firmer ground now, and with wine inside her had gained confidence. 'I'll admit, he's a handsome young buck, but he don't carry on decent. He'll ruin you, child, given half a chance. Look to yourself.'

Edgar reappeared, laughing. 'Master won't be back this evening, by the look of it. Out all day, up all night——'

Bessie cuffed him soundly, and Edgar consoled himself with a cup of wine.

'You told her?' he murmured to Bessie, then smiled at Eloise.

'It's all for the best, girl. You don't want to get mixed up with him like that. Stay with us. Keep quiet as a mouse and don't give him any encouragement. That way you'll keep out of trouble.'

Eloise thought of possible rebellion to come, and wondered what their understanding of trouble was.

The games went on noisily for some hours. Tired after the day of riding when so long out of practice, Eloise found no difficulty in slipping into sleep.

Only minutes later, it seemed, she was awoken. Rapid footsteps in the night-silenced hall outside, a tearing at the curtain door and De Sable strode into the room. Afraid of what she might see, Eloise kept her head tucked well down.

De Sable was clearly in no mood to talk, or even bring himself to be civil. Amid the thumps and crashes of the master getting ready to retire, Eloise heard Edgar ask quite politely if there were anything the matter. He was told to shut up in no uncertain terms, and after that and a crunch as De Sable threw himself down upon his bed, all was silence once more.

Eloise drew herself further under the sleeping-rug and wondered. Perhaps even the great De Sable wasn't always as irresistible as he considered himself.

De Sable took breakfast in his room the next morning. Bessie and Eloise sat quietly beside the hall fire mending linen, with a good view of all that went on.

First Lefèvre appeared and, puzzling at the absence of his guest, paced about nervously. At length he approached the fire. Ignoring Bessie, he addressed Eloise, enquiring whether the lord De Sable had passed a comfortable night.

'That I would not know, my lord. There was certainly some little disturbance in the early hours.'

Eloise wondered if Lefèvre thought her more worthy of his attention than Bessie, and disliked him even more for it. Looking up, she noticed several women descending the stairs, including Lefèvre's sister and the flashy redhead. All were deep in whispered conversation, which dissolved suddenly into giggles and rueful laughter.

'I hope my lord Richard is not ill...' Lefèvre said half to himself, then hesitated. De Sable had emerged from the guest room. The women immediately fell silent, which was worse in its way than the whispering that Eloise had endured the previous day.

He strolled across the hall to Lefèvre, looking neither at the cluster of women nor to Eloise and Bessie. Instead he paid heed only to Lefèvre. The hall might have been empty of all others.

'Good morning, my lord. Another night made enjoyable by your most excellent hospitality.' He silenced a whisper among the women with a rapier glance. 'Unfortunately, I fear we must be on our way if matters are to progress with all speed——'

'Surely not, Richard?' Lefèvre burst out. 'We were going to get out the maypole. You must stay for the celebrations...'

'Pagan rites,' De Sable said crisply. 'The Lord Gamberon would not care for such heresy, although you may, of course, do as you please. At present.'

He pulled on a new pair of gauntlets, white kid with gold embroidery. Taken at face value he was all politeness, but Eloise was already learning to read the signs. The deepening of faint lines at his mouth, a brittle ice in his eyes. De Sable was not pleased.

'If you will not stay, of course I cannot detain you. Perhaps some other time...? We would only be too glad——'

'Thank you, my lord, but no.' De Sable managed a little warmth in his voice, but when he spoke to Eloise and Bessie there was no pretence at good manners. 'Edgar is packing. I suggest you both stop wasting time. Go and help him.'

'I'll have a wolf steak and make it snappy,' Bessie grumbled as she packed up the mending. De Sable was upon her in a flash.

'What did you say?'

Eloise immediately jumped to Bessie's defence. 'She was merely commenting upon your ill humour, my lord. And quite reasonably, too, I would say.' She stood her ground and watched De Sable's momentary fury subside like a settling hawk. 'And, whatever the urgency, I suggest that my lord make time to take a camomile infusion before we leave. To settle your nerves.'

He frowned at her furiously, but said nothing. Eloise and Bessie took their leave, and took care not to speak to each other before they were in the privacy of the guest room.

'You'd better make it quick with that infusion, child. I've never known him stop short of violence before, when he's been in a mood like that. Today must be a lucky day.'

Eloise took a mug and a muslin sachet of dried camomile from the chest before it was locked up. While Edgar and Bessie finished the packing, she went in search of water to boil. De Sable and Lefèvre were still beside the fire, and still under scrutiny by the ladies of the castle.

Silently she went about her work, boiling the water then pouring it over the sachet of dried flowers. At once a powerful scent rose with the steam, strong and sickly. After counting to twenty, Eloise stirred the infusion briskly for a minute and discarded the soaked sachet.

'My lord?'

De Sable was so intent upon ignoring the whispers of the women that he had blotted out her voice, too. Eloise stood up.

'My lord, the mixture will only work if you sit down
to drink it. I suggest that you go to your room now, and
take the infusion while it is still hot. It will only take ten
minutes or so to work. The same length of time that it
will take Bessie and Edgar to load up the cart and fetch
the horses.'

She set off towards the guest room, and after a few
yards heard De Sable grudgingly take his leave of
Lefèvre. As they entered the room Bessie and Edgar were
just carrying out one of the large travelling-trunks. Eloise
pulled the curtain door closed behind them and turned
to face De Sable.

'Sit down. Drink this, then you can lie on the bed
until it's time to leave.'

'I'll stand.'

He put his hand out for the mug but Eloise kept a
firm grip upon it.

'You must sit down to drink it, my lord.'

Mutinously he sat down on the bed, looked at her for
a long time, then drank the infusion in one draught.

'It tasted perfectly normal.' He sounded slightly
surprised.

'Of course.'

'So it wasn't poisoned.' It was a statement, not a
question. 'I thought at the very least you would try to
save your friend King William Rufus a tiresome task,'
he finished bitterly.

'I do not know the King personally,' Eloise said
briskly, then sat down beside him. 'Now, my lord, Bessie
and Edgar have given me the Egyptian's warning about
you. Don't think that you can appeal to my feminine
weakness with a tale of fantasy. Just tell me what has
served to bring you to this ill-humoured pass——'

'What?' He looked at her, cold anger replacing quiet bitterness. Standing up sharply, he began to pace about the room. 'You can sit there and ask me as nicely as you like what ails me? I was never under any illusions about my task. One way or another it will probably lead to my death, either honourably on the battlefield or with the dishonour of failure. No, fear for my life has never cost me any sleep. But now I have a far greater worry.'

He stopped abruptly. Eloise watched him sort and sift words in his mind, toying with the hilt of his sword as he did so.

'I cannot reveal everything. Nor even a sand grain of the knowledge that I must as yet keep to myself. More especially because you have made your feelings about my mission quite plain. My mission cannot possibly be allowed to fail. And yet——'

A rapping on the door-frame announced Edgar's return.

'Ready to go, my lord.' He eyed Eloise suspiciously, then went back out to wait. There was an uncomfortable pause, then De Sable decided that his conversation with Eloise was at an end.

'So. All speed to the nearest convent, then. With the hope that we don't meet anyone that you can reveal me to along the way.'

He strode out quickly, leaving Eloise to gather up her cloak and follow.

The summer day was clear but not too hot. The little party drove out of Lefèvre's castle, De Sable leaving behind both safety and a brave but plainly disappointed Alisaun.

Over a period of hours they worked down fro.
uplands into a wooded valley. Here insects buzz.
through the greenery and the succulent leaves of bluebells carpeted the woodland. Within weeks the fragile
bluebells had bloomed and faded. Soon all trace of them
would have disappeared, until the next spring.

Bessie drove the ox cart while Eloise sat beside her.
The two men rode one each side of the oxen to direct
them. No one seemed to be in the mood for talking, so
Eloise had plenty of time to think.

The first song that she had composed had been a
success with Lefèvre and his party. Now she had another
idea for a song, suggested by the frail, passing beauty
of the bluebells. While the party travelled on Eloise
juggled words, phrases and notes in her head.

She wondered how many songs she would need to
become a proper performer. There could be no going
into this career with a half-hearted attitude. Once she
had denounced De Sable, she would have to succeed on
her own.

At the thought, Eloise looked up to watch De Sable
riding before her. He certainly did not seem like a man
with a problem. As the party rolled along the woodland
ride so he looked about him at the trees, the sky and
the wide, tussocky track ahead.

A faint admiration for him crept up upon Eloise before
she could stop it. He was practically under sentence of
death, but remained calm and unruffled. She held the
power to destroy him at any time. He knew it, but would
not worry either Bessie or Edgar with the prospect yet.

They stopped for refreshment, and the atmosphere
eased a little. Eloise was wary, expecting De Sable to try
and win her over to the cause. He did nothing of the

sort. Instead he behaved as he usually did. There were no hole-in-the-corner whisperings with Edgar, and no suspicious glances.

The warmth of the day had made the horses and oxen particularly thirsty. They drank all the water that had been brought for them, yet still looked about for more. After she had finished her mug of milk, Eloise collected the buckets and went off to the nearby stream to fetch more water.

The stream was only a little way distant, but Eloise had to pass by a tangled bramble thicket to reach it. As she neared the bushes there was a frantic, jingling rustle from the other side. Something small was making much mischief.

Eloise put down the buckets and crept a little way into the undergrowth. The bramble canes were long and whippy, and trembled at the rough treatment they were receiving.

As she edged through the prickly barrier, Eloise saw the cause of all the commotion. A young merlin had seen a tree stump in among the brambles and tried to land. The leather straps at its feet had tangled in the bramble canes and it now hung upside-down, panting in a brief lull in its struggles.

Falconry was another passion that poverty had forced Eloise to forgo. Moving out of the thicket, she quickly took off her stockings and wrapped them around her hands. Now she was able to untangle the bird without fear of either of them coming to harm.

In a few moments she had freed the bird and held it safe in her hands. There was no identifying mark on either bewits or bells, but a thin voice calling from the other side of the stream announced that the owner was

not far away. Eloise withdrew from the thicket and went
to the waterside.

A young woman seated on an expensive-looking grey
mare came into view. Seeing Eloise she hesitated, plainly
wondering whether to risk speaking, but then she saw
the little merlin.

'Jack! Oh, thank goodness!' In agitation she wheeled
the horse about the bank, but was too nervous to cross
the stream. Eloise slipped off her shoes and, holding her
skirts up in one hand and the bird in the other, splashed
across.

The young woman was older than Eloise, nearer De
Sable in age. Her pale blue outfit was cut to show off
her enviable figure, and fine wisps of pale gold hair escaped from beneath a richly embroidered veil. Despite
a good upbringing, she could not conceal the obvious
relief in her voice.

'Thank you. I take it you will be eager for some
reward?'

She began to probe in the gilded purse at her waist,
but Eloise waved that kind of gratitude away.

'It was nothing. Birds are lost and found all the time.'

The woman looked agreeably surprised at the sound
of Eloise's voice.

'So you're one of us? I'm sorry—the dress—and the
bare feet . . .'

Eloise settled the merlin on his owner's wrist, then
shook out her stockings. 'We aren't all as lucky as you,
my lady.'

'No. No, quite.'

She looked uncomfortable, unused to conversing with
the lower classes. Eloise dried her feet and ankles as best

she could under the embarrassed scrutiny, but could not bear the silence.

'Have you caught anything with the bird, my lady?'

'Oh, no. He was after a lark, but it was too swift for him.'

Eloise wondered what the lady's falconer was about, letting her enter a young bird so early in the season. After its fright, it might lose heart forever.

'Perhaps he is still a baby, my lady. A few more weeks might make all the difference. The old larks will be moulting then. He'll have a better chance against them.'

A petulant frown crossed the lady's beautiful features, but then she smiled. 'You sound exactly like old Joseph, girl. If he were to find out that I'd flown Jack after all his warnings...well, it's a good job he need never know.'

Eloise opened her mouth to say something, but a rustling on the other side of the stream silenced her.

'My lady?' De Sable arrived at the waterside and executed a graceful bow to the newcomer. 'I hope that little Eloise is not troubling you?'

Eloise scowled, but De Sable had eyes only for the woman on the horse.

'Not at all, my lord. She merely returned my hawk to me.'

Falcon, thought Eloise blackly, furious at the idiocy of people who had too much money to really care about their sport.

'It seems a lonely place for one so fair to ride alone, my lady. I am surprised that your husband does not accompany you.'

'Oh, he's back at home.' The lady gestured idly with a flick of her hand. 'He never wants to come out, or do anything exciting.'

Eloise watched De Sable. He was appraising the lady intently, without bothering to conceal the predatory look in his eyes. For her part the woman smiled, and smiled again.

'I think perhaps it might be as well if you were to have an escort, my lady,' De Sable said slowly, his voice sweet and full. 'There are some wicked types about these days.'

'That I don't doubt. But I am afraid that I failed to catch your name...'

'Richard De Sable.' He bowed again. 'At your service, my lady.'

'Melisande Artois.' The woman inclined her head graciously, but her smile was sly. 'At yours.'

Eloise remembered Bessie's warning. It was true—De Sable obviously wasn't safe with women. What was worse, they seemed to like his unctuous good manners, and fell for his charms.

They must be mad. Couldn't they see that it was all an act?

CHAPTER SIX

ELOISE was sent back to fetch De Sable's horse and then explain that the young master would be travelling on ahead. By the time the other animals had slaked their thirst and the cart was moving, De Sable and Madame Artois were quite a considerable distance on their way.

As Edgar guided the unwilling oxen through the stream and up on to the opposite bank, Bessie made her feelings plain.

'It'll be the end of him, you mark my words. All it takes is the sight of pretty curls, or a well-turned ankle, and he's away. One of these days——'

'Ah, reckon so.' Edgar nodded to where De Sable was leaning indulgently towards Madame Artois, as though hanging on her every word. When she laughed, as she often did, Madame Artois would keep putting out her hand to pat him confidingly on the arm.

'That's the first sign. She's hooked. Now all he has to do is reel her in, like a little fish.'

'Edgar!' Bessie was shocked. 'Not in front of our Eloise! Pay no mind to him, child. He's an evil-minded old man, and no mistake.' She nudged Eloise, but Edgar merely laughed and winked at her mock disdain.

'There's some that won't get a chance to grow into evil-minded old men. Destined to be cut down afore their time. Reckless and foolhardy, that's what they are.'

He watched De Sable and Madame Artois for a moment, but Eloise was more interested in where they were headed.

'Oh, look! That's what I call a real castle!'

The Artois castle reared high and imposing above the surrounding countryside. Although by far the most important building in the area, the castle was only part of a much larger community.

A patchwork of tiny allotments embroidered the forest clearing about the castle. These ran right up to a palisade fence enclosing a high, grassed mound. Formed by the sweated labour of peasants to provide a high vantage point, the castle had been built on top of the mound. It had a good view in all directions, and in times of danger the villagers and their stock could be gathered within the protective confines of the castle yard about the mound.

Madame Artois led De Sable through the castle yard and they both dismounted at the foot of a flight of steps cut into the grassy mound. Bessie brought the cart to a halt in the yard. Here De Sable's three servants waited for formal admittance before presuming to enter the domain of their betters.

It was some time before they were called up. A thin, pasty figure emerged and came slowly down the steps. After a brief word with Edgar, he led the oxen and cart away while Bessie, Edgar and Eloise dragged De Sable's belongings up the steps to the castle.

All castles were built on the same lines whether of stone, like this one, or made of wood. A store-room for provisions formed the ground floor, with a flight of steps running up the outside of the building to the first floor. This consisted of a large main hall where the family in residence lived and ate. Their servants also used the hall and slept there at night, all huddled around a large hearthstone in the centre of the room.

A fire burned on the hearth night and day, and as the only outlet for smoke was a louvred shutter in the roof the atmosphere ranged from draughty to a thick, smoky fog.

At one end of the hall was a wooden gallery, reached by a sturdy ladder. Here the lord and lady slept, away from the common crowd below. In the Artois household this gallery also provided guest accommodation, tapestry hangings curtaining off one corner.

Bessie was not impressed by the surroundings.

'Her ladyship might give herself airs and graces, but she's not got that much to crow about. We've stayed in better places.' She wiped her nose on her sleeve and urged Eloise to hurry with unpacking the master's bedlinen.

De Sable was nowhere to be seen. At the sound of girlish giggling from one of the offices beneath the gallery, Edgar went to investigate. When he came back it was with a rueful smile.

'Boss is engaged, meeting the master of the house. Her ladyship's laughing like a drain at every word he says. Seems that she should be a pushover, at any rate.'

'Looks a flighty piece to me,' Bessie grumbled, cracking a clean pillowcase with a flourish. 'Here's to be hoped that my lord Artois is a heavy sleeper.'

Eloise blushed at the thought of De Sable and his assignations. She would avoid denouncing him to the Artoises until she could discover whether or not De Sable was able to win them for his cause. If they were unsympathetic, as she now realised her old master Gilbert must have been, Eloise would act. If they were sympathisers with the Duke of Normandy, she would have to keep her silence. Let De Sable do the risky work first.

He arrived in his room suddenly, while the preparations were still incomplete. Although Bessie and Edgar fussed that things were not even half ready, De Sable was not interested in the domestic arrangements. Instead, he winked at Eloise.

'The lady Artois wishes to go out riding. You can accompany us, Eloise.'

'Me?' Eloise automatically put a hand to her hair, then to her plain working-dress. 'Oh, I couldn't possibly——'

'You will,' De Sable said shortly, tightening the belt of his white and gold tunic. 'Young Alisaun kindly donated the riding-habit that you wore at the Lefèvres'. I stuffed it in a corner of that trunk, somewhere.'

He stood in the doorway, his light, athletic body outlined against the heavy darkness of the tapestry drapes. The gold embroidery on his tunic was repeated on his gloves and sword belt, which all shimmered in the leaping candle-light of the gloomy hall.

Eloise wondered whether she was being taken along to safeguard Lady Melisande's honour or De Sable's. No woman could fail to be impressed by his immaculately dressed charm and easy manner. From the way the Lady Melisande Artois had been simpering at De Sable as they journeyed towards the castle, she was more than impressed.

There was little enough privacy in the guest room to change, and Eloise refused to do so until De Sable and Edgar had both stepped outside. Bessie promised to alter the riding-habit at the first opportunity, but for the moment Eloise would have to gather in the excess material. She chose a silver cord from what she called De Sable's 'dressing-up box' and used it as a belt. Her only gloves were gone through at the fingertips, but as the day was fine she could go without.

She had neither ornament nor veil to cover her hair, but secured it in a demure roll at the nape of her neck and hoped that the Lady Melisande would not notice. After all, it isn't as though I will be riding up with them, Eloise thought. As a servant I shall be out of sight, behind.

'Ah, the Lady Eloise!' Melisande rushed forward, excited as a puppy. Eloise was negotiating the ladder, one arm full of her long skirts, and was quite taken aback at her welcome.

'I must say, you and Richard aren't very alike, are
you?'

Eloise looked at De Sable quickly, and he turned away
just as rapidly. Not before Eloise had seen the grin on
his face, though.

'You would be surprised at how we differ, Lady
Melisande,' she said with taut civility. De Sable did not
turn around.

'Well, now we're all three here we can set off. Eddie!
You're not still doing those boring old accounts? Come
out here and meet Richard's little sister.'

A tapestry curtain was pulled back and Artois himself
appeared. He was tall and angular, with a quiet dignity
lent weight by a shock of white hair. He was one of the
oldest men Eloise had ever seen—near sixty, she guessed.

Artois approached and bowed, taking her hand and
brushing it lightly with his lips. If ever there was an ill-
matched pair, then it was the Artoises. He was as restrained as his wife was excitable. She bobbed about,
swishing her generous skirts through the fragrant herbs
scattered over the floor.

'Do hurry up, Eddie. We want to be off.' Lady
Melisande pouted, then giggled as she squeezed De
Sable's arm. 'I'm going to take Richard all around the
boundary. And Eloise,' she added, as an afterthought.

Edward Artois smiled indulgently and patted his young
wife. 'Run along, then. But don't be late for dinner.'

With a brief nod of farewell to De Sable and Eloise,
he returned to his office and the accounts. Only when
Lady Melisande had skipped on ahead to organise horses
did Eloise get a chance to round on De Sable.

'What on earth do you think you're doing? Telling
them that we're related! Oh, the shame of it!'

De Sable was already smiling and now laughed openly
at her rage. 'If you could have seen your face!'

'I think you are cruel, and spiteful, and——'

'Why? Because I'm giving you the chance to get out and about with those of your own class? Letting you ride? Enjoy yourself? If that makes me cruel, then to accept the offer but complain makes you ungrateful, little nightingale!'

He slipped his arm around her playfully but Eloise shook it off.

'There was no offer involved. You made it perfectly plain that I was to accompany you, and that there was no alternative.'

She pursed her lips in a thin, resolute line but De Sable tweaked her ear, still laughing. 'Your trouble is, you can't take a joke!'

'No, indeed. And I doubt if the King's men can, either.'

At once De Sable looked troubled, and stopped touching her. They had nearly reached the stable block before he could regain some of his cheerfulness and turn on his most winning smile.

'Come on, Eloise. Can't we be friends? Forget all this wretched business and agree to disagree?'

'The country is threatened by an uprising. You want to see the man who is the root cause of all my country's troubles set on the throne here, and expect me to ignore such a little inconvenience?'

His look of puzzled exasperation was almost the undoing of Eloise. When De Sable looked like that, all other things faded away. It needed all of Eloise's resolve to harden her heart.

'No, my lord. At the first opportunity I shall denounce you as the traitor you undoubtedly are.'

That gave De Sable pause for thought. As Eloise entered the dark of the stable he hesitated outside. Lady Melisande soon bustled out to see where he was, and dragged him inside by the hand.

'Come and talk some sense into old Joseph, Richard. He says he won't let me take Jack out to play.' Melisande

looked at De Sable with liquid brown eyes. Here was a
child who had never grown up, and had been allowed
anything and everything she wanted.

The falconer, old Joseph, was adamant. As Eloise had
suspected, he knew very well that the bird had flown
already that morning. He didn't take kindly to it and
was determined that the Lady Melisande should not get
the better of him.

She pouted and tugged at De Sable's arm, but her
pleas were in vain. Both he and the falconer knew birds
too well. They were not toys to be paraded by the un-
caring. Joseph pointed out that appeals to her husband
would meet with the same result, and Eloise breathed a
sigh of relief for the young, ill-used falcon.

Finally, Melisande saw that she could not win. With
a last stamp of her small foot, she scowled at Joseph
and called for the horses to be taken out. Turning on
her heel, she swept out, ignoring both De Sable and
Eloise.

De Sable and Eloise both had more sense than to an-
tagonise their hostess further. There was an awful silence
as all three mounted their horses and started off out of
the castle yard.

At last De Sable rode up alongside Lady Melisande
and risked a comment about the weather. She snorted
dismissively.

'Perfect flying weather for Jack. I bet that even now
Joseph's taken him out somewhere. I'll show that
peasant. I'll get even with him.'

De Sable looked back at Eloise, who was hanging
behind on purpose. 'Servants! Who would bother with
them, that's what I say.'

In a flash Lady Melisande lost her ill temper and took
on an air of coy delight. 'Oh, Richard, you say the
funniest things!'

'He keeps us all in fits,' Eloise added with sarcasm.
When De Sable turned round in his saddle to give her

a quizzical stare, Eloise poked out the tip of her tongue at him.

Despite the fact that De Sable urged her to ride alongside Melisande instead of a few yards behind, Eloise continued to follow in their wake. She felt no inclination to disturb their cosy pairing when they were getting on so well together.

Eloise made the best of the ride, although that wasn't hard. The weather was beautiful, bright but not too hot. The greenwood had not yet taken on the parched, dusty look of late summer and the grassy lanes were cool and shady beneath the trees. Melisande pointed out where her husband and the men had killed an enormous dog-wolf. Even though it had happened many years before her time, she said, the thought still made her shiver. Eloise noticed that the lady drew a little closer to De Sable as she spoke.

The grassy track sloped down gently for a mile or so until suddenly the wood opened out and they were in a small, treeless valley. A stream trickled along the valley bottom, a lush succulence of the last kingcups and flag irises the only greenery in a wasteland of snagged tree stumps.

'Eddie makes them get our firewood from down here, so that it doesn't spoil our view from the castle. It's a good job they're well away from the house—all the noise and the bonfires they make.'

Eloise couldn't help wondering what Melisande's servants thought as they dragged her firewood uphill for a mile.

They halted at the edge of the stream. For a moment all was peace, and Eloise could enjoy the silvery cadences of a bird hidden in the forest edge. Nature had as much charm for Melisande as it seemed to hold for De Sable, and it did not take her long to start chattering again.

'I do so love flowers. Especially in the hall. Why don't you pick some for me, Eloise? A nice big armful.' A curl of wheaten hair escaped from beneath Melisande's veil and she squinted up charmingly at De Sable as it blew into her eyes. 'Richard and I can sit in the shade and busy ourselves with grown-ups' talk,' she finished, leaving Eloise with no room for argument. She knew when she was not wanted.

Eloise walked a little way upstream, wondering how best to waste time. There would be no point in picking the flowers yet. They would wilt quickly enough in the warmth, without having to wait for the happy couple to finish their 'grown-ups' talk'.

The valley bottom was a real sun-trap, the murmur of bees about the waterside plants very soothing. Across the stream a little chalky track squiggled away out of sight behind the shoulder of a small hillock. Had the heavy formality of Alisaun's dress not weighed Eloise down in the heat, she would have liked to have explored. As it was, she sat down in the thin shade of a pollarded willow and lay back.

She did not sleep. The sound of bees and remnants of birdsong delighted her too much. Eloise could have stayed there all day, humming snatches of the songs that she was developing or drifting amid her thoughts.

There was no urgency to get back to De Sable and Madame Artois. When Eloise judged a quarter of an hour had passed she stood up and shook the grass seeds from her gown, ready to pick the lady's flowers as instructed.

Eloise found little pleasure in picking the flowers. She knew that they would have a much longer life where they were, and most would be dead before they reached the castle. Nevertheless, orders were orders. She took care to pick as few flowers as possible, making up the bunch with sprays of pale green, almost translucent beech leaves. That was when she heard the scream.

Immediately Eloise started to run towards the sound. After only a few yards and time to think she hesitated.

Did she really want to see what was going on? If De Sable had decided to play rough there would be nothing that she could do about it.

Despite her misgivings, Eloise went on. When she was almost in sight of the place she crept into the greenwood, and made her way quietly through the undergrowth.

They were standing in a small glade, a few yards from the main track. The Lady Melisande was whimpering, but De Sable was unimpressed. He was shaking Melisande by the elbows. His face was like thunder, cold lightning flickering from his blue eyes.

'Stop it! Unless you want another slap!'

Melisande crumpled against him, but he thrust her away roughly. She wilted to the floor in a heap of fine linen, tiny sobs trickling into the peace and quiet.

'But Richard... I want you...'

De Sable turned his back in disgust. 'What about your husband?'

'Eddie? He doesn't mind. Honestly.' Her sobs stopped suddenly as she brightened. 'He likes me to have friends. That's why we have so many people to stay.'

'Kind host he may be, but my gratitude doesn't extend in that direction, lady.' De Sable snorted, and stalked off towards his horse. Quick as a flash Eloise slid through the undergrowth and reached the stream-side again before he rode into view.

'Come on. We're going.'

'Oh, I haven't finished picking the flowers——'

'Leave that. It's time we got back.'

Plainly, he was in no mood to be crossed. His jaw had the firm determination that Eloise had learned to be wary of, and he pulled on his gloves savagely. Without a word, Eloise picked up her skirts and walked to her horse with careful dignity. He might have frightened Melisande into tears, but he would never intimidate Eloise.

Melisande accepted the small bunch of greenery and flowers that Eloise had been able to snatch up, and with a sarcastic sneer took up a position beside Eloise for the journey home. De Sable was most definitely out of favour. He had to ride behind, and there were no more loving glances or little giggles for him from the Lady Melisande.

Eloise would have been happier if the ride back had been completed in silence. The artificial conversation that Melisande tried to engage her in was even more embarrassing than unspoken tension would have been.

Every comment had some barbed message for De Sable and his rejection of her. All along the steep, winding lane that led back towards the castle, Melisande related tales of the fine young men that they had entertained in the past. All of them had been so charming, so grateful. She asked Eloise if ingratitude ought not to be regarded as the greatest sin, and cast a crafty look at De Sable over her shoulder.

Melisande confessed to Eloise that she enjoyed the company of the most handsome of the young men that her husband entertained, but then she went too far.

Turning eyes as limpid as forest pools to Eloise, she idly pushed a strand of hair back beneath her veil and said, 'Life is so much more interesting when a girl has the freedom to take lovers. My first husband was such an old stick-in-the-mud. Mummy and Daddy soon bought my way out of that one, thank goodness! Isn't it a good job that Eddie is so much more reasonable?'

Eloise did not even try to reply. She knew that no words would have come, leaving her opening and closing her mouth like a carp in a stew pond. Fortunately Melisande did not seem to require replies to keep her talking.

'Oh, just wait until you're safely married off, Eloise. That's when the real fun begins.'

She reached across and patted Eloise's arm. For her part Eloise blushed furiously and turned her head away.

When they arrived back at the castle Edward Artois was waiting. He looked relieved, but after a veiled threat from Melisande De Sable merely fumed wordlessly. It was plain that his fury was never far from the surface.

'Good to see you back so soon, my lord Richard. I trust that your expedition was a pleasant one?'

'Indeed.' De Sable accepted a goblet of wine as he stood at the fire, flanked by Eloise and Melisande. 'I wondered at the wisdom of letting a party of only three travel about the countryside, but now I see that your fair lands are free from all but the most pleasant diversions.'

Artois looked away and nipped at his lip thoughtfully.

'Ah, yes,' he said at last. 'No wolves, no brigands...although rumour has it that there are ruffians of a type roaming the country.'

'Oh?' De Sable said innocently, smoothing a little dust from his breeches. 'What type is that?'

Artois laughed self-mockingly. 'Oh, I don't rightly know...out here in the sticks, the gossip gets a trifle garbled. Some nonsense going about in Gloucester that— oh, what's his name—the King's brother...'

'Robert of Normandy,' Melisande sighed, her eyes quite dewy at the thought of the Duke's reputation.

'That's the chap. Evidently he's heading back here from Crusade, reckoning to invade and make himself King of England. Some say spies and traitors have already landed. Hmm. I don't know...' He chuckled softly and Eloise shot De Sable a knowing glance.

'Perhaps England is ready for a change,' De Sable said casually. 'Who knows?'

The kitchen staff started to arrive in a bustling rattle of pots and pans. If Edward Artois answered De Sable's question, Eloise did not hear.

Dinner was pleasant, made all the more enjoyable for Eloise by the sight of De Sable trying to fend off the Lady Melisande's secret caresses beneath the table, while

he was trying to converse politely with her husband.
Before the final course he dealt a particularly fierce
rebuff, and it was all Eloise could do to continue in her
own conversation with the Artoises' other guests.

Melisande made an excuse and went to lie down,
missing the remainder of the meal. De Sable suddenly
found the full range of his charm and eloquence again,
soon having the audience enraptured with his tales of
the Crusade.

Eloise watched him, realising that it was all a
performance to win their confidence. When he had them
where he wanted them, that was the moment to turn
them towards the Duke's cause. She might loathe everything that Robert of Normandy stood for, but there had
to be a sneaking regard for De Sable's technique.

He began with how the Princes of the West had massed
their hordes at the Pope's call to arms. Names that had
already grown into legend: Raymond, the mighty
Bohemond and his nephew Tancred, gentle Godfrey de
Bouillon and Robert of Normandy, the knight that no
one, Christian or Infidel, could unhorse.

Several of the dinner guests became restless at the
mention of the Duke's name. The rumour had not only
reached the ears of Artois. De Sable continued without
pause, but now his tales were of Raymond's tantrums,
redeemed when he returned just in time to save his companions from death at Dorylaeum, and Tancred's unfortunate mistake at the Al Aqsa mosque. The diners
were soon laughing heartily at the thought of a good
old-fashioned massacre. Only then did De Sable tell the
story of how Duke Robert had refused to accept the post
of King of Jerusalem, even though miraculous signs had
shown that he was the candidate endorsed by heaven.

Eloise felt certain that De Sable must surely commit
himself now. Instead he began to describe how oranges,
the most exotic fruit imaginable, grew on every roadside.
The fruits were so common that even an army marching

under the hot Mediterranean sun could find enough to quench their thirst.

Finally, he sat back and took a long draught of wine. Despite eager requests for more stories he waved them away indulgently, promising more excitements over supper that evening. The more Eloise saw, the more she had to admit a grudging regard for De Sable. He had left the audience eager for more, and looking forward to that evening's entertainment. It was a trick that ensured that he did not outstay his welcome, or alert people to his motives.

Artois had a quiet word with his honoured guest, then thanked him publicly for such an entertaining diversion. As the dinner guests straggled off, De Sable broke away from the knot of his admirers and approached Eloise.

'My lord Edward heard about the Lady Melisande's disagreement with the falconer this morning. He wants to make it up to her. We are to accompany them on a hunt this afternoon.' He straightened his tunic, then stopped and looked at her intently. 'What's the matter, little nightingale? Don't look so downcast!'

He lifted her chin with his finger, but Eloise was not beguiled by the soft light in his eyes.

'Even if I did not despise being forced to keep company with you, my lord, I should be shamed that I have no other decent clothes to change into.'

De Sable laughed and ran one hand through the honey gold of his hair. 'Is that all? Deus, I thought it was something really important! I'll have to learn to live with being despised, and as for clothes—well, I can't see what's wrong with what you've got on.'

At her cry of dismay he continued quickly, 'All right! If it matters that much, I dare say that the Lady Melisande could find you something——'

Eloise rounded on him, but kept her voice low in the busy hall. 'Doubtless the lady is generous. With some things,' she added sharply, but he did not rise to the bait. 'But I cannot see how she can be expected to provide clothes for—for a gentleman's sister!'

De Sable retreated. He was still laughing, but now there was a more self-conscious air in his amusement. Eloise had hit a raw nerve with her reference to his deception.

'I see. Well, if this means that you would really rather not go, I am sure that you can take the Lady Melisande's place on a bed of pain. I'm sure she'll be only too eager to keep me amused in your absence. I can make some excuse for you. Come, while I change for the hunt, you can tell her of the arrangements.'

Needing no further bidding, Eloise strode off to the ladder and went quickly to the upper floor. She knocked on the wall beside the tapestry curtaining that served as a door to the Artois bedchamber, but there was no reply. Eloise was half conscious of De Sable arriving at the entrance of his room, but was more interested in listening for Melisande's reply.

She turned back one edge of the tapestry for a peep, but the bed inside was empty. At that exact moment there was a harsh exclamation from De Sable next door and the unmistakable sound of the Lady Melisande's giggle.

Things were getting beyond a joke. Why did women have to play the fool for him? Eloise wondered. De Sable emerged from his room, and Eloise had to laugh at the expression on his face.

'You look as though you have dropped a coin and found a button, my lord!'

'Quiet! Go and find Edgar. This is ridiculous,' he said, half to himself. 'We can't stay here. It is a madhouse.'

'I'll go for Edgar,' Eloise said, then added matter-of-factly, 'I expect he's had lots of experience in throwing young ladies out of your room.'

De Sable caught her quickly by the arm as she skipped past. 'No. No, forget Edgar. He'll only think the worst of me, even if he says nothing. You go in and speak reason to her.'

'Me? Why don't you? You were the one that was happy enough to flirt and encourage her when it was on your terms——'

De Sable was horrified. 'But she's not just in there—she's in the bed...with no clothes on...'

'Don't make me laugh. After what Bessie and Edgar have told me about you, there's no point in playing the innocent. Come on.'

Eloise ripped back the curtain and confronted the pink and giggling Melisande. 'Ah, my lady. I think you had better be quick if you are to join your husband in the hunt. With luck, you might even have persuaded him to make Joseph let you have Jack.'

A spasm of pain crossed Melisande's face, but it soon changed to a hard glare. 'There is no Jack any more.'

'What?' Eloise was puzzled, unable to make sense of the words.

'He was no fun. Now he's dead and Joseph will get the blame.' A faint light of pleasure began to filter through her features.

'Dead? Why?'

'Because he didn't do what I told him to.'

There was a coldness in her voice that Eloise hoped De Sable could hear outside. Like him, the Lady Melisande was not one to be crossed lightly.

'Never mind, Lady Melisande. I dare say your husband will provide you with another bird, or two or however many it takes to keep you happy. Now, I'm afraid I have rather a bad headache. As hostess I'm sure you won't begrudge me a quiet lie-down here while you go off to enjoy yourself with Richard and the hunt.'

This was truly madness. Far from denouncing De Sable, Eloise found herself getting him out of a jam of his own making. Why? She didn't know. Eloise watched

Melisande slide under the tapestry partition between the two rooms. All she did know was that Lady Artois might well be determined enough to wreak a revenge of her own on De Sable, without any help at all from Eloise.

CHAPTER SEVEN

ELOISE did not waste her time while De Sable was away. She changed into a work-dress, then found Bessie to beg anything that might be made into a new, formal dress.

De Sable's travelling lifestyle meant that there was no room for non-essentials in the baggage. The only thing that was anything like suitable was a pair of heavy linen curtains, which were kept in case private arrangements for the master were unavailable. They were of a coarse, dun-coloured slub, dull and plain, but never used. Bessie was reluctant about the whole venture, but Eloise reasoned that what De Sable had never used he would never miss.

One of the curtains would not provide sufficient material for a dress, and that was all Bessie would let be sacrificed. Eloise was undaunted, and by removing the side panels of Alisaun's hunting gown and adapting them found just enough spare material.

While Bessie cut out the pattern of a plain, round-necked dress from the curtain, Eloise stitched the hunting gown back together. Removal of the spare material would make it a better fit, but what De Sable would say if he found out that his goods had been used to make a dress Eloise was not keen to find out. Bessie was dubious of the whole affair. Passing a servant off as his sister—no good would come of it. He'd soon show his true colours towards Eloise, Bessie said, and added darkly, 'If he isn't doing it already.'

After the pleasant morning and early afternoon, cloud began to blow up from the west before dusk. The party returned, hot and tired, just as the dull rumblings of a thunderstorm began murmuring in the distance.

Eloise had only that moment finished the last seam of the reshaped hunting gown when De Sable came up to the room.

'There's some entertainment required. I told them that you would play.'

Eloise shook out the hunting gown and pursed her lips. 'It would have been nice to have been asked first.'

'It is what I pay you for,' he said curtly, and turned to go. 'I shall expect you in the hall in five minutes.'

'Yes, brother dear,' Eloise called after him, much to Bessie's delight.

What he had said was perfectly true, whatever Eloise might think privately. De Sable paid her tuppence a week more than she had received at Gilbert's. There her soft heart had cost her dear—everyone had gone to Eloise when they had been short of cash, and she could refuse no one a loan. The fact that the money had so rarely been repaid had not mattered to Eloise.

Bessie and Edgar were as careful with money as Eloise was, and there had been no calls on her wages. Eloise had been hoping that by forgetting the tuppence pay rise and managing on her old amount she would be able to put a little by in readiness for launching her solo career. When De Sable spoke to her in his current tone of voice, Eloise wondered whether she would be able to stand him long enough to save any money at all.

Eloise changed into the hunting gown and went out. A low murmur of appreciation greeted her, and several people asked whether she had recovered. De Sable had told them all the same story—how his poor little sister was sick at home. Their concerns seemed genuine enough, however, and Eloise answered them all gladly.

She ran through a popular medley of songs, interspersing one or two compositions of her own. These were all well received, but Eloise was uneasy. As she paused to accept a refreshing drink from one of the company, she realised why. Apparently unnoticed by the company, a group of Artois' men had slipped into the hall and now stood quietly at the back. They were ranged behind Artois and De Sable, who were deep in conversation. Eloise didn't like it. The soldiers looked too well armed to be music-lovers.

She concentrated on her drink as Artois looked up at her. 'Another song? If my lady is refreshed?' Artois spoke kindly, clapping his thin pale hands together.

De Sable grinned at her and gave a wink. Eloise ignored him and pretending to be absorbed in tuning her psaltery, waited for a request. Artois offered De Sable the choice but he declined, so Artois cleared his throat. There was a short pause and Eloise looked up. The soldiers had moved in closer, and now stood only feet away from De Sable. He did not seem to have noticed them, and appeared more interested in studying the Lady Melisande. She had ceased her pursuit of him and now merely smirked at her husband like a cat in a dairy.

At once Eloise understood. De Sable wasn't stupid enough to have exposed his true motives to the Lady Melisande. More likely she herself had seen a way to get even with De Sable. Furious at his continued refusals, she was evil enough to point the finger of accusation at De Sable. A few stray ideas must have been planted in her husband's mind, which was already primed with worries about Duke Robert's spies. All De Sable had to do now was walk into the trap that must have been set for him.

Artois made his choice of song. 'How about "Weeps Still the Green Willow?"'

'Er...' Eloise continued to work upon the psaltery, playing for time. In a few seconds she could be free of De Sable for ever. A sudden thought struck her—she was recognised as his sister. They must both be implicated in the plot! If she denounced him now, she too

would be arrested and tried. 'It is the sultry weather, my
lord. It affects the strings——'

Her mind moved like the lightning that flickered
through the purplish sky outside.

'It is a long time since we were back home in Brittany,
my lord, but I think I can remember the song that you
request.' Eloise gave De Sable a piercing stare, but he
paid no attention. She began to sing.

> Weeps still the green willow in coppice and lea?
>   Sighs still the salt breeze as it comes from the
> sea?
> Do cliffs still resound to the cry of the birds?
>   Oh, homeland, my homeland is dear beyond
> words.
> Tall poplars stand guard at the sweet meadow
> edge
>   While little birds flute from the copse and the
> sedge.
> Through pastures and byways my mind wanders
> free,
>   In groves of green willow my heart waits for
> me.

After several more verses of similarly dull stuff,
cobbled together as she went, Eloise finished the song
with a flourish. She smiled sweetly up at Edward Artois.
He looked genuinely delighted and led the applause.
Feeling sufficiently confident to add a little comment of
her own, Eloise did so despite the intensity of De Sable's
stare.

'Thank you, my lord, and everybody. It is an old song,
not much sung in our country nowadays. I fear that the
hateful Normans have taken to using it for their own
foul purposes,' she finished, with relish. Artois smiled
all the wider. Outside the thunder rolled nearer, and
several of the ladies looked about apprehensively for
male protection.

'Bessie hates storms. She will be hiding under the bed again. Perhaps you had better run along and comfort her, Eloise,' De Sable said softly, leaning back in his seat.

'Of course.' Artois drew his wife to him and she snuggled into his embrace with a little too much eagerness. Eloise stood up, curtsyed to her audience and went as quickly as she dared. As she swept past De Sable, he caught her by the arm and said quietly,

'Be sure to stay with her until I come.'

He was a little slow in loosing her hand, and in the end Eloise pulled away from his grasp. As she did so she caught a glimpse of the look in his cornflower-blue eyes. Had she not known of his reputation, Eloise would have imagined that it was all for her.

It was some time before De Sable returned to his room. Eloise sat with Bessie, who jumped like a frog with every clap of thunder. Only when the rain came, sluicing across the roof above them, did Bessie relax. At least if a bolt of lightning hit the settlement now, heavy rain would douse any fire that resulted.

When the pause between thunderclaps became greater, and the intensity of the storm decreased, they heard De Sable's light footsteps on the ladder outside.

He entered the small, stuffy room, already stripping off his sword and belt. 'Arrange a bath for me, Bessie. I can't go in to supper like this.'

He stripped off his tunic and ran his hand wearily through his hair. As soon as Bessie had left, however, his manner brightened considerably.

'Who's a clever girl, then?' He hesitated, then went to Eloise. 'Changing the words so quickly. Thinking on your feet. That's what I call real initiative, and it ought to be properly rewarded.'

Before she knew what was happening, Eloise was pulled into a fierce embrace, all protests stopped by his mouth pressed urgently to hers. Feeling not only the strength of his desire, but also strange unspoken feelings stirring within her, once more Eloise panicked and struggled to free herself.

The more she squirmed the more his urgency increased, until he freed her mouth to taste the delights of her throat and neck.

'Take your hands off me! At once!'

With a ferocity of determination equal to his own, Eloise tried to thrust him away. De Sable stopped, then laughed and released her.

'After the little nightingale rescued me, she refuses the reward? Now, that is hardly fair!'

Eloise scowled at him. 'I did it to save my own skin, not yours.'

'I was ready for you to give the word to Artois and his men. Why didn't you?'

'Because, as your "sister", I could hardly be seen as wholly innocent, could I?'

'I hadn't thought of that,' De Sable said, with a false air of innocence.

Eloise looked at him, the merry light in his blue eyes and the firm, handsome mouth that had so recently been pressed against hers.

His shirt had fallen open in the struggle and Eloise watched him lace it up methodically again. Seeing her expression, he stopped and spread the neck of his shirt wide, laughing.

'Ah, do you see something that you like, Eloise? It is all there, for the asking!'

She turned away, both embarrassed and ashamed. 'I suppose that we will be leaving straight away, my lord?'

'What? While we still have a comfortable billet and before I have thanked you properly? Oh, no. We'll stay tonight, and move on tomorrow. There's plenty more time for fun before then.'

Eloise watched him scoop up a clean towel from the pile and go off in search of his bath. De Sable was a most unpredictable character, that was for sure. He seemed reluctant to force his attentions upon her in the presence of Bessie and Edgar, yet he knew that he could rely on them to turn a blind eye on his indiscretions. Instead he always waited until he could get Eloise cornered, on her own. She wondered whether inflicting fear was the only way that he could add excitement to his life. Having tired of a degenerate lifestyle, he might be in search of more subtle pleasures. She felt suddenly warm at the memory of his hands and lips upon her, but immediately stifled the feeling. He was the enemy, after all.

The rest of the day passed off without incident, but Eloise was conscious that the Lady Melisande might still be up to something. She no longer pestered De Sable, but clung closely to her husband. Although she pretended to hang on his every word, Eloise could see that the Lady Melisande's mind was elsewhere. Was it running on ahead for other tricks? Eloise wondered.

The weather did not improve overnight and by morning the rain was as heavy as it was persistent. Eager to be away, De Sable and his party spent the morning ready and waiting in the hall. Eloise and Bessie put the finishing touches to the new dress, while De Sable would occasionally leap up and stride to the open door, looking for a break in the sullen rain clouds. On one occasion he did look queryingly at the material in the new dress, but made no comment.

Their departure was delayed until early afternoon. Eloise watched De Sable, but throughout the long wait he showed no sign of the nervousness that she felt. He displayed only the typical irritability of one trapped by the English weather.

At last they were on their way. Eloise wondered if Bessie and Edgar were as relieved to be making their escape as she was. Neither of them seemed at all worried, and nor did De Sable. Perhaps this sort of tension had

become altogether too common for them to spend time
worrying about it.

The track from the castle was thick with mud, and
they made slow progress. Heavy with belongings, the
cart made deep ruts through the sludge, the oxen sinking
almost to their knees with every step. In two hours they
had covered barely half the distance that might have been
expected.

The sky cleared, sunshine pushing back the drab
greyness, and steam started to rise in the sudden heat.
Wisps of it came from the oxen and the smell of hot,
wet livestock was thick enough to cut with a knife.

The afternoon was turning out to be very hot and,
after a few more damp, uncomfortable yards, De Sable
called a halt. They hauled the cart off the track and into
the shade of the overhanging trees, a bow-shot or so
from the road. Here, cold drops dripping from the leaves
after the rain provided refreshment and they all sat in
silence, grateful for the rest after such a toil on the road.

Suddenly De Sable looked round. From back down
the road that they had travelled came the sound of galloping hoofs. Several horses were coming towards them
fast—using the wide grass verges rather than the churned
track. It must be important. The verges were to be spared
wear and tear except in the most dire emergencies.

There was no mistaking the red square decorating the
knights that galloped full speed towards them. It was a
party of men from the Artois castle. Bessie stifled a cry,
but Eloise was too stunned to do anything. As the men
drew nearer she waited for Edgar and De Sable to draw
their swords, but neither moved. They merely stood
beside their horses and watched.

The leading horseman slithered to a halt in a shower
of grass. He nodded to De Sable, and when he spoke
his voice was more apologetic than threatening. 'The
Lady Melisande's missing some small item, my lord, and

seems to think that it might have found its way in among your belongings.'

'How very novel,' De Sable said drily.

'Not really, sir,' said the captain of the guard. 'You'd be amazed the number of times we get called out for exactly this sort of thing. Now, if you wouldn't mind...'

He waved his men forward and, as Eloise and Bessie watched helplessly, they began to search methodically through the cart, first removing each trunk and putting them down on the grass. When they tossed Eloise's sleeping-roll out, a small silvery object bounced on to the grass and lay glittering in the sunshine.

'Ah. The Lady Melisande's bangle, if I'm not much mistaken.' The captain dismounted and retrieved the chased silver bracelet. Eloise was horrified.

'It wasn't me! Honestly...I'd never do such a thing——'

The captain looked from Eloise to De Sable and back again. 'Oh, I know that, my lady. You're as innocent of this as the day is long. It's him.' He cocked his head towards De Sable, who was watching him keenly. 'The Lady Melisande can't bear to let any young man go without a token of her esteem. Isn't that right, sir?'

De Sable shrugged. 'And I thought that I must be the first to refuse her generous hospitality.'

The captain laughed and bid his men re-pack the cart. 'Afraid not, my lord. The first time she had us fooled and I'm afraid the gentleman suffered for our loyalty. Word soon gets around, though, and it didn't take us long to realise that it was the penalty for being a gentleman, as you might say, sir. I thought we'd cured her, coming back saying that the last search turned up nothing and putting whatever it was back in her trinket box, secret, like. But no. Seems like she's up to her old tricks again.'

'And you can't say anything to your master?'

The captain and his men laughed ruefully. 'No, my lord. The Lord Edward is nothing if not doting. The best we can do is stick together, and protect ourselves.' His attention was diverted to the restacking of the cart for an instant. 'Careful there, lad——'

It was too late. One of the men had cracked a trunk against the side of the cart. With a clattering slither, a panel in the base of the cart opened, casting a treasure-trove of money and valuables on to the grass. Eloise recognised some of the pieces that had been donated at the Lefèvres'.

There was a long, horrible silence. Finally De Sable said lightly, 'Looks as though you've struck lucky after all.'

The captain looked at De Sable long and searchingly, then got down from his horse and went to the pile of coins and jewellery. Eloise saw a glance pass between Edgar and De Sable, but neither moved nor spoke.

'Now this,' the captain said thoughtfully, 'is very interesting. Very interesting indeed...' He ran his fingers through the pile which chattered musically at his touch. 'There's been talk of funds being collected by travelling folk. Funds for an uprising.'

Eloise didn't think it was possible for so many people and so many animals to be so quiet. The captain stood up and went back to mount his horse.

'I'm afraid I'm going to escort you and your party back to the castle, my lord. You and this little hoard are going to be kept nice and safe until we get the answers to a few questions.'

'I wish you'd keep him under lock and key forever!' Eloise burst out suddenly, to Bessie's horror. 'Mother said you wouldn't manage to get me and the dowry to St Hélène. She said the task was beyond you——'

'Oh, shut up!' De Sable bit back savagely, and Eloise shrank into silence. 'If you hadn't been so wilful, you could have been married back at home, then I wouldn't have been trapped into bringing you all this way!'

'You? Trapped?' Eloise squeaked, bouncing back. 'I like that! It's the first time you've ever done anything poor Mother asked. And now all you do is moan, moan, moan...'

'Can you wonder the old lady couldn't marry her off? God help the convent she's headed for, that's all I say.'

Edgar murmured to the captain as Eloise continued to berate De Sable for his stupidity and ingratitude. At the mention of a convent, the captain moved his horse back a pace, but still regarded them all with suspicion.

'So you reckon this is all a gift to the convent, to make them take her on?' He pushed his leather cap back on his head, still not wholly convinced by the little performance.

De Sable rode up between Eloise and the captain, giving her a sharp flick on the arm with his riding crop as he did so. She bridled, still full of loathing and unspoken insults.

'Bide quiet, girl!' De Sable pulled a face of great suffering at the captain, then quickly unscrewed the silver tip of his crop. 'There we are—dear Mother's letter of introduction, complete with an item-by-item breakdown of the dowry.' He removed a furl of papers secreted in the hollow crop. Waving them casually beneath the captain's nose, he handed him just one of several sheets.

'All those bits refer to that?' The captain scanned the papers that De Sable offered with the nervous curiosity of an illiterate about to be found out.

'No,' De Sable said, looking wary. 'This is for the stuff that you haven't found. Yet.'

The captain cast his eye over the squiggles on the parchment before him, wondering what it all meant. Finally he sighed and handed the sheet back to De Sable.

'Don't suppose there's any chance of seeing the rest of it, my lord?' he muttered, asking rather than demanding.

'Oh, dear. Is that an order?' De Sable slipped reluctantly from his horse, but the captain stopped him, shamefaced.

'No—no need to trouble yourself, my lord. Not on our account. It's just that me and the lads don't get much chance to see this sort of money and things. I thought it might be something to tell the nippers...'

'Oh, no. Not just now. Walls have ears.' De Sable hopped on to his horse. 'You all look honest enough, but who's to say who might overhear when you're back at base, eh? Anybody with less than honest tendencies, I mean. Give me a few days to hand the money and the wench over before you tell your tales. I don't want to feel a robber's stick brought down on my head!'

Everyone laughed, except Eloise. She stared straight ahead, knowing that she had saved herself, but at the cost of betraying her family's memory. De Sable would get his come-uppance in the end. She would see to that.

Still laughing, the captain ordered his men back to the Artois castle. Only when they were out of sight did De Sable breathe a sigh of relief. Edgar and Bessie started chattering and laughing, congratulating Eloise on her performance. Seeing that she was ignoring them pointedly, De Sable held up his hand for silence.

'A change of plan. Another five minutes here, then we make a start directly for Bristol.'

Eloise gasped, startled out of her silence. 'You're going to get a ship back home from Bristol, aren't you? Well, you can leave me here. I'm not going back to Normandy, with you or anyone else.'

De Sable sighed, pushing his hair out of his eyes with a weary hand. 'Nobody's asking you to. Home for us is Brittany. And I shan't leave you here or anywhere else. We're all four together in this, now.'

Roughly he commanded Eloise and Bessie to get down and help Edgar collect the spilled valuables. Once the false panel in the cart was secured and the contents hidden again, the cart was heaved back on to the track. Progress was slow, but with every hour the track dried out and the mud receded. When dusk fell they pitched camp to the sound of wood owls and nightingales on every side.

It was a fine night, rain clouds now far away. Stars pricked the dark velvet of the sky, and despite the excitements of the day Eloise had to admit that sleeping in the open on nights such as this was pure pleasure.

De Sable was quieter than she had seen him before. He spoke little on the journey, said nothing over supper and retired to the edge of their woodland glade when the meal was done.

Bessie and Edgar muttered together as one collected the plates and the other got ready to turn in for the night. Eloise busied herself cleaning the plates with damp grass, but could not help overhearing what they said. They were both concerned for De Sable, that he was not himself. They were less interested in his personal welfare than their own, as he held the key to their safety. One false move by De Sable and they would all be faced with disaster.

With a sudden murmur they were silenced. De Sable had turned and was wandering slowly back to their little group. He crouched down beside the fire, but only spoke to wish Edgar goodnight as the servant went to his bed beneath the cart.

'It is your bedtime too, little nightingale. No songs tonight.' He stirred the fire into leaping life and fed it with dry brush. When Eloise did not move immediately he looked up, fixing her with a look that made her tremble and look quickly away. 'Go now. I wish to speak with Bessie.'

Eloise got to her feet, but as she reached the cart De Sable spoke again in the same sweet, low voice.

'I must thank you for saving me again. I suppose you will say that you were once more only acting in your own interests?'

'Of course,' Eloise said coldly. 'You may be sure that the authorities will be informed as soon as I can get to them without your interference.'

De Sable laughed quietly in the darkness. 'That is what I thought you would say. Is there no compassion in you, little nightingale?'

Eloise paused, watching the firelight flicker over his strong, handsome features in the same way that his lips had so recently flickered over her.

She had no reply. Ducking under the cart, she curled up on her mat and hoped for sleep.

The murmur of talking between De Sable and Bessie went on for a long time. Eloise heard the odd word, caught the odd whisper and wondered if they were talking about her. The next moment she was waking, remembering dreams of De Sable abandoning her in the depths of the forest, or leaving her to die in a boat cast adrift on the Channel.

She lay for a minute while the fears of the night receded. The owls were still calling, but a chill of early dawn was in the air. Looking out through the spokes of the cart wheel, Eloise could see that the fire had long since crumbled into ashes. Bessie was snoring quietly beside her, as usual.

Suddenly there was a rustle of movement from the river bank, thirty or forty yards distant. While still tensed with fright, Eloise recognised the tall, lean silhouette that emerged from the waterside trees. De Sable had been swimming. She heard him blowing through his teeth at the chill, and push the fire awake with hissing handfuls of kindling.

There was no movement from Bessie or Edgar, so Eloise judged that it was not officially time to get up. She lay listening to the sounds of De Sable coming to the cart, drying himself vigorously with a towel, then the rustlings and other small noises as he dressed.

There was a soft click, then the sound of liquid splashing into a pan. De Sable moved away, towards the now cheerful fire. Eloise watched him heating wine for a warm drink after his swim. What she could not have guessed at was what he would do next.

After taking a few sips from the pan, De Sable poured the rest into a mug and came towards the cart. Eloise quickly closed her eyes as he approached and feigned sleep.

She felt him kneel beside her, the other side of the cart wheel. Forcing herself to breathe deeply, she pretended to be asleep. After a moment he put out one hand and touched her shoulder lightly.

Eloise did not move straight away. She waited for him to touch her again, more uncertainly this time as though he had lost conviction. Only then did Eloise stir as though waking.

'My lord?'

'Ssh!' he whispered, keeping one hand on her shoulder. 'Come out. The sun is about to rise, and I have warmed wine.'

Eloise thought of her dreams, where De Sable had thought to rid himself of her. She snuggled down forcefully. 'No.'

He paused, even more uncertain. Eventually he spoke again. 'Why not?'

'Because I'm not stupid. I'm set to ruin you, so you mean to do away with me. What better place and time than now?'

'I ought to, that's for sure. Never has a woman plagued me as much as you have,' he snapped bitterly. There was a tense moment, then at last he said, 'But I shall always be grateful for your quick thinking over these past days. Even if it was always carried out for your own preservation.'

Eloise turned her back on him irritably, making plain her need for sleep. He was nothing if not persistent, and prodded her gently in the back.

'What?'

'Aren't you going to come out and see the sun rise, then? I'll warm up the wine again for you.'

'Don't bother, my lord.'

'Then you aren't coming out?'

'Alone with you? No.'

He paused again, and she heard him swill the wine around the mug and take a drink.

'You have this situation all wrong, Eloise. Don't imagine that all of us are savages, like the men you tangled with in Brionne. I want to make you understand—to see why the old order in England must be changed. We don't want bloodshed, only peace.'

He took another drink. Eloise saw the distant sky beginning to show streaks of lemon, peach and apricot, and smelled the soap and clean linen smell of De Sable. He was very close, and she could almost feel his wary uncertainty.

'Are you going to kill me?'

'Oh, no!' He said it with such fervency that Eloise immediately believed him, despite all earlier doubts. She was not unreasonable by nature, and, though trapped into the situation by allies of an enemy she despised, realised that both sides of the story ought to be heard.

'I shall come out only if you promise to put your sword safely in the cart.'

He muttered uncomfortably about risks in the countryside, but Eloise was adamant. Finally he agreed, then went to reheat the wine while Eloise pulled on her new dress, crouching beneath the cart.

When she arrived at the fireside, he poured the wine out again and handed her the warm mug. There was silence between them as she took a sip, only the soft reeling of a churn owl hidden among dead wood in the forest. Then at last De Sable started to speak.

CHAPTER EIGHT

'BESSIE suggested that it was high time I spoke to you. Properly.' He spoke quietly, uncertainly at first. Gradually his enthusiasm began to bubble over, suffusing his words and animating his gestures.

He explained how Duke Robert and his mighty force would sweep into Southampton, ready to dazzle the land with their promises of a new beginning under England's rightful King.

Duke Robert was adamant that there should be no unnecessary bloodshed. William Rufus was to be approached with honourable terms. Only if he put up resistance was there to be any attempt to fight. Robert was most eager that his brother should be spared undue distress.

Eloise was impressed that De Sable felt so strongly for his lord, but still felt that the cause was hopeless, and a waste of time and money. 'Life may be difficult here sometimes, but it is remarkably untroubled in comparison to how Normandy was when I and my family had to flee.'

'Things are different now.' De Sable threw aside the empty mug of wine and grasped her hands. 'Don't you see? Duke Robert had his faults then, letting bad councillors advise him. Now that he has spent four years away from the influence of the Lord of Montgomery and his like, the Duke has a much better grasp of things. With the Lady Sibyl to help him and trustworthy advisers, everything will be different—better. There will be unity between Normandy and England, and together, who knows what can be achieved?'

Eloise watched mares' tails of cloud slowly light up in shafts of sunlight. 'I agree that it seems a wonderful idea. In theory,' she said at last. The sun lit a patch of blue sky in the east, almost as intense as De Sable's eyes as he watched her. 'But what you are helping to arrange is anarchy, none the less. I had to flee for my very life from the regime of Duke Robert in Normandy. How can you guarantee—guarantee, not promise—that things will be any better if he comes to rule here? And what will happen to King William Rufus? He's not the sort to step down without a fight. This country has been good to me. The treatment I have received here must have something to do with the King's strong rule of law, just as much as the chaos in Normandy was the fault of Robert. I owe loyalty to the country that took me in.'

'The King will be well looked after, be assured of that, Eloise. Your loyalty is touching, but it is pointless. Honest men can achieve nothing in the England of William Rufus, but when the Lord Robert comes to rule...'

He paused, and in the half-light Eloise felt him let go of her hands. A turmoil of emotions rioted within her. If he made another approach, would she be able to resist as she knew that she had to? In her mind Eloise repeated the warning that Bessie had given her. De Sable was not safe with women. Especially not with the likes of her, a servant that could be cast aside at the first inconvenience.

She could not move. Even when his hand was laid upon her shoulder, feather-light. When his touch slid down her spine and encircled her waist Eloise knew that her will-power was ebbing. This time she would be unable to fight against the tide of desire that he unleashed in her. She had to get away before it was too late.

Longing for the touch of his skin upon hers, she already ached with the guilt that such pleasure would bring. As De Sable bent to kiss her, she summoned every fibre of her being and turned quickly away from him.

He had not held her fast this time, and escape was as simple as that turning away.

'Eloise? Don't go... not this time...' he said softly, but did not pursue her as she ran back to the cart.

Part of Eloise had wanted to stay with De Sable, only common sense forbidding it. Now that she had seen exactly how devoted he was to his cause, she respected rather than reviled that part of his conscience. De Sable was silent as they started the morning's trek, and Eloise knew that it was to do with her latest rebuff.

They stopped at a ford to let the beasts drink. Bessie dozed in the summer warmth, lulled by the hum of bees in sheets of wild thyme about the banks. Edgar went on ahead to see if there were any likely villages in sight. Eloise sat on the bank tugging at grass stems while De Sable stood at the edge of the shallows with his horse.

Eloise turned words and phrases about in her mind, but this time they were not for a new song. There was something troubling her, and now seemed as good a time as any. The task would be more unpleasant the longer she delayed. At last she stood up and cast the grass stems aside. De Sable showed signs of hearing her approach, but moved away rather than turning to her. She went to his horse and made a great fuss of it before saying rapidly, 'I am sorry, my lord. I should not have accepted your offer this morning. It is something that every girl learns at her mother's knee—all men are weak in the face of temptation. I should not have tantalised you——'

De Sable, too, spoke quickly as if he had been preparing a speech also. 'The fault was entirely mine. I have been uncouth and unfeeling, and it will not happen again,' he finished roughly, concentrating on some distant point on the far bank.

'I——' Eloise began tentatively. When she did not continue he transferred his attention to her, watching her embarrassment with a guarded curiosity.

'I wonder—if we might not be some sort of friend to each other, my lord. We cannot agree upon certain things, but to be honest I cannot really bear to think of myself informing upon you, and that is the truth.'

She looked up at him shyly from beneath her lashes and saw him frown.

'Then you don't hate me quite as much as I imagined?'

'I do not hate you at all, my lord.'

A slow smile spread across his face and Eloise felt the warmth rise to her cheeks. It would not do to encourage him overmuch.

'That does not mean that I do not dislike your politics or your morals,' she said, with a stiff dignity that belied her true feelings.

'I think that I can probably live with that,' he said quietly, and, easing his horse round, swung himself into the saddle. 'We must talk about your future, then.' He frolicked his horse out of the water and up on to the bank beside the cart. 'But not today.' He tapped Bessie on the shoulder, startling her from sleep, and went off in search of Edgar.

Eloise was not impressed. De Sable might have lost his air of glum depression, but he had started talking to her as though she were a child. There was no simple communicating with the man.

They reached the port of Bristol in the heat of the afternoon. Approaching it from downwind, they found that the smell of stale fish and brackish water greeted them a mile or so distant. So did the beggars. No sooner had the cart rolled into view than a whooping, tattered throng charged forward. When they reached the cart, their hands were everywhere until Bessie had to bring it to a halt while De Sable and Edgar shouldered the crowd away with their horses.

'Tuppence for the one who can provide me with the best lodging for my animals!' De Sable called, and at once the beggars charged on ahead to do his bidding.

As the little party worked its way along the river bank, the smell was almost solid enough to cut with a knife. Fouled by hundreds of inhabitants and their livestock, the water was green and sluggish. In one place a fallen tree had partly blocked such flow as there was. The remains of a cart and a dead cow had found a resting place there, wreathed in a cloud of flies.

They entered the town in the shadow of the castle building. Here a narrow dark lane between overhanging houses was choked with a log-jam of people, horses and carts.

Two dogs had taken a violent dislike to one another, and started an almighty scrap. What made matters worse was that each had been harnessed to wooden sleds packed with wine barrels coming up from the quay. Broken barrel spars and hoops littered the cobbled street, which was ankle-deep in wine. A huge crowd had gathered to watch cursing merchants try to twist the fighting dogs apart.

No traffic was moving, many people making matters worse by stopping to stare. Eloise was horrified by the filth and squalor of Bristol, and turned to say as much to Bessie. She saw a small hand come up from the crowd and reach for the purse at Bessie's waist. A sharp cry alerted the old woman, who brought the ox whip down smartly on the head of the hopeful cut-purse.

Eloise put her hand to the purse at her own waist and held it tight. There might not be much in it, but it was all that she had. She leaned forward and tugged at De Sable's tunic. He was busy laughing at the argument in progress.

'My lord—we shall lose everything if we do not move soon! The crowd is full of rascals!'

'Indeed? Then it would seem that I have come to the right place! I shall be quite at home here.' He responded to a beggar's tap on his thigh with a few words in English and a couple of coins. Backing his horse until he sat level with Eloise, he paused to explain.

'It seems that we cannot go much further in any case. Heavy traffic is banned from the centre for fear of damage to underground storage tunnels. A short cut up this side-alley will find us good lodgings, so I'm told.'

Eloise clutched her purse even tighter and looked up the side-turning. If the main thoroughfare was dark, the alley was worse. Reckless building had caused the shanties on either side of the cobbled track to lean in upon each other wearily. There was hardly a glimpse of sky to be seen between their touching roofs.

'Are you sure it's safe?'

De Sable moved closer to her, and for once she did not move away.

'As sure as I can be, little one. The ruffian gave me the name of an acquaintance whom I trust. It should be safe enough there.' He called to Edgar and together they guided the ox cart off the main thoroughfare and into the shadowy lane.

Eloise hated the journey. The air between the shanties was hot and stale. In every doorway lurked heaps of drunks and cripples who lunged out at the travellers, demanding money. Pigs and dogs scavenged through piles of waste that all but choked the open sewer running down the centre of the lane. A woman came out of one of the shanties and hurled a bucket of vegetable waste into the lane, then stopped to stare at them suspiciously. She watched them until they had turned a corner and emerged into a large, open square.

Here the houses were sturdier, and limewashed. There seemed to be at least an idea of civic pride. House-holders were out sweeping the dusty cobbles, or scrubbing down their house fronts.

De Sable took them towards a building on the far side of the square. While he went inside to arrange terms, Eloise and the others looked about them, relieved that their first experience of Bristol had not been typical. There were no pigs in the square, only dozens of cats. They lay in the sunshine or played about the buildings, and Eloise wondered how many mice it took to keep all those cats well fed.

'Don't you worry, miss. They're only a precaution.' A small, fat man had come out of the building with De Sable. 'Folk have heard tell as how mice bigger'n half-grown cats is coming in on the ships from foreign parts. Don't know if I believe it, meself, but it pays to be safer'n sorry!'

They all laughed and De Sable introduced the man as servant to a Breton merchant. He was in charge of the town house while his master was back at home in Brittany. De Sable's party would be made more than welcome, and could stay as long as they liked while the master was away.

Puffing and panting, the servant bent to unlock the great double doors that took up most of the front of the house. They opened to reveal a large, clean stable where the cart and oxen could be lodged. At the back there was a sturdy wooden staircase leading up to the living quarters. While Edgar saw to the animals, De Sable, Bessie and Eloise followed the servant upstairs.

The first floor was neat, clean and functional. A scrubbed oak table was surrounded with four expensive carved chairs, rather than the more usual wooden benches. Chairs were a rarity, and to see four together was a sure sign of great wealth. Another sign of prosperity were the windows. Here, simple holes in the wall had been covered with thin sheets of flattened horn. This let through a dim, milky light and would not let out heat in winter like a normal window. Eloise approved of the new arrangement and was shown how ventilation could be altered by opening and closing the horn screens at will.

The servant was delighted to have someone to show how good a housekeeper he was, and took them up to the top floor where the master slept. Eloise had assumed that they would all be sleeping in the stable downstairs, but the servant insisted that they make themselves completely at home.

'As long as the place isn't broke up, I'll see master finds it clean and tidy. No sense in staying in a place if you aren't going to make proper use of it, is there?'

He grinned at De Sable and Eloise in turn. For her part Eloise was too engrossed in what lay up a further staircase in the corner of the room. The servant urged her to go up, following on behind with Bessie and De Sable.

As they reached the top of the stairs they were conscious of a strong scent of roses and a pinkish glow from a bedchamber doorway. Entering the room, Eloise saw that curtains had been drawn over the windows. Forgetting her manners, she rushed forward to open them, but her sandals did not clatter across the wooden floorboards as normal. An enormous woollen tapestry had been laid on the floor, muffling all sound.

'I keep it dark so as not to fade the colours,' the servant said, amused at her wonderment. 'Go on, miss—open the windows, too. If you'll be sleeping in here tonight, it'll need a bit more airing.'

When light flooded in from the uncovered windows, Eloise was enchanted. The room was hung with tapestries similar to the one on the floor, all figured and embroidered in shades of pink and gold. Pottery dishes of dried rose petals stood on the window-sill, perfuming the air.

Instead of a straw mattress placed on the ground, the bed was a proper wooden one, like the one her parents had slept in at home. Curtains were hung around it from a rail set into the ceiling, and the bedding itself looked soft and sumptuous. No rough straw here, but feather-stuffed mattress and bolsters. Only the finest for a man of evident taste.

'I'll fetch you some water.' The servant bustled forward and took up two large water jugs from a table at the bedside. 'I take it you'll be off to the entertainments this evening, my lord.'

De Sable looked delighted. 'What's this? Fun and games?'

'Oh, indeed, my lord. Held up on the hills overlooking the town as a general rule. To get there, well, it's right across town from here and with this hot weather and having to cross the river...' He waved his hand across his nose descriptively. 'So now a lot of the quality goes out on to the plain, just the other side of the town wall from here. Masking, dancing, that sort of thing.'

He left in search of water. De Sable threw himself down on to the bed and bounced appreciatively once or twice.

'Well! Only in town for five minutes and already we're learning where the bright young things are. How's that for business?'

Bessie chuckled indulgently, but Eloise was troubled.

'You won't work here, surely? With so many people? It would be madness.'

'Whatever I do you would say was madness, little nightingale. I'm so used to sizing a place up that I do it automatically now. No, we'll all go out tonight and have some fun. I know how interested you are in my moral welfare.'

He winked at Eloise, but she was not amused even though Bessie laughed. Eloise was only too eager to go down and help unload the cart. While she and Bessie carried the trunks up to the top floor, the older woman provided yet more advice. They stopped at the first floor for Bessie to catch her breath and mop her brow. As Eloise sat on the top step, waiting for the order to continue, Bessie began.

'The young master's reckless, but he has a good heart, child. He's reckoning now that an end to his gallivanting's long overdue.' She caught her breath at last. 'Even so, he's been that wanton in the past I've my doubts as how he'll ever settle. But that's as maybe. You just be certain to take my advice. There is no certainty—outside o' marriage.' These last words were accompanied by a knowing touch to the side of her nose and a wise nod.

Eloise stood up and took a hold on the linen trunk again. It was comforting to know that Bessie was keeping an eye on her welfare, but she anticipated no further trouble from De Sable. They had sorted matters out quite amicably between them.

After washing away the dust of travel, De Sable strolled out to take a ride around the town. While Edgar cleaned and checked the saddlery, Bessie and Eloise spent their time preparing De Sable's clothes for the excursion that evening. Although the day outside was hot, a pleasant draught rippled through the top-floor room, and with the sound of house-martins beneath the eaves and pleasant conversation the afternoon soon went.

When De Sable returned he was in high good humour, and hurried them all along to get ready for the entertainments. Edgar was wary of leaving the cart unattended so would only spare an hour away, but Eloise and Bessie were more than ready for some diversion.

It was only a few hundred yards to the plain, so De Sable left his horse behind and walked with Bessie and Eloise. He pointed out the street of cheese-makers as they passed, each disreputable hut with a mangy cow and calf tied up outside. The broken barrels from the accident that they had seen still lay scattered in the street, but would soon be collected as firewood if nothing else.

As they joined a general flow of well-dressed riders out of the gates, Eloise studied the fashions carefully. She wore the dress that she and Bessie had put together, but that was sadly outdated here. The fashions were more in keeping with the things that she had seen in Alisaun's collection. Bright brocades and velvets, overdresses with pointed sleeves so long that they hung almost to hem-level.

Many people stared at De Sable, amazed at seeing a well-dressed, handsome young man reduced to walking like a serf. It was a well-known fact that anyone who was anyone rode on horseback. Walking any distance at all was for the poor and foolish.

'Know anything about horses, Eloise?' De Sable said lightly, waving to the curious riders as they passed. 'There's a horse fair up behind our lodgings. I've got some spare cash burning a hole in my pocket and thought you might like to come and help me choose one tomorrow.'

It was a reasonable request. Any common cut-purse might make off with cash, but a ruffian would think twice about walking past the local sheriff leading a quality animal. Eloise agreed, eager for a chance to be taken seriously.

The crowd spilled out on to a broad, grassy plain, grateful that the breeze was blowing the town and river smells away from them. Hucksters had already set up their stalls offering views of freaks to a gullible public. Bessie handed over a halfpenny to be taken into a tent housing a 'man eating fish'. She returned disappointed, telling not of some deep-sea horror, but of being shown a man sitting at a table, nibbling at a cod's head.

Eloise was more careful of her money, but was still intrigued by the signs for bearded ladies, mermaids and sea monkeys. She did not take thrift to extremes, however, buying sweet almond biscuits, a pot of honey with the comb still inside and four fresh, glistening trout. These came with the assurance that they had been caught well away from the foul town waters.

'Anybody watching will think I don't feed you. You'll be sick all night!' De Sable laughed, offering to carry her prizes. Eloise gave him a withering look.

'As if I'd eat all this! It's for all of us. It's about time we had a change from cold meat and rye bread for supper every night.'

As they wandered through the throngs of stalls and their audiences of the well-to-do, Eloise kept her eyes open for more treats. Seeing a barrow-man selling fruit, she slipped away and returned a few minutes later with a small basket of cherries. De Sable was talking to a stranger, and by the way Bessie was edging back from the newcomer he was to be regarded with suspicion.

Eloise went to stand beside Bessie, a respectful distance from De Sable. The stranger looked up at her arrival and grinned, showing teeth rotten and missing.

'That looks a bit of all right.' He nudged De Sable, who responded with pained resignation. 'What would you take for it?'

'Eloise is not for sale,' De Sable said tartly, but despite his tone the newcomer approached Eloise stealthily.

'Lend her to me, then. Only for a night or two...'

As he drew nearer, Eloise recoiled from the stench of long-unwashed body and nameless odours of decay.

'Roger, leave her alone, there's a good chap. She's mine and that's an end to it.'

Roger paused to push a lank lock of black hair out of his watery eyes, and peered at Eloise hungrily. 'Go on, Richard. I haven't had any fun in months.'

Years, more like, Eloise thought, horrified of spending even a second alone with the putrid, slug-like Roger.

'Belvas, I've told you once. Go away. I won't have you worrying my staff.' De Sable was determined now and took a quick step forward. At once Roger Belvas shrank away like a snail from salt, melting back into the mêlée of people about the stalls. De Sable continued to Eloise's side.

'I'm sorry about that. A nasty piece of work. Nobody takes any notice of him. He won't be at the reception.'

The words made no sense to Eloise, but she accepted them without question. Whatever reception it was would concern De Sable and not her.

They wandered around the pleasure ground, laughing at the maskers and their plays, performing dogs and the dancing bear that shuffled about sadly on its hind legs. Its owner beat a drum and the bear in equal measure. The animal moaned half-heartedly and tried to twirl faster, but, already giddy, dropped to all fours and suddenly charged to the extent of its heavy iron chain. With screams and yells all the paying customers scattered, even though the bear showed no signs of chasing them. It had thrown itself on to the floor, panting, small round eyes misting with exhaustion.

As the owner went to kick it upright again, Eloise rushed forward.

'Don't!'

The man stopped, amazed. Eloise continued, even though De Sable had moved in quickly behind her.

'The poor thing's exhausted. He's too old—look, he hasn't even got any teeth left...'

The bear had rolled on to its side and lay with mouth open, tongue lolling. In the warmth of the evening it smelled nearly as ripe as Roger Belvas had done, but Eloise reasoned that at least the bear couldn't help it.

'Come on, Eloise. Let's go home.'

'Not yet! Tell him he's not to ill-treat this poor animal. If he can't look after it properly, then he should find it a decent home.'

'Oh, he's going home, all right. I've had more'n enough of 'en. It's off up the castle for him now.'

The bear man had recovered his wits sufficiently to snarl at Eloise. Before she could work out what he had meant, De Sable had grasped her by the arm and was steering her masterfully back to the town gate.

'Does that mean——?'

'It's off to the home of rest for retired bears.'

'Don't patronise me!' She shook off his restraining hand but did not rush back to the bear as he had expected. 'I'm not a child. They'll bait it with dogs, and kill it that way.'

De Sable straightened his tunic and tightened his belt, not expecting the straight talking. 'Look, let's go home, enjoy our supper, and then tomorrow you've got the horse fair and the reception to look forward to. It's a shame about the bear, but it happens all the time...'

'What reception is this?' Eloise stopped and was immediately suspicious. If De Sable wanted to give a reception in the merchant's house, then that would mean a lot of work for her and Bessie.

'Oh, did I forget to mention?' De Sable said carelessly. 'There's a ship due in from Italy tomorrow. The town is holding a reception. Earlier this afternoon I met a man who invited us both.'

'Both? Who do you mean?'

'Why, you and me, of course. Who else?'

De Sable was astonished that she should have thought of anything else. Eloise was equally astonished that she should be invited to such an occasion.

'I haven't got anything to wear...' she wailed, looking at Bessie for support. The older woman merely laughed, but De Sable looked grave.

'Yes, indeed. We can't have you arriving at a formal dinner in a confection of old curtains, can we?'

Eloise blushed to discover that he had known full well where her new dress had come from. She stepped back in confusion, but De Sable was already making arrangements with Bessie.

'I haven't said I'll go yet,' Eloise risked in a small voice. De Sable laughed and ruffled her hair cheerfully.

'You'll come. And you'll love it.'

Eloise was not at all sure about that. Bessie was no support. She was more interested in warning Eloise not to show herself up in good company.

There was a mercer's stall within the town on their way home. With an expansive wave of his hand, De Sable instructed her to choose what she liked. Eloise was horrified. To pass her off as his sister had been sinister enough, but now to ply her with clothes when he knew she was too poor and threadbare to refuse was too much.

'I'm not going to stand and argue in the street,' he said mildly, as the stall-holder spread out the rich, colourful materials before them. 'You'll be grateful and choose, or go in the dress that you're wearing now. Either way, I have said that I will be accompanied by a young lady and it would be the height of ill manners for you to be absent.'

Eloise was cornered. She would never want to be seen as ungrateful, even by De Sable. She looked nervously at the materials, then at Bessie, and back at the materials. Every colour of the rainbow was represented, or as near as the dyer's art could obtain. After a long while, during which the mercer shook out bolt after bolt of material, Eloise twisted her fingers and looked up at the expectant De Sable.

'What will you be wearing, my lord?'

He threw back his head and laughed. 'Now you're wasting time!'

'No, my lord...I have a mind to choose the rose damascene, but if my lord wishes to wear his red tunic we might look a little odd together...'

'And that would never do! Have it, then. I'll bow to your choice, my lady. And what else?'

'More?'

'Take the whole lot if you like. Every last lace and furbelow. There's nothing I like better than spending money!'

After consultation with Bessie, Eloise took a dress length of damascene, the same of cream linen, five yards of serviceable cotton cloth, several hanks of thread and a fine gold hairnet set with tiny pink beads.

The final bill was eleven shillings and seven pence three quarters. Eloise was aghast—that was more than De Sable had paid for her! If that weren't enough, he handed over eleven and eight pence, then stopped the mercer nipping a quarter from one of the pennies to hand back as change.

'All that money...' she whispered faintly, but De Sable merely shrugged.

'I like spending money. Call it a hobby of mine. The only one that can be mentioned in decent company!'

He laughed, and, giving Eloise back the things she had bought earlier, took charge of the latest purchases. All the way back to the lodgings they were accompanied by the smell of fruit, honey, fresh fish, new materials and De Sable's humming. He was evidently very pleased with himself.

Eloise was becoming extremely suspicious of his motives.

CHAPTER NINE

SUPPER that evening was most refined. They all sat to the table and dined off fish poached in wine, almond cakes with honey and fresh cherries. De Sable sent out to the vintner for a bottle of good wine, so even Edgar was coaxed into having a change from ale.

When the meal was over and cleared away, Eloise and Bessie began work on the new outfit. Fine needlework would have to wait until the light of day, but together they could manage to make a start with cutting and tacking.

The well-scrubbed floor began to disappear under lengths of fabric, and wherever De Sable sat seemed to be under siege on all sides. He soon made an excuse and left.

'He'll only stay down in the stable with Edgar,' Bessie said, as though Eloise would be interested. 'He won't go out drinking now.'

Bessie and Eloise worked on with quick enthusiasm. When dusk fell they found fat, scented candles in a chest. Mindful of the great expense, they marked each candle an inch from the top and agreed to finish work when the wicks had burned down to that point.

Sleep did not come easily to Eloise that night. She lay on her mat beneath the window, seeing the faint dots of starlight spread by the sheet of horn. She wondered if De Sable would remember his offer to take her to the horse fair. If the dress would be ready in time, which hardly seemed possible given the amount of work still to be done.

She was still wondering if the reception would be spoiled by the weather when she closed her eyes for a minute, then awoke to find it suddenly morning.

Someone was crashing about downstairs, and Eloise heard the muffled tones of Bessie. It must be very late. She hated being last to use the washing-water.

Jumping up, Eloise went to the corner and washed quickly in cold, soapy water left in the basin. I must have slept soundly, Eloise thought, not to have heard De Sable's usual performance. The tapestry on the floor was damp and cold where he had splashed about. Eloise found that her bare feet were tinted pink with dye from the carpet, and she wondered why men couldn't use flannels.

De Sable had not forgotten his offer. He had breakfasted early, and Bessie had got up to make a start on the dress, so the hour was not as late as Eloise had feared. When the stable doors were opened the morning air was still cool and frail, dawn only then beginning to give it strengthening warmth.

Edgar led De Sable's horse out into the square, while De Sable pulled on his gloves and took the reins.

'Will you ride up in front or behind, Eloise?' he said, swinging into the saddle and settling himself carefully.

Eloise was dubious of giving De Sable any encouragement. 'How far is it?'

'Miles. Far too far for you to walk. Quickly! I want to have a good look around before the best animals are snapped up.'

She elected to sit behind him. Her reasoning was that, while she might have to hang on, that was a better prospect than being sat in front where De Sable would have the advantage.

Edgar cupped his hands to make a stirrup and De Sable put his right hand behind his back for her to grasp as she hopped up behind him. The horse side-stepped at the unusual sensation, but quickly settled at De Sable's touch. Edgar strapped De Sable's sword to the front of the saddle, where it would not inconvenience Eloise, and they were off.

'You aren't hanging on, Eloise.'

'I have my balance,' she said, knowing full well that balance alone was not enough.

'Very well. But this horse is a little nervous. He's inclined to——'

The horse skittered on the cobblestones and Eloise flung her arms around De Sable's waist in terror.

'You did that on purpose! You——'

'Ah, careful now, Eloise! Where's your proof?'

Clutching tightly at him, face pressed into his back, Eloise felt the bubbling of his concealed laughter. When the horse had settled, she let go of him and instead caught hold of his belt with both hands and hung on that way.

Her humour was not restored when she found he had lied about the distance. The horse fair was held barely a bow-shot from their lodgings, and would have been hardly five minutes' walk. Eloise determined to stay cross with him, but it was not to be.

His knowledge and love of horses was evident as he walked among the animals for sale. That alone made him a better person in Eloise's eyes.

After they had discussed the merits of half a dozen destriers, Eloise confessed herself a little overawed by their sheer size and strength.

'They have to carry the weight of a knight in armour, Eloise. That takes some doing. They need to be workmanlike, but are no more frightening than a lady's palfrey. Like this one, for instance.' He paused to caress the muzzle of a light chestnut mare. 'Perhaps she would be more to your liking, little nightingale.'

Eloise shook her head. 'Too flashy, my lord. Besides, days spent in the idle pleasure of riding are over for me.'

De Sable tapped her playfully. 'Oh, come on! It's me you're talking to, remember? I don't treat you so badly, do I?'

'No, my lord. A little too well, if anything.'

'Then stop playing the martyr. Use your imagination—which ones have taken your fancy?'

Eloise scanned the rows and rows of horses that they had both studied so carefully. All shapes and sizes, all ages and colours. There must have been hundreds of pounds' worth of quality horseflesh standing before Eloise, but her eyes kept drifting back to one non-descript little animal in particular.

'The close-coupled cob. Over there, by the monastery wall.'

'The little hogged grey? He'd be tormented by the flies with no mane to flick them away. You'd have to keep him inside all the time. What good is that?'

'You said I could use my imagination. Anyway, elder lotion would keep a lot of the flies away. And it wouldn't be a problem in winter. Only summer.'

De Sable began to stroll off, whistling, and Eloise went after him dutifully. He cast a casual glance over the lines of horses, stopping here and there to inspect one missed on their first circuit. Dealers appeared from nowhere when he began to run his hands over a horse or open its mouth. In every animal he found some fault—it was too old, too nervous or, more often than not, too expensive.

Within a few minutes they had reached the monastery wall and the stalls of saddlery and other equipment. Eloise was immediately drawn to a cart hung about with the trappings of falconry: bells and bewits of German silver, leatherwork in all sizes from tiny white and gold jesses for a merlin to great thick leather straps for the largest eagle. De Sable tapped her on the shoulder.

'I thought you came here to look at the horses!'

'If my lord has seen nothing that suits, then I was merely filling in time until you wish to leave.'

'In that case, why don't you go and say goodbye to your little grey friend over there? I doubt it will be more than a few minutes before some fool is persuaded to part with hard-won cash for him.'

Reluctantly, Eloise left the stall and wandered down the line of ponies and smaller horses. They were all appealing, mealy muzzles pushing at her hands and snuffling for treats. Typical of ladies' horses, Eloise thought, fed too many tit-bits and all fat as barrels.

The grey cob was different. He stood a little apart from the others in case the sweet-itch that he suffered from transferred itself to the more saleable animals. As Eloise approached him he moved forward, eager to use her as a scratching-post for the unbearable irritation about his head and neck.

Eloise pulled his ears and laughed as he tossed his head and lipped at her fingers, looking for sweetmeats.

'Aren't you lovely?' she said softly to him.

'Typical woman,' De Sable observed to the horse dealer that had appeared at his side. 'Never look to the practicalities, only the outward appearance.' He stepped forward and looked into the horse's mouth, shrugged, then bent to pick up one of the animal's feet. With a shake of his head he let it drop and ducked under the rope to look at a hind foot. Here the news was even worse. With a sharp intake of breath, he clicked his tongue in dismay.

'Never seen a worse case. Cat's meat,' he muttered to himself. The horse dealer began to shift nervously from foot to foot.

'He don't like travelling, sir, and that's the truth of it. Unsettles him, y'see...'

'A horse that doesn't travel? That's as bad as a hawk scared of heights!' De Sable laughed and turned to go, but the dealer caught at his arm.

'I mean he needs a rider, sir. He likes to be directed in what to do——'

'Aha! Stupid as well as being a chronic invalid?'

'No, no, sir, you're taking me all wrong,' the dealer wheedled. 'Let the lady take him up and down for a little test ride——'

'Oh, no,' Eloise said firmly. 'Leave me out of this. The horse is far too small for you, my lord, and I'm not getting dumped on my head for you to prove a point.'

'Staff these days!' De Sable threw up his hands in despair. 'Get that animal out here this immediate moment or you go back to the gutter, where I found you,' he threatened darkly, eyes narrowing.

'Yes, my lord.' Eloise had no choice but to do as she was told. De Sable was of such uncertain temperament that she trembled at the threat and did not wish to put him to the test.

The horse had no saddle, but stood patiently as Eloise vaulted on to his back. She was painfully aware of the people moving about through the horse lines, all of whom might shortly get a good laugh at her expense. With a mutinous scowl at De Sable, she walked the horse out to the centre of the horse fair where a long strip of beaten earth provided a clear trial-ground.

The fair was on a slight slope that ran down to the harbour several hundred yards away. Eloise started off in a walk, hoping that the animal wouldn't suddenly charge off and dump her in the water. It seemed responsive enough, but also quiet and obedient. Eloise risked putting the horse into a trot. With such a short back, the increase in speed gave it a choppy, bustling action. After a few painful bounces, Eloise got into the rhythm, and found it unusual, but fun for all that.

With the harbour getting closer every moment, Eloise tried the brakes with some trepidation. The horse slowed beautifully, fell back into a walk and stopped exactly when Eloise wanted. She was in love.

When Eloise asked the horse to turn it did so, bending neatly around her inside leg. She sighed, wondering if the horse's new owner would appreciate riding it as much as she had.

De Sable had called it 'cat's meat'. If only Eloise could discover some reason in the horse to make it less painful to lose.

'Perhaps you've got no speed. Move like a rheumatic snail, is that it?' She bent forward and pulled one of the soft grey ears that had swivelled at the sound of her voice. 'Come on, then—let's see what you can do, if anything.'

The horse went straight into a canter when asked, then into a full gallop with a smoothness that even Eloise had not expected. Although it could not cover much ground with each stride, the horse made up for that deficiency by twinkling its short legs with great speed. It made little of the rising ground, and within seconds Eloise was back where she had started. Once more the horse showed perfect manners when asked to stop, and followed Eloise meekly back to its position in the line when she'd dismounted.

'A daisy-cutter,' De Sable was saying dismissively. 'Apt to trip.'

Beside him the dealer was moving from foot to foot distractedly. 'Two pounds, then. But that's as low as I can afford to go. With a wife and fourteen nippers——'

'But at least I'd be taking one endless source of expense off your hands. One pound and ten shillings.'

Eloise looked at De Sable with wide-eyed astonishment. This was going too far. The dress had been one thing, but a horse as well? What would people think—De Sable spending such money on his servant? It was more than shocking—it was immoral!

De Sable looked at her sharply, then nudged the horse dealer. 'Come on. Sell that animal as fit to ride and I'll have the town sheriff down on you like a ton of bricks.

It's only fit for the stew pan. Let my staff eat well for
once in their wretched lives.'

Eloise didn't know whether to cry or heave a sigh of
relief. She knew that she could never bring herself to eat
a morsel of the beautiful, gentle horse, but on the other
hand the title of 'Kept Woman' would no longer be hov-
ering over her head.

Once the money had been handed over, De Sable was
only too eager to leave the horse fair. Eloise trailed along
behind him, leading the cob. The horse had none of her
misgivings and, when they were halted by a press of the
crowd in front, it would lean forward and nuzzle her
gently.

'We won't stop here for a saddle. I wouldn't want the
horse dealer to accuse me of sharp practice, would I?'
De Sable turned to Eloise with a laugh.

'Then you were buying it for me!'

'You might as well have it. I'm too tall.'

They passed through a patch of sunshine that fell between two shanties and Eloise noticed how the light
rippled over his corn-gold hair. That one so fair could
be so devious...

They collected De Sable's horse then went back
through the town gates. Here they stopped at the saddler's small, open-fronted shop. Dozens of saddles rested
in racks about the walls, each with a matching bridle
laid across it. Eloise stood by, trying to look invisible as
De Sable asked for the horse to be fitted out. Seeing
wealth in the young man's appearance and attitude, the
saddler was only too pleased to help. While De Sable
held the horse the saddler spread a cloth over its back,
and after checking one or two sizes found a saddle that
fitted perfectly.

'There!' De Sable took the matching bridle and fitted
it quickly over the cob's head. 'Well, Eloise? Aren't you
going to try it out?'

Eloise nodded dumbly and climbed into the saddle. The new leather squeaked as she tried a few turns and manoeuvres, the little horse even more responsive now that it was properly equipped.

The saddler asked whether the goods should be delivered, but with a quick look at Eloise De Sable shook his head.

'We'll take it as it is. I don't think my lady will get down now, even if I were to ask her!'

Eloise knew that she was headed for ruin. No decent girl would ever allow herself to be trapped in such a situation. A man had passed her off as his sister, bought her clothes, and a horse, and now he was going to introduce her into society. No good could come of it.

She could hardly eat all day. Instead she and Bessie concentrated solely on their dress-making. Finally, as the town bell marked the hour of four, Bessie heaved a sigh. Everything was finished. Now came the time to see if all the hours of cutting and stitching had been worthwhile.

De Sable and Edgar were made to stay down in the stable while Eloise took her bath in the upper room. It was hard work carrying buckets of well-water upstairs in the heat, but well worth it.

Eloise had steeped some of the dried rose petals from the window-sill. She used the scented water to wash her hair, then bathed long and carefully. She emerged pink and softly perfumed. In the afternoon warmth her hair dried quickly when spread in a thick curtain of curls about her shoulders.

Bessie helped her to dress. First came a stiff bodice and petticoat, made of the white cotton. Then an under-mantle, high-necked, with long, tight sleeves and cut perfectly plain from the cream linen. Finally, Bessie held up the rose damascene overdress.

With a rustle of fine material and the heavy scent of newness, Eloise wriggled into it. They had put in all the things that Eloise had so admired in dresses that the fashionable ladies had worn to the fair the day before. Cut tight to the waist, the pink overdress flounced out into a long, full skirt. The sleeves too were fitted, but at the elbows widened until they fell in folds and points to the floor. The neckline was cut in a deep V, revealing the fine linen undermantle.

Bessie knelt to billow the hems this way and that, settling the layers of material over one another. Finally she sat back on her heels, regarded their handiwork minutely, then said, 'Reckon that'll do.'

'Are you sure?' Eloise bit her lip uncertainly. If only there were a looking-glass.

'There's one way to find out. I'll see to your hair, then we'll get another opinion.'

She pushed Eloise into one of the chairs then set about her with comb and pins. By the time the beaded net was securely in place over her curls, Eloise was surprised that she had any hair left. Bessie was unaware of the agony that she had inflicted, and seemed quite pleased with herself. Without another word she went to the doorway and called down for De Sable to come up.

Eloise heard him come up the stairs in a few bounds. By now, she felt painfully self-conscious and wished that she had never even heard of De Sable. Things had gone far beyond any joke. It was a ridiculous pantomime, and he expected her to act it out now as his sister. She could not bring herself to look at him.

De Sable did not laugh, as she had expected him to. Neither did he make any immediate comment. Instead he waited until he had walked all around her slowly, and stood directly before her.

'Bit long, isn't it?'

Eloise looked down to where her much-repaired stockings and slippers were concealed beneath the generous folds.

'I believe it to be the fashion, my lord.'

'Won't be able to do much walking about in that.' He sounded doubtful. Eloise looked up sharply at Bessie's laugh.

'She don't want to do any walking—standing there's as much as these fine ladies d'do!'

'No dancing? Oh, then I shall be sorry about that.' He lifted her chin and she saw that he too was dressed in fine new clothes of his favourite colours. The calf-length white tunic with gold embroidery and matching gloves was not the work of a mere day, as her outfit was. He was wearing new soft leather boots, also in impractical white. That showed how much he knew of getting things clean, Eloise thought.

He was still looking at her, as though waiting for her to say something. Eloise felt herself blushing and looked away, but there was no time for modesty. Downstairs Edgar was already leading the horses out into the square.

De Sable sauntered off to the stairway and went down. Eloise followed, but needed Bessie's help to hold the yards of skirts up out of the stable straw. Once out into the sunlit square, De Sable got on to his horse and circled it about.

'If we leave now there will be no need to hurry. A quiet, gentle ride across the town, and no embarrassment at being the first to arrive.'

Eloise took her time arranging herself aboard the new horse. When at last she was ready they said goodbye to Edgar and Bessie, who waved them cheerfully out of sight.

'Well, now, little nightingale. A whole evening of entertainment lies ahead of us. What are we going to talk about?' He slipped one hand inside his tunic and withdrew a slim leather case.

'My lord, I may have no option but to accompany you, but we did agree to be friends. We can talk about anything and everything, with one exception. I do not intend to become your plaything. You can put all thoughts of that nature out of your head this instant.'

He looked irritated at first, but then his usual air of amusement returned. 'Then I take it that you will not be willing to accept this as a gift?' He handed the leather case to Eloise, who turned it about in her hands without opening it.

'Go on—open it,' De Sable said, his irritation returning. 'Don't think of it as a gift, then, if that would compromise your morals. Take it as my express wish that you wear it this evening, and that you will not disobey.'

Eloise undid the catches and the case sprung open. On a bed of grey velvet lay the most beautiful necklace that she had ever seen. A filigree of gold was set about with tiny butterflies and flowers in bright pink enamel.

'My lord—I——'

'You can't refuse it,' he snapped, 'as it is no longer a gift.'

All resistance dissolved under his steely glare. Eloise stopped her horse and waited for De Sable to turn in alongside her. He did not, but continued along the street. Eloise was forced to call him and, when her voice was drowned by street noise, to trot after him in deep shame.

'My lord,' she said quietly, coming alongside him again. 'I thought you would at least offer to fasten it for me.'

De Sable looked down at her quickly, then reined in his horse. 'Of course. That was most ungracious of me.'

With a rapid movement he snatched the necklace up. As Eloise bent forward, he fastened it about her neck, amid curious stares from the townspeople. Without a word he took the case then rode on, leaving Eloise to catch up as best she could.

They continued in silence after that. Following the line
of the town wall, De Sable led the way through bustling
crowds. He kept away from the dark, narrow lanes and
within a few minutes the smell of the dockside greeted
them.

Eloise kept close beside De Sable as they rode along
the quay. A clutter of ships jostled each other in the
harbour while shouts from their crews and the ever-
present seagulls rang through the air. Carts drawn up
beside the ships were loaded with wooden boxes and
barrels of all shapes and sizes. Wine from France, fancy
goods from Spain, spices and exotics from furthest
Outremer.

The whole scene was alive with sound, scent and
colour. Dogs barked, gulls cried, women laughed and
men sang while the tang of salt-seasoned wood and tarred
rope filled the air.

A never-ending procession of carts wound slowly away
from the quayside. De Sable led Eloise past them as they
toiled slowly up the hill from the docks, heavy-laden.
At the steepest part of the hill De Sable turned off left
to take a route around the shoulder of the wooded
hillside. His horse pranced nervously over the sacks laid
down to give draught animals a better grip, and frolicked along in excitement for a few yards. Eloise kept
well clear.

'Come on! We can at least get there before all the
food is gone,' he said crossly. Eloise was at a loss to
know why he was so disgruntled. Perhaps, having seen
her in the new dress, he had realised that the whole ad-
venture would be a disaster, and now wished that he had
not brought her. She looked down at the beautiful new
dress and wished that she were back at the lodgings, in
her comfortable old clothes and safe in Bessie's company.

'We're here now,' he said shortly. 'You might at least
make some effort to enjoy yourself.'

They were approaching a face of the slope that had a panoramic view of the town below. Already people were mingling happily on a large green field, bright with fluttering banners and enclosed with garlanded ropes of flowers and greenery. Servants arrived to help Eloise from her horse and lead the animals away. As though in a dream, Eloise thanked them then followed De Sable as he strode across the grass.

He knew several people, nodding to them and exchanging the odd word. Eloise knew no one. Never before had she felt so uncomfortable and out of place. The long folds of her skirts hampered her and more than once De Sable had to wait for her to catch up.

'I don't wish to inconvenience you further, my lord. If you would prefer that I wait in one of the marquees until your business here is over...'

'Business? Do you think that I would go to all this trouble for business?' He rounded on her savagely, blue eyes flashing. Eloise shrank, and began twisting at a handful of her skirt in agitation. Surely she hadn't done anything so dreadful that it deserved such anger?

'Then—what would my lord wish?' Eloise ventured hesitantly, half afraid for his answer.

'A little polite conversation would have been nice.'

Eloise relaxed a little, but the pink damascene had already been crushed into knife-pleats beneath her nervous hands. 'Very well, my lord. What would you like to talk about?'

He would have spat out an oath, but he stifled it as a servant came between them with a salver of drinks. Eloise took one to give her courage, but De Sable snatched it roughly from her, shoved it back on the tray and grasped her by the wrist.

'Richard!' a cheerful voice called out, and De Sable's expression softened at once. He turned away to greet the newcomer and Eloise managed to free her wrist from his grasp.

'And who's this?' The newcomer finished greeting De Sable and moved towards Eloise. He was near De Sable in both height and age, but his features were merry and generous instead of classically handsome.

'Eloise Emeron. From Brionne. A...friend,' De Sable muttered, and the newcomer laughed knowingly. Eloise cringed with shame. De Sable was surely a man who had a new 'friend' for every occasion.

'I am Hugh. Delighted to make your acquaintance, my lady.' The newcomer took Eloise's hand and pressed it to his lips. Eloise replied politely as she had been taught so many years ago, sinking into a deep curtsy. When she rose, the tousle-headed Hugh was looking at her with a searching gaze.

'My lady Eloise... I wonder if I might steal Richard from you for a moment or two. A fair lady such as yourself should not be left alone in the open, so perhaps you will let me first escort you to a place of refuge. There are sweetmeats and the like set out in this little marquee. Wait here until I return.' He took her firmly by the elbow and propelled her towards a small red and white striped booth.

'If you would care to wait in here, my lady, I shall not detain Richard long. Gentlemen's talk, you understand...'

Eloise stood on the threshold of the marquee, with its overpowering smell of crushed grasses. De Sable was pulled away out of sight by Hugh, and Eloise wondered what was so important. She wandered into the marquee and suddenly remembered how long ago her last proper meal had been. And how terribly hungry she was now.

A long trestle-table draped in white cloth ran the length of the booth and Eloise joined the queue that was inspecting the food on offer. The line of people snaked forward at a shuffle, so Eloise was able to manage her long skirts without arousing any comment. At the end of the line there might be a bench where she could sit down and not have to worry about gathering up her skirts with every step.

Thin wooden platters were piled here and there along the table. Eloise took one and looked at the wonders on display.

A horn of plenty spilled out sun-dried fruits from the Levant. Figs, raisins and corinths lay dark and tempting over the white cloth. A large bird, of what type Eloise couldn't recognise, had been roasted and laid on a salver, surrounded with hard-boiled pigeons' eggs. Nibbles of green hazelnuts and sprouted wheat grains stood in silver dishes, each of which nestled in an arrangement of cornflowers and creeping Jenny.

Eloise chose a small pastry turnover that looked interesting, a handful of dried fruit and two cheese and parsley scones from a large heap in the centre of the table. She looked longingly at tiny marzipan fruits in their woven marzipan baskets, but did not want to seem greedy.

There was a bench at the end of the marquee, and Eloise sat down between two ladies who admired her dress and complained about the heat. Eloise made polite conversation, but was more interested in her food. The pie was a pleasant concoction of savoury mince, and the rest of the party food was also tasty and unusual. A servant approached with goblets of heavy red wine, but her companions sent him away to fetch the 'Irish wine' and urged Eloise to try it.

At first she was not very impressed. There was only a splash of the Irish wine in each goblet, not a real cupful. The stuff had an unusual smell too—harsh and bitter. Eloise took a sip. It burned like fire, and she felt it wriggle in a hot glow all the way down inside.

She paused for a moment, trying to decide whether she liked it. Perhaps another taste might help her to decide. It was very strong stuff, as the second goblet convinced her. She would have no more, but just sit quietly until De Sable came to fetch her. Or Hugh. Whichever. The 'Irish wine' had her happily confused already, and she giggled to herself.

Eloise sat in a warm haze, enjoying the hum of civilised conversation around her. People came and went, talked and laughed with her about the weather, their aching feet and the tedium of official receptions. Although she was shy and ill at ease among so many strangers, Eloise repaid their friendliness with polite good humour, and even began to enjoy herself.

She badly wanted to go outside and see what was going on. Afraid for her reputation, she dared not venture out into the open without a male escort. Despite this she refused several requests to accompany handsome young men outside for a dance. Society was fickle. Eloise had no one to advise her who was an acceptable partner and who was not, and did not intend jeopardising her good name.

She had finished her meal and was just popping the last corinth into her mouth when an arm slid about her waist in a gale of evil musk. She cringed away from Roger Belvas, who had spotted a tiny gap beside her on the bench and pressed himself into it.

'All alone today? Richard's a fast one—bringing his servant to a bash like this. Thinking of hiring you out, is he? Hoping you'll bring him in a bit of extra cash?'

Eloise squirmed away from his cruel grasp and leapt up. 'I regret that I do not appreciate your attentions, my lord. Kindly keep your hands to yourself.'

Belvas stood up and moved towards her. Although his tunic was new and obviously expensive, it could not conceal his stale, unwashed condition. Small eyes quick and cunning, he approached, tongue flickering around his lips for a second in anticipation. Eloise backed away, unwilling to make a scene, but Belvas crept nearer.

'You don't have any choice, my fine lady.' He spoke the words with a sneer. 'You're only Richard's serving-girl. Nothing. Giving men pleasure, that's all your sort are good for.'

Moving closer, Belvas was forcing Eloise to retreat towards the rear entrance of the marquee. He was trying to frighten her into making a dash for the door. Once they were in the open it was but a short distance to the woodland edge. If he once managed to get her away from the crowds, there would be no one to hear her cries over the music and gay laughter of the reception.

CHAPTER TEN

ROGER'S plans were thwarted. Eloise could not have run anywhere in her billowing skirts, and took refuge in the only place she could. A small group of people were conversing quietly in the centre of the marquee, and with relief Eloise recognised one of the women that she had sat with earlier. Throwing all caution to the wind, she stood at the edge of the group and cleared her throat.

'Excuse me, my lords...ladies...'

The group turned to her with indulgent smiles.

'My—er—escort is detained at present and my lord Belvas is——'

'Making a nuisance of himself again?' A large, jolly man interjected, bringing rueful laughter to the whole group. Belvas skulked closer, like an outcast dog.

'She's only a common serving-wench,' Belvas snarled, raking Eloise with a barbed stare. 'One of De Sable's women.' He spat out the final word as though it were the worst of crimes. The group that Eloise had joined fell silent, and she felt their indulgence turn to curiosity and laughter.

'De Sable?' she heard one of the women whisper in flat, accentless French. 'But she's doesn't seem his type...far too gentle...'

'She ain't one of his type.' An elderly lady took a few faltering steps forward and leaned heavily on a cane of polished wood. Her skin was yellowed and dry with years of following the hunt. She shook her head, studying Eloise minutely. 'In fact, she looks all right to me. Fine bones. Long flanks. No wench, this. What's your name, girl?'

Eloise felt her mouth go dry, and tried to flatten out her Norman accent. 'Emeron, my lady. Eloise Emeron.'

'Not one of the Berkshire Emerons?'

'No, my lady. The Gloucestershire Emerons.' Eloise crossed her fingers within the folds of her skirts. It wasn't exactly a lie. The old harridan was greatly impressed, and patted Eloise on the arm.

'Better. Much better. Now you won't remember this, child, but your father will have been there. Gloucester— the Christmas court of '85. Ah, I remember it as though it were yesterday. Ran a tight ship, did the old Duke of Normandy——'

'King William the Conqueror, that's what you must call the mean old buzzard, Mamam! "Duke of Normandy" has rather unpleasant overtones these days...'

There was laughter at the tubby man's words, but the old lady was insistent and wagged her cane at the group.

'Mean? William? Never. Careful, thrifty with money maybe, but at least we knew where we stood with old Duke William. Christmas really was Christmas in those days. Proper religious festival, set between work and more work. None of this reckless expenditure on trifles that goes on nowadays.' She brandished her cane towards the table of sweetmeats. 'Clean living and hard praying. Fresh air, exercise and hard work. Honest Norman values. Never hurt anybody.'

The group laughed again, but in deference to the old lady Eloise merely murmured politely.

'Gone to pot nowadays, though,' the old lady continued, while the group closed in to finally exclude Belvas. Losing interest in his mother and Eloise, the tubby man turned to his companion.

'I hear old Gamberon's gone to earth in your part of the world, Enzio. Any trouble with him?'

Eloise pricked up her ears at the mention of 'Gamberon'. Duke Robert of Normandy, and not men-

tioned in a friendly tone of voice. She only half heard
the old lady's tales of Christmas '85, for her mind was
trying to sift information from the hum of talk about
Italy. The man Enzio was short, slight, expensively
dressed and neatly manicured. He was a merchant, just
back from Apulia, and related tales of Duke Robert and
his crusaders, who were resting there on their way home.
Enzio was dismissive enough of rumours that the Duke
would invade England, but his tubby host was not so
amused.

With growing horror Eloise realised that this was how
mass panic would spread. People like the tubby host had
livelihoods to protect. They couldn't afford civil unrest.
Nothing could be allowed to ripple the pools of their
wealth. She listened, hearing his immediate plans to set
his own private army on alert. Any spies would get short
measure at a pitchfork's end.

Now Eloise was really worried. All it needed was a
few people to be as easily inflamed as the tubby host,
and it wouldn't only be spies that came under attack.
Anyone who still kept land in Normandy while living in
England . . . who had any sort of connection with Duke
Robert . . . even poor musicians, dragged along unwillingly in the train of a spy . . .

The old lady suddenly gripped her arm with greater
intensity and started towards the doorway. 'Hugh! Yes,
Hugh De Sable! Where's your rascal of a brother? I want
a word with him!'

She had seen the tall figure of Hugh striding past the
marquee and her stern voice brought him to a halt. He
came forward at once and bowed politely.

'Lady Maud? I see that you are acquainted with the
Lady Eloise.'

'Your manners don't make up for Dick's fancies. What
does he mean, bringing out a nice young girl then abandoning her with a bunch of old fools? Be the gentleman
and take her about, Hugh. Might as well show the poor

child a little sophistication before Dick ruins her forever.
And none of your brother's tricks. No trying to pass her
off as a long-lost cousin.'

'No, Lady Maud.' He looked a little distracted as the
old woman placed Eloise's hand on his arm, but resumed
his immaculate manners as Eloise looked up at him.

'I'm afraid Richard is in the usual place, Lady Maud.
Dicing at the tables. But at least he was taking money
on board as though it was going out of fashion when I
left him. It is when he loses that it is time to worry.'

With a laugh the old lady hobbled back into her group,
satisfied that she had done her part. Eloise was desperate to pass on the news, but Hugh seemed more
interested in the lines of horses parked at the far side of
the pleasure ground.

'I am afraid I shall have to leave you, my lady. I am
needed urgently at home, and cannot escort you——'

'My lord—does your brother tell you everything—ab-
solutely everything?'

Hugh looked down at her, and smiled kindly. 'Why,
no. In many matters he plays his cards very close to his
chest. Does this mean that my lady is in some kind of
trouble?'

'It is not what you think.'

'No. Indeed not.' He was still smiling, but Eloise
thought that there was pity in the deep grey eyes. She
could not risk telling Hugh what she had heard. She had
to speak to De Sable himself.

'Do you know the Lord Roger Belvas?' Eloise looked
about her, afraid that the hideous Belvas was lying in
wait somewhere, and would leap out as soon as Hugh
left her alone and unprotected.

'I'm afraid so! Everyone knows Roger. He wasn't invited tonight, but I see that he has gatecrashed his way
in, as usual.' Hugh wrinkled his nose in disgust.

'I am afraid to say that he has been making a nuisance of himself. That is why I had to take refuge with Lady Maud and her group...'

Hugh sighed, and Eloise took his impatience as an indication of something quite different. He patted her hand briskly and turned back the way that they had come.

'No matter. Roger Belvas is an insect, nothing more, but you should not be troubled in that way. I shall take care to leave you with Richard, then, before I depart. But mind, if he should give you any trouble I want to know about it!'

He laughed easily, and showed no slyness in his humour. Eloise had liked the look of him from the first, and despite the urgent business that caused him to look back towards the horses now and then he was the perfect companion. Never walking too fast for her, keeping up a polite conversation and introducing her properly to the many that stopped to speak to him, he was totally charming. Eloise wondered why De Sable couldn't take a leaf out of his brother's unblotted copybook.

De Sable did not acknowledge them as they approached the dicing table. He leaned forward, waiting for the next throw with the delighted anticipation of a true addict. Only when the table roared with delight as he bankrupted another poor idiot did De Sable lean back to grin up at his brother.

'Back already, Hugh? That was quick. Oh, and you've got—Eloise, isn't it?' The crowd of young men around the table cackled like animals, each seeing her as yet another of the feckless Richard's conquests. He stood up slowly, filling his money pouch with coins and leaving the table with an air of regret.

'Belvas. Causing a commotion.' Hugh spoke to De Sable with a crisp urgency that surprised Eloise. He gave Eloise's hand to De Sable and with a swift goodbye left at last to go and find his horse.

De Sable walked away from the crowds with Eloise in tow, and she tried to avoid tripping up in her long skirts. Finally, she was forced to say something. 'I wish you were a gentleman. Like my lord Hugh.'

De Sable stopped and gave her an unfathomable look. 'Indeed. But I shouldn't get too fond of my little brother, Eloise.'

'Why not?'

'Because I say so. That should be reason enough,' he retorted sullenly. They had reached a place where the grasses grew taller, stretching up to reach the sun from beneath a thin canopy of birches. There was no one in sight now. He stopped and turned to face her, both hands on her shoulders.

'Eloise...'

'No, my lord,' she said firmly. 'I do not have the inclination, and neither of us has the time now. The merchant Enzio has brought news of Duke Robert's plot and we must get away——'

'Oh, that...' he said, idly brushing a strand of hair from her forehead. 'Old news. Don't talk to me of plots and danger. We're here to enjoy ourselves.'

His eyes were very blue, his hair a golden halo in the evening sunlight. Eloise took a deep breath and tried to prepare herself to repel his advances.

'You don't understand, my lord——'

'Richard. Call me Richard, if only for tonight...'

'My lord, it will mean wholesale slaughter. The majority will turn on those who might have even the slightest links with Duke Robert of Normandy. No one will be safe! I am afraid, my lord...'

'Eloise...my little rosebud. Has anyone told you how very beautiful you look tonight? A delicate pink rosebud with a soft, creamy heart——'

A giggling couple frolicked past them and disappeared into the depths of the greenwood.

'Why do you think that I have treated you so well, spoiled you with presents, brought you to meet all the dignitaries and notables? Eloise...'

'I can guess, my lord. And although it will seem ungrateful, I feel the time has come that I should put a stop to this ridiculous charade once and for all. We are both in mortal danger, my lord. We must leave the town at once, I must go straight away into a convent and you— well, you must fare as best you can.'

His hands were straying down towards her waist but as she pulled back he did not press her with his attentions. Instead he stood by silently as she fiddled with the catch of the pink enamelled necklace. Releasing it, she handed it back. Without a word he withdrew its leather case from his tunic and replaced the necklace on its bed of velvet.

'I did not realise how much you despise me, Eloise. You must find all this a great embarrassment.'

'Indeed. But it could be worse. I might have given in to your selfish, foolish desires and become merely another notch on your tally. I am sorry if all your expense has been in vain. Perhaps you will take care to choose a willing partner next time. You should be able to get a little money back for the clothes and the horse——'

'Hope I don't find a buyer so keen for a bargain as I was,' he said, with an attempt at a smile.

'Playing on my sympathies won't work, either, my lord. Kindly take me back to the lodgings and we can make our escape from there.'

De Sable caught her hand as she moved away. 'Oh, not yet! Listen—the musicians have started to play.' He listened to the faint music drifting from the hillside above. 'A Spanish measure. I insist upon your company.'

He swept into a deep bow and Eloise was confused. He was under sentence of death, and at any moment hordes of enthusiastic spy-hunters might descend upon him, but De Sable was as calm as a summer sea.

'I—I have never danced it, my lord. Only watched others...'

'Then now is your chance to excel, as I am sure you must do in all things.'

She followed him up the slope to the dancing place and took her position at the end of the line of women. Her long skirts were not a handicap in the slow, stately movements of the dance, but the nearness of De Sable was most off-putting. He held her far too close in the promenade and squeezed her hands in a most familiar fashion whenever they had cause to touch. Eloise spent her time staring at the grass and blushing, imagining that all the little whispers and giggles were directed at De Sable's disgraceful behaviour.

Eloise hurried from the dancing ground before the final strains of music had died away. De Sable followed her, but was able to catch up without hurrying himself overmuch. The tussocky grass was difficult for Eloise to negotiate as she held up handfuls of her skirts while trying not to reveal her threadbare slippers.

De Sable summoned a servant and took two goblets of wine from his tray. One of these he held out to Eloise. 'Stand still and take it, then.'

'There isn't time—we must get away!'

He moved quickly to stand in front of her, barring her way. 'Do you see me hurrying? No. It's no good. If the game's up, well, we might as well just stay here enjoying ourselves for what little time we may have left.'

Eloise looked at him, her eyes wide with amazement. 'You're throwing your life away!'

'I'm surprised you're that interested after some of the things you've said to me.' He smiled ruefully and pushed the wine goblet at her again. Several passers-by looked and laughed, and Eloise realised that they must be used to seeing De Sable in such situations. There would be little point in making a scene.

'If you're captured then there will be little enough chance for me, or Edgar, or Bessie. That is what I'm concerned about. You're a big enough rogue to be able to look after yourself.'

He laughed and patted her head, which pulled at her hairpins cruelly. 'That's my little nightingale. Always ready with a few kind words!'

Eloise took a steadying draught of wine and gave him back the goblet. 'If we leave here right now there will be time to pack up everything and be on our way before the reception is over. There must be a convent here somewhere that you can leave me, while you three get well away under cover of darkness——'

'And miss a moment of this most excellent entertainment? No, little one. If you are so keen to be locked away in a convent for ever more, let us make the most of your last few fleeting hours of freedom!'

He dropped their goblets on a nearby table and swept her back to the dancing ground. Eloise was powerless in his grasp. She could do nothing but follow De Sable, and the dances.

When there was a break for refreshments De Sable took her firmly by the hand and they went once more into the red and white marquee. Belvas was still skulking around the food table. He softened scones in his wine so that his few remaining teeth were not loosened further on hard pastry. De Sable showed no signs of acknowledging Belvas, but the social outcast was not so easily put off.

'It won't work, you know, Richard,' Belvas sneered loudly. 'People might be saying that she's the real thing, but you won't be able to keep up the deception.'

Eloise had little enough appetite for more sweetmeats, and lost it completely at those words. De Sable squeezed her hand and motioned for her to keep silent.

'And how do you know that Eloise isn't "the real thing", as you so quaintly put it?'

Belvas spat a tough piece of scone crust out on to the grass. 'Everyone knows you won't marry. And no decent family would have their daughter seen out with you.' He sidled up to Eloise and pinched her cheek painfully between dirt-grimed fingers. At once De Sable threw out his hand and struck Belvas on the arm. He shrank back, sallow complexion flushing an ugly red. For a moment Eloise thought that the two men were really going to come to blows. The crowd began to edge away, half fearful, but the breathless return of Hugh gave Belvas a chance to slink off when De Sable wasn't looking.

'Hugh, welcome back. Had you left the back door open?' De Sable said mildly, handing his brother a platter and indicating the food set out on the table.

'No, after all that. But I had to go back and check, all the same.' He smiled down at Eloise, and shrugged. 'I wish I hadn't. A message has arrived from Maman. She wants us both to go back home immediately, Richard. She's been hearing all sorts of things about your reckless behaviour, and want us both back where she can keep an eye on us.'

De Sable helped himself to several cheese and parsley scones, dropping one on to Hugh's plate in passing.

'Ah, well. I'm afraid she'll have to wait.' There was a murmur of disgust from an eavesdropper or two in the crowd about them at De Sable's words. 'I'm having far too much fun here.'

'Richard! Maman's letter was quite specific. We're both to start for home right now. She's worried to death. Both she and Papa are imagining all sorts of things— that you'll bring shame upon the family, and lead me astray...'

The eavesdroppers murmured their support for young Hugh, who seemed to be genuinely well liked. His brother was merely tolerated as a charming rogue.

'Look, Richard, I'm leaving right now and I strongly suggest that you come with me. You know that Maman isn't very strong, and shouldn't be worried...'

There was a sigh of reproof from the crowd, but they fell into silence at a stony glare from De Sable.

'Eat your supper, drink your wine and then go, Hugh. If we meet up on the road to Southampton, well—so be it.'

Hugh nodded, his mouth full of hurriedly eaten scone.

'If we meet, all well and good. If not—if I'm "otherwise engaged"—then don't wait for me. Better Maman has one son home safe and sound than that both of us should go missing!'

He laughed, and with plate loaded up with food moved away from the table, towing Eloise behind him. Once they were all three out into the open, Hugh took Eloise's hand once more.

'Remember what I said, Lady Eloise. Should Richard not treat you kindly, then let me put an end to all his tricks.' He bent and brushed her hand lightly with a kiss. When he stood up again it was to cuff De Sable companionably. 'Watch yourself. Don't go talking to any strange men. I've heard Montgomery's men are on the prowl!'

He skipped away to the horses with a wave, and was gone. For the first time Eloise noticed a shadow of doubt in De Sable's expression as he watched his brother ride off.

'My lord—you're hurting my hand...'

'Sorry,' he said faintly, and loosed his grip.

'Let's go after him. You have a valid excuse for leaving.'

'No,' De Sable said sharply, then bent to whisper in her ear with a soft laugh, 'No one would expect me to! I'm Jack the Lad—a wicked chap who couldn't be expected to give a thought for his own poor mother, let alone anything else!'

Eloise thought for a moment, then looked De Sable straight in his laughing blue eyes. 'Your brother Hugh's in this as well, isn't he?'

'Right up to his neck.'

'And all that—what he said—none of it was true?'

De Sable led her a good distance from anyone who might possibly overhear and pulled her down to sit beside him on the still sun-warmed grass.

'It was a device to provide us both with an alibi for leaving town in a hurry. He will go directly, I will leave a little later.' He brushed at the feathery grasses that grew about them, sending puffs of grass seed into the air. 'I cannot possibly leave you here now, Eloise. It is far too dangerous a place. If the merchants are becoming jumpy then it is no place for anyone with your honest nature. Try to help them with information and your reward would be a slit throat. Besides, I do not like the latest news,' he said, half to himself.

'What is the matter?'

'Events are running on too fast for my liking. Montgomery's men coming in could prove a two-edged sword...'

De Sable was plainly too preoccupied to pose a threat to her now. If Eloise was endangered, too, she wanted to know all the details. 'Who are these "Montgomery's men"?'

De Sable plucked at the dry grass-stems and gave a mirthless laugh. 'If ever there is mischief, then you can bet that Montgomery and his merry men are behind it somewhere. Duke Robert must be kept from his evil influence. Doubtless Montgomery was behind all the wickedness that you say went on in Normandy.'

Eloise shook her head, memories of the fear and slaughter bringing a sudden chill to the warm evening. 'No, my lord. I do not recall the Duke of Normandy sending anyone to us but the Lord of Belleme.'

De Sable lay back on the grass, looking at the dusk-dusted sky. 'The Devil has many names, Eloise. The Lord of Belleme, Scion of the house of Talvas—and now he has assumed charge of his family's lands of Montgomery. They are all one and the same wicked fellow.'

From the tone of De Sable's voice, Eloise was left in little doubt that increased power for Belleme—Montgomery—meant increased evil. 'He is unnatural. My father used to say that Belleme was in league with the Devil.'

'Hardly that, little one. But he is an evil man, to be sure, hand in hand with overpowering ambitions. Duke Robert will rue the day if he takes up with Montgomery again.'

Eloise looked towards a thin line of heather-purple hills in the far distance. As the light began to ebb away, very slowly, she spoke. 'Then we are between a rock and a hard place. If King William or his henchmen learn of your mission, then we are dead. If all goes according to your plans, you have no guarantee that the Lord of Belleme will not be as ruthless here in Duke Robert's name as he was in Normandy.'

'That,' De Sàble said with a heavy sigh, 'is about the size of it.'

Words seemed inadequate for a long time after that. Eloise sat in silence until she felt De Sable's hand fall lightly on to her back. She turned and saw him watching her through half-closed eyes.

'What are you thinking about, little nightingale?'

Bats flickered through the growing dusk about their heads and Eloise sighed. 'About all the things that I shall miss in life.'

At her tone, he laughed and sat up. 'My word, it doesn't take much to pull you down, does it? I've been in much tighter corners.' His hand ran softly up and down her back, and for once Eloise did not resist. Suddenly she wanted him to kiss her, and to let herself yield beneath the firm touch of his hands. Almost before she had acknowledged the frightening, sinful thought he stood up. Offering her his hand, he started off towards the refreshment tent again.

'People have started to leave. It's time we stocked up again, little one. Tonight is going to be long and difficult.'

She followed him in a half-dream, aware at last of what she had fought for so long. Despite her hatred of his mission, Eloise needed De Sable now, and could not think to be parted from him. From deep inside her a small voice warned that she had been ensnared like a thousand others, but she didn't care. She was doomed—they were both doomed—and nothing else mattered any more.

De Sable filled her a plate from the never-ending supply of party food. When Eloise protested weakly, he countered that it might be a long time before they had the chance of free food again. As soon as they could slip out of the rear entrance of the marquee, De Sable wrapped the food in a napkin and stuffed it inside his tunic. Leaving the platter on the grass, they went to the horse lines and while a servant went to fetch their animals there was an agonising wait.

De Sable had a face like thunder as he queued impatiently for their horses to be brought. Eloise was beginning to realise that his quick changes of mood might owe more to self-preservation than an unstable temper. Showing irritation at an evening interrupted would be expected from the feckless character that De Sable liked to play.

Once they were safely aboard their horses, De Sable set off at a sharp trot. Eloise followed him, fearing that the horses would slip on the hill, but once they were safely away from the pleasure ground he slowed his pace.

'Carefully down the hill, then as quickly as we can out of the city. They won't have got far in the time we've spent partying.'

'You surely aren't after Montgomery's men?' Eloise was horrified.

'No, silly!' He laughed, waiting for her to catch up at the bottom of the hill. 'The others. Hugh got to hear the rumours before you did, and it was sheer luck that he happened to spot us. He went back to get his household on the move and told Bessie and Edgar to get going, too. They're used to sudden changes of billet.'

Eloise tried to keep up as De Sable's great destrier surged on towards the harbour. When they turned right rather than left to leave the town by the south gate, Eloise felt a pang of regret.

'What is it, little nightingale? No songs, only a sad face?'

'It was such a pretty house. Almost like being at home again,' she finished wistfully.

'I'm afraid it will be a long time before you can rest in such a peaceful place again,' De Sable said, but not unkindly. 'Perhaps there is an even more beautiful house waiting for you somewhere. One day.'

They met another river, smaller and scruffier than the main one. After crossing it on a rickety wooden bridge they followed it for some time. The evening was drawing on now, and as a steep, wooded hill reared up on their right De Sable changed places so that Eloise was a safe distance from the greenwood edge.

That was not necessarily an advantage. The oily dark river gulped and guzzled eerily in the growing darkness. Water bats flittered about the willows and alders and the banks were full of their own secret noises. Eloise kept her head down, looking to neither left nor right. She didn't want to see what was making all the noise.

De Sable touched her shoulder, bending down to whisper. 'A light up ahead. Stay here while I ride on and investigate.'

There was no time for Eloise to protest. He was gone, with a soft thud of hoofs on the well-worn track. Eloise

did not like it, alone in the dark. She had spent her whole
life in the company of other people, and now she was
alone. What if De Sable didn't come back? If he was
murdered by bandits? If——?

Eloise shook herself. Imaginings were the way to
frighten herself to death. There was nothing to be done
but wait. And wait.

When De Sable finally returned he was out of breath
and laughing. 'No money for the turnpike gate. Would
you credit it? You'd think people would set out with
their money already sorted.'

'Is it Bessie and Edgar?'

'No, they're held up by the idiot in front. The toll-
keeper's going to heave his cart off the track to let us
through. That will take quite a while. There's no point
in hurrying for a minute.'

Eloise turned her horse in to ride on beside De Sable.
As they moved slowly on towards the light of the turnpike
gate, De Sable cleared his throat.

'You didn't give us away to Enzio.'

'No, my lord.'

'Thank you for that.' He paused, the jingle of the
horses' harness disturbing a moorhen that barked into
the night. 'It was because you could not implicate
yourself, I suppose. Like the last time—at the Artoises'.'

Eloise did not answer immediately. She was too confused. Guilt and resentment at her feelings for De Sable
had thrown her mind into a whirlpool. Then there was
fear for Hugh, that one so young and kind could be
drawn into such a business. Bessie and Edgar, too—their
lives also depended on her silence.

The matter of a plot against the King had seemed so
clear-cut at first, her instinct to inform so right. Now
Eloise realised that nothing ever happened in isolation.
One word from her and people, too many people, would
perish.

CHAPTER ELEVEN

THE delay for the turnpike was agonising. Even a day before, Eloise would have been eager for such an opportunity. She would have jumped down, told the toll-keeper everything and finished all the wretched deception.

Not now. Eloise said nothing. Sitting quietly on her new horse in her party clothes, all of which De Sable had provided for her, she could not bring herself to reveal him as the spy he was. That was what he was banking upon.

Once he had handed over the toll money and the little party was safely through, De Sable started whistling cheerfully.

At last Eloise could stand it no longer. 'My lord, don't! I do believe you want everyone to hear us as we travel.'

'Of course!' De Sable bent down to her as she rode beside him. 'What could be more natural than a knight and his lady travelling home after an evening's entertainment? If we should be riding in company with two honest country folk and their cart—well, then, it is only because there is safety in numbers.'

Bessie and Edgar laughed, but Eloise was amazed at his cool nerve. 'You really are the most wicked, scheming——'

'Ah, and the fun is barely started yet, little nightingale.' He withdrew the packet of food from his jacket and threw it into the cart. 'Hugh has a good start on us and is not so heavy-laden. With luck he will reach the meeting place we arranged secretly by dinnertime tomorrow, but it will not be safe for him to linger there long. Our little party must make all speed to spare him needless danger.'

'Where are we to meet him, my lord?' Eloise asked innocently. The information might be useful, although she doubted that she could ever bring herself to use it.

It was De Sable who was the wary one now. 'You can't ensnare me like that, little one. Let me only say that it is a very long way indeed from here.'

They journeyed on at a good pace for several miles. When the track dropped down a hill to cross a narrow river, they stopped to let the animals drink.

'Time for the party finery to be cast aside,' De Sable said, taking the reins of Eloise's horse. 'Such pretty things will cause comment in the boring light of day.'

Eloise got down, but it was with little enthusiasm. De Sable had already thrown his white and gold tunic into the cart and stood stripped to the waist in the cold night air.

'Hurry up, then. You can't parade about the country-side in such an outfit.' His voice was sharp and uncompromising.

'I confess that I cannot bear to lose such a beautiful dress, my lord.'

Pulling on an everyday tunic, he gave a soft chuckle and advanced, but Eloise backed away.

'Indeed, and I would not ask you to. You may place it in one of the trunks containing my clothes. It will be safe enough there. My dear staff keep everything clean and beautiful, and the dress will not be spoiled.'

His humour was not unkind now. Still Eloise hesitated, uncomfortable at the thought of changing so close to the meagre hamlet that straggled about the river banks.

'Change against the side of the bridge.' Guessing at her uncertainty, De Sable led her towards a shadowy area. 'I shall keep watch.'

Reassured, Eloise changed quickly into a work-dress, while Edgar tied her new horse to the back of the cart.

Folding the pink and cream dresses, Eloise wondered aloud whether there would ever come another chance to wear the outfit.

'Why not?' De Sable answered airily. 'Until then, you have at least one nice new petticoat to enjoy.'

'You looked! You looked at me when I was changing!'

Her rage only served to amuse De Sable further. 'I was charged for five yards of good cotton cloth the other day. I merely wanted to ensure that my investment hadn't gone to clothe the poor and needy of the parish.'

Eloise stalked off towards the cart and packed her party clothes away. When De Sable crept up to her with a cheeky whisper of, 'You kept woman, you!' she ignored him and went to sit beside Bessie on the cart.

They moved off to the sound of De Sable's merry whistling. The summer night never grew completely dark, and Eloise was grateful for that. They passed such strange things on the road. The worst were the fetid bogs. Mist wreathed a hill-circled hollow where outcasts camped. All about them were the tumbled ruins of great houses, thrown down by wind, weather and time. As the ox cart rumbled past great carved pillars and smashed statues, Eloise wondered what giants had once lived in that stinking, sulphurous place.

The road continued, passing through small valleys between rounded hillocks. Mile after mile passed without any slackening of pace. As dawn unravelled the ragged edge of night, Eloise realised from the position of the sunrise that they were travelling roughly south-east. Looking at the sky she noticed several strange pinpoints of light streaking across the horizon. They seemed to hesitate, then slid away over the shoulder of a hill.

Eloise drew in closer to Bessie. No one else had remarked on the lights in the sky. Perhaps lack of sleep was playing tricks upon her. At last she must have dozed, nodding against Bessie's comfortable shoulder.

Jolted out of uneasy sleep by a roughening of the track, Eloise awoke to find a very different countryside. Instead of close-crowding hills, the land was becoming more open and windswept.

'Men say that there is a pagan evilness about this plain,' De Sable said quietly. 'We will wait here at the edge until we can cross in full light.'

There was a cluster of rough huts ahead and they stopped in their shelter. The locals were shabby and threadbare but refused the travellers' offer of a share in their meagre rations.

As they ate the party sweetmeats and shared a skin of wine, De Sable had a warning for them. The track they were to take across the plain followed a river. It was rumoured to be bewitched. While De Sable was not superstitious by nature, he did not intend putting local beliefs to the test. Edgar could take the animals over to drink where the local people did, but once on the plain proper no one was to go near the river.

They did not need any urging to obey. The plain and its sullen river looked lonely and formidable indeed.

When the animals were rested and the sun giving stronger light they set off again. A chill breeze cooled them at first, but very soon the sun's strength began to grow.

Eloise wondered at the change in De Sable. He had not slept, but kept watch all the time, whether the group was resting or travelling. That alone would account for his reserve, but Eloise considered that there was some other reason. Perhaps he had realised at last what a trap his foolish loyalty to Duke Robert had led him into. Despite her hatred of the Duke, Eloise felt more than a pang of regret for the brave, generous souls that did his bidding.

'My lord.' She leaned forward to touch him gently on the arm as he rode beside the cart. De Sable shook himself as though to wake.

'I can ride beside the oxen, my lord. Rest in the cart.'

He shook his head. 'Something is not right. I can sense it. We must keep alert.'

They rode on for another hour, then a small group came into view. Still some way off, they were stopped at the side of the road. De Sable shielded his eyes from the sun and stared at them.

'Deus! I knew it. There must be trouble.'

As they drew nearer, Eloise recognised Hugh and his small party. The younger De Sable was already galloping his horse towards them, and in that deserted landscape did not need to contain his news.

'Montgomery's found out! He's sent over shiploads of men. They're moving outward from Southampton. Salisbury Town is already crawling with them, like leeches. They've come to take matters into their own hands. The game's up, brother...'

'Not until it's over,' De Sable said wearily. 'Did you get as far as Salisbury yourself?'

'No. Tavern gossip saved us from that.' Hugh leapt down from his horse and paced about frantically. 'What are we to do? Who will save the Duke once he has fallen into Montgomery's clutches?'

'Or us,' De Sable muttered. 'Who will save us?'

Eloise had been listening carefully. When De Sable covered his face with his hands to order his thoughts, she spoke out.

'My lords... If Duke Robert has not yet reached England, could not Montgomery and his men be prevented from meeting up with him?'

'Eloise,' De Sable reached across and patted her hand, 'the lord Montgomery has been scheming since his cradle. He will have long since put a watch on all possible ports and landing places.'

'It is rumoured that he himself is lying in wait at Rouen, in case the dear Duke should go home first before

coming to England.' Hugh slumped back against his
horse in desperation. Eloise was not so easily beaten.

'Surely you two are not working alone in this collection business?'

The two brothers exchanged a wary look, but Eloise
continued.

'Then you must find some way to meet up with the
rest of your allies. You said yourself, my lord, that there
is safety in numbers.'

Again the De Sables looked at each other, then at last
they both spoke at once. 'Headquarters?'

It was agreed. Everywhere was equally dangerous for
them now, but at least there might be a chance against
Montgomery's scheming if they could band together with
others.

Within half an hour everything was arranged. The
carts would follow at their own pace, but Hugh and
Richard De Sable would ride on ahead. Their destination was the castle of Lord and Lady Braceur, hidden
away at the edge of the New Forest.

To the surprise of Eloise, her master removed the
saddle of the horse that Hugh lent him. She was even
more surprised when he ordered her down from the cart.

'It is a fair journey, and I need sleep. You will take
care of the riding while I rest behind you.'

Eloise looked at Hugh for support, but he laughed.
'I regret my horse is not fit enough to carry both my
brother and myself, Lady Eloise. It is a common enough
practice on campaign, although I declare that never
before have I heard of a lady doing the driving!'

'Shut up and ride,' De Sable snapped, lifting Eloise
on to the destrier's broad back. Flinging himself up
behind her, he paid no attention to Eloise's complaints
as his arms wound about her waist. At the same time
his head was laid on her shoulder, but by then Eloise
knew further argument was useless. Even in that un-

comfortable position, his warm breath was already slow
and steady against her neck. He was asleep.

They made good progress. Horses were much faster
than draught oxen, even though Hugh took care not to
force the pace and dislodge his sleeping brother.

Eloise discovered that the more she talked to Hugh,
the more she liked him. He was as loyal to his brother
Richard as he was to Duke Robert, although he did acknowledge that Richard had his faults.

She was painfully aware of the nearness of De Sable—
his warmth, and the light, unshaven prickle as his face
rested against her neck. It was not decent. It was not
right, Eloise thought. They would not even be on the
same side if any battle was to be fought. He was a spy.
She was an honest girl. He murmured and stirred in his
sleep, and without thinking Eloise caught at the arms
about her waist. What if he should fall?

For several hours there were no sounds more threatening than rustles in the greenwood. Hugh began to relax
and lose his hunched attitude of fear and urgency.

'Only a mile or so to the Braceurs' now, Eloise. No
sign of the enemy. It looks as though we're going to be
all right!'

Scarcely had his words been spoken than a low rumble
like thunder rose up from ahead. Jays flew scolding from
the wood, but a magpie laughed out loud. He flew escort
to four horsemen, whose mighty warhorses plunged and
rattled towards the travellers.

'Dear life,' Hugh whispered, clutching at Eloise's arm.
'Richard—Richard, this is it!'

The thundering grew louder until the very earth shook
with fear. Clad in black from head to foot, each holding
a mighty spiked shield, the approaching knights were
ready for action. Their swords were already drawn.

Eloise had seen such devils before, and cried out at
the memory. De Sable's arms tightened around her, his

hands grasping the reins as the borrowed horse started to wheel in fear.

'Stay still,' he hissed, cutting through Eloise's terror. 'They will not dare hurt you while you are with us.'

Neither Hugh nor Richard drew their swords. They stopped and waited.

'Good day to my lord of Montgomery's men!' De Sable greeted them affably as the cohort screeched to a halt, barring their way.

Eloise forced herself to look up at the knights. They were the same brand of cut-throats that had murdered her friends and destroyed her homeland. Now they were to set up Duke Robert as their puppet king and wreak the same havoc in England. Their black, concealing helmets allowed speech but not recognition. They were faceless, nameless horrors.

De Sable was not overawed. He settled his horse and gave Eloise a reassuring squeeze. 'Is my lord of Montgomery hereabouts, then? Hunting, perhaps? How fortuitous. I should so like to renew our aquaintance.'

'That a threat?' one of the black knights snapped suspiciously. 'There'll be a welcome for you back at the Chief's, mind, if you threatens.'

The speaker's companions cackled with glee. Many had entered the horrific castle of Belleme, but no guest had ever emerged alive. Or even in one piece.

'Threats? How can you think of such a thing? No, gentlemen. My brother and I knew the lord of Montgomery when he was nothing but a little black imp. The last time we crossed his path, however, was a very long time ago.'

'Thank the good Lord,' Hugh muttered under his breath.

'Brothers, you say?' Eyes glittered within the row of faceless helmets. The knights looked from one to another. 'What's your names, then?'

Hugh introduced them both quietly, but made no mention of Eloise. She tried to shrink into invisibility within the shelter of De Sable's arms. It was to no avail.

The four knights muttered among themselves, but sheathed their swords. Then the leader shoved his horse a pace nearer. 'Two De Sables are on our list, right enough. But what's that?'

He tipped his head in the direction of Eloise. Even sunlight shied away from the stern darkness of his helmet.

'Oh, only something I picked up on the road. A new servant.'

Eloise was too terrified to baulk at De Sable's words. She cowered beneath the towering shadow of the four horsemen.

The leading knight circled about his three victims. When he drew level with De Sable, he leaned forward and said crisply, 'Where's the cash?'

His three companions yelled with laughter. The De Sables had not been able to conceal a fleeting expression of shock at the words. For once Eloise was glad of De Sable's arm tightening about her. Any support was welcome in the face of the awful reputation of Montgomery's men.

'What cash?' Hugh asked innocently.

At a quick nod from the leader, one of the ruffians rode to Hugh's side. There was a flash of grinning white teeth beneath the sinister helm. In a split second he had wrenched Hugh's head back and was pressing a well-used dagger against the young man's taut throat.

'There must be some mistake,' De Sable said levelly. 'We are simply visitors to this delightful country. We rely on the hospitality of our kin and have no "cash"——'

'No. You're the ones who've made the mistake, trying to convince the old Duke to go it alone. When the Chief found out old Gamberon's glory boys were passing round the hat, he got a bit upset. We don't like it when the Chief gets upset. We're here to put things right.' The leader dropped his voice to a growling whisper. 'We know who's involved. We got a list. Hand over the money.'

He transferred his attention to Eloise, rolling words off his tongue with relish.

'Ever seen a man have his throat cut, chicken? There's a powerful lot of blood—pumping and throbbing and gurgling as he starts to drown——'

Hugh gasped as the knife was pressed harder against his neck. Eloise hid her face in her hands.

'Oh, really!' De Sable removed his gloves as though in a fit of pique. 'I was looking forward to dinner at the Braceurs' until you started that nonsense. If material things mean so much to you, the ox carts with all our belongings are travelling along some way behind.'

After a moment's hesitation the sign was given that Hugh be released. De Sable tucked his gloves into his belt as the four knights drew back a little.

'Right,' their leader called out. 'We'll take you on to the Braceurs'. Then we'll collect your goods. And if it's not up to scratch—well, I hardly need to tell you the rest, do I, my lords?'

The black knights kicked their horses into action, surrounding their victims. With one in front, their leader behind and a horseman on either side, Eloise and her companions were forced onward.

When Eloise felt that neither she nor their horses could go much further, a castle came into view. Had she not been in such terror of the four shadows about them, Eloise would have been enraptured. Instead it was left to De Sable to hug her still tighter with a cheerful comment.

'All these garlands and bunting! See what celebrations there are in our honour, little nightingale. I dare say Lord and Lady Braceur cannot wait for our arrival!'

'They got plenty of company already,' a knight
snarled. 'We only needs half a dozen more of you collectors before we got all the names what's on the list.'

De Sable ruffled Eloise's hair with a merry laugh.
'We'll be among friends, then, little one. We won't do
so badly.'

Eloise was not so sure. She looked at Hugh. Though
unharmed, he was still suffering from his rough hand-
ling. What hope could she have?

They entered the Braceurs' castle through a gateway
festooned with greenwood boughs and forest flowers.
The small, forlorn figures of Lord and Lady Braceur
stood in their castle yard as loose herds of knights milled
about them. Some wore the threatening black livery of
Montgomery. Many more were ordinary, sun-browned
young men, as merry as Richard and Hugh De Sable
were when not escorted by ruffians.

Cheerful shouts greeted their arrival. The De Sables
seemed to know everyone and replied in kind. Hugh went
to make their introductions to the Braceurs and the four
Montgomery's men went off in search of the ox carts.
De Sable got down from the horse then helped Eloise.
His strong arms made little of her frailty, and when her
legs threatened to subside with the terror of it all he held
her firmly.

'Bear up!' His blue eyes were twinkling. 'We're not
dead yet. If it weren't for Montgomery's vultures, this
would be a fine billet. We're among friends. Come and
meet them.' He led her to a group of men playing cards
around a horse trough. Eloise clung to his supporting
strength gratefully. 'We were all at Nicaea together. This
is Gregory, and Miles, and that's——'

Eloise heard none of the cheerful greetings. The afternoon heat, exhaustion and the overwhelming fear of
Montgomery's men finally proved too much. She
swayed, faltered and felt herself falling.

The next thing she knew, Eloise was enveloped in De Sable's strong, gentle arms again. She heard Hugh and others directing him to a room in the castle. There was no chance to protest, nor any strength left in her to do so. It was altogether easier to keep her eyes closed and leave everything to De Sable's quiet calmness.

They were on the top floor, sunlight streaming through a high window. The room was light and airy, with a cool breeze fanning her face.

'Don't wave your handkerchief about like that, Hugh. She doesn't want your germs.'

Eloise stirred herself to stop the hasty words, but, with a further sharp exchange, De Sable dismissed his younger brother.

Feeling fingers at the laces to her dress, Eloise opened her eyes in horror. De Sable laughed at her expression and held up both hands.

'Loosen tight clothing for a faint—that's what they say! I was only doing my duty.'

'Thank you, my lord. I think I am recovered sufficiently.' Eloise struggled to sit up, moving away from any danger at his questing hands.

'Hugh doesn't think so. He thinks I've ruined you forever, and that now I shall cast you aside like all the rest.' De Sable was still laughing.

'Your brother is a good and honourable man, my lord. And very brave to withstand being threatened by those wicked men. Please do not make fun of him if his only concern is for my welfare.'

De Sable tweaked her nose, then arranged a light sheet over her. His expression was grave now, but the blue eyes were still merry.

'You might not think him either good or honourable if you knew what he thinks ails you, little nightingale.'

'Is he a physician, then, my lord?'

De Sable laughed and stood up, moving towards the door. 'No. Only a brother, which is often worse. Do not worry yourself. His diagnosis is wide of the mark.'

He took the ring of two keys from the door lock. 'I must leave you now, and look to Bessie and Edgar. I shall secure the door against Montgomery's merry men, but you will have the spare key. Doubtless I need not urge you to stay in here safe from the ruffians, though. From now on, make sure that you stay in company. Montgomery's men are not so brave when a lady is escorted.'

He removed one key from the great split ring and handed it to her. Before his long strides took him to the door, Eloise called him back.

'Wait, my lord—I have suffered nothing more than a faint, but what does the Lord Hugh think ails me?'

De Sable stopped short, turned, and thought for a moment. With a wicked smile he decided to tell. 'It is a good thing that my brother Hugh is the heart and soul of discretion.' He looked down and Eloise thought she saw a flush suffuse the pale amber gold of his skin. Then he looked up, speaking now with only devilment in his expression. 'Little brother is not at all happy. He suspects that I have given you the nine-month sickness.'

It was the turn of Eloise to flush and turn away. 'Oh, my lord...the disgrace of such a thought...'

'Why? There is no shame in it. The chance of a son is the greatest gift a man can expect.' He folded his arms and grinned at her horror.

'Yes, but only a legal husband can expect that, my lord!'

'Deus, it looks as if Hugh's nagging must make a husband of me yet!' De Sable began to back towards the door. 'La, there seems to be nothing for it but to marry you, then, my lady!'

Eloise did not reply. Instead she twisted the sheet covering her with nervous fingers, unwilling even to look at De Sable. Only with the soft click of key in lock did she realise that he had left her alone at last.

Eloise was glad that there were so many people about. Hugh and his two servants shared the large room with them, which meant that there was always company of some sort. Montgomery's men snooped about everywhere, distrusted by everyone and even by each other. Squabbles were always breaking out among them, discontent never far from the surface.

When the trunks were brought up, their contents had been searched. Everything was tumbled into bundles, crushed and creased but mostly undamaged. The money was never mentioned in Eloise's hearing. Whether any or all of the collection had been found she was not told.

Safer that way, Eloise thought, as she pressed her rumpled pink and cream outfit. What I don't know, the Montgomerys can't torture out of me.

There was a pleasant surprise at supper that night, even if Eloise did think it rather odd. In Duke Robert's new empire, all were to be equal. Once work was finished, master and servant would dine together. Eloise had her doubts about how long the wonderful ideal would work. Bessie and Edgar had no such misgivings, and were delighted at the chance to eat with what they called 'the quality'.

As most of the collectors had made for the Braceurs' castle, the place was packed. With the addition of all their staff, the overcrowding at dinner was almost unbearable. Diners even sat on the floor, or wedged their platters on any ledge about the walls.

'I notice it's the masters who have seats at table,' said Eloise, arms practically pinned to her sides as she sat squashed between De Sable and Hugh.

'Not all of them. Look, Montgomery's men have to stand.'

De Sable grinned and pointed to the patrolling knights. While all other men were out of armour, Montgomery's men were still in their working clothes. Several of them glowered over the terrified Braceurs.

'Then it looks as though the brave plan has failed, my lord. The Lord of Montgomery has moved in to manipulate events as surely as he will manipulate poor Duke Robert.'

There was no reply from De Sable. He was watching a small servant scuttling between the black knights to speak to the Braceurs. A message. Those about the Braceurs fell silent, and heads turned towards the door.

Two of Montgomery's men drew their swords. Coarse oaths from their leader brought the ruffians to order, but did nothing for the growing disquiet among the crowd.

Braceur got to his feet. He was a pale, insubstantial figure with a matching voice, and Eloise could not make out his words.

Hugh could. He slapped down his knife and pushed aside his plate. 'Dear life. It gets worse. Prince Harry has arrived here now. He wants to stay here before going on to visit his brother, King William Rufus. We really are finished now.'

De Sable leaned behind Eloise and tapped his brother on the shoulder. 'None of that kind of talk. Harry might delight in playing his two brothers off against each other, but there's no one he hates more than Montgomery. Perhaps we can use him against our black-hearted companions.'

'Oh, it's no use, Richard! No one can hope to organise this great tribe. The world and his wife are here,' Hugh finished, looking pointedly at the barely touched meal before Eloise.

There was little time left to worry. People crouching near the door jostled, then stood. A wave of movement rippled out from the doorway as all acknowledged Prince Harry's arrival.

He bustled in, flanked by an oppression of knights. Harry himself was as short and undistinguished as his bodyguard was large and impressive. Only his eyes marked him as something special. They were narrow and shifty, regarding everyone with deep suspicion as he scanned the room.

'Food, wine and a woman. Quick!' Prince Harry shouldered his way to the top table. Normal people shrank from his approach—they melted away. Only Montgomery's men dared stand their ground.

In the silence that followed everyone held their breath. Harry and his satellites sidled to within inches of the black knights surrounding the Braceurs.

'Won't dear brother William be delighted to learn that Montgomery's little army are on the move again?' Harry paused for effect. 'That'll get him here quicker than money would.'

The opposing forces sized each other up like seasoned tom-cats. Only after some time did one side appear to back down. With slow, deliberate movements, the leader of Montgomery's men removed his gauntlets, and signalled his men to do likewise. Then he lifted off his fearsome black helm. Montgomery's men had kept these on despite the summer heat, but as the men followed their leader's example the effect revealed was even more horrifying. Hot, sweating gargoyle faces and lank, wet hair showed that the lord of Montgomery did not choose his men for their looks.

'No army here,' the leading black knight sneered slowly. 'Sir.'

Prince Harry turned and grinned slyly at his henchmen. 'Oh, good. Lots of fun and games and no thought for the morrow, then. It will be just like home life at Robert's.' He grabbed a passing servant-girl and heaved her off to where food and wine had been hastily set out for him.

'Don't trust him, little nightingale,' De Sable whispered in amusement. 'Not even to betray us!'

Eloise did not answer. She had already decided not to trust Prince Harry an inch.

CHAPTER TWELVE

ELOISE'S resolve was difficult to maintain. Prince Harry was friendly enough, in a roguish sort of way. Within hours he had chatted to each person, roaming about and delighting in all the gossip. When he had cornered Eloise for the second time, De Sable stepped in and steered her away with a plausible excuse.

'You should not let men compromise your honour by speaking to you so,' De Sable said with tight-lipped anger. He was hurrying her along the corridor to their allotted room, but at his words Eloise stopped and shook off his guiding hand.

'It meant nothing. Prince Harry has a reputation to keep up. He is supposed to be seen compromising ladies. I am not foolish enough to encourage him any further.'

She started off towards the room once more, leaving De Sable where he was, fuming.

'He called you "Sixpence".'

Eloise stopped and looked back over her shoulder at his furious tone. Standing straight and tall, one hand on the hilt of his sword, De Sable was every inch the threatening crusader knight. And he was jealous.

'Prince Harry calls all the girls "Sixpence". It saves him having to remember their names.' She turned with a swish of long skirts on the flagstones and continued on her way. 'I am surprised that it matters to you, my lord.'

'I have no wish to see you taken advantage of.' He covered the distance between them in a few lengthy strides.

'Yet you used me as an attraction to gain funds for your cause? You were quite happy to take advantage of my musical talents when it suited you, my lord.'

De Sable grasped her roughly by the shoulders and forced her to face him. 'That was different——'

Before he could say more, Hugh emerged from the doorway of their room to complain about the noise. De Sable waved him away, but Eloise was not so easily silenced.

'If you think I'm going to be a pawn in this foolhardy enterprise any longer you are much mistaken, my lord. I'm going to——'

'You're going to what, little nightingale? Prince Harry never does anything unless there's money in it—and plenty of it—for him. This castle is rock-solid behind Duke Robert and his claim. And I can't see you appealing to Montgomery's men—well…not in that way…' He laughed, and loosing her shoulders caught up her hand instead. 'I have you well and truly trapped, little nightingale. Only I hold the key to your freedom.'

Slowly he raised her hand to his lips. Eloise was helpless. Light from torches set in the walls flickered over De Sable's fine features and ignited stars in his blue eyes. Eloise felt herself falling under his spell. As so many others must have done, she thought to herself, half in a dream.

De Sable kissed each of her fingertips in turn, his eyes never leaving her face. Only when he laid her hand against the coolness of his cheek did she come to her senses. Snatching her hand away, Eloise ran to the refuge of their room, where the company of Bessie and Edgar and the others would keep her safe. She no longer felt safe alone with Richard De Sable.

Eloise was unsure where that first day at the Braceurs' ended and the next began. Certainly, festivities went on long into the night. She was woken several times by a drunken racket outside the room, then it seemed no time at all before early-morning waking noises: the shifts changing for the look-outs above on the roof; servants slopping cold water as they ferried it to the many guests.

They ate breakfast in their room. It was well and truly crowded now, as a couple of Harry's staff had been squeezed in with the two De Sable parties.

The brothers thought that this was a sinister turn and advised their staff to guard their tongues. Eloise laughed at their caution. The castle was packed, and people had to be fitted in where there was room. She laughed and joked with Prince Harry's men, much to De Sable's fury. Eloise paid no attention, and told Prince Harry's men to do likewise.

Eloise did her best to make their lodgers feel part of the group. Even so, something stopped her short of any careless talk when their conversation strayed towards the Duke of Normandy. Was it De Sable's unspoken anger, which crackled from his eyes each time she caught him looking at her? No. There was something else—but Eloise did not want to acknowledge it.

After breakfast De Sable and Hugh gave their staff the day off and went their separate ways. Eloise agreed to go out for a walk with Bessie and Edgar. She wanted to get away from the crowds and most of all the shadow of the black knights. Prince Harry's arrival had quelled their ambitions a little, but Eloise still felt weak and sick whenever she saw one. Fresh air would restore her.

Her plans were ruined, but from an unexpected source. As she crossed the great hall with Bessie and Edgar, Harry strode towards them through heaps of hounds sleeping about the empty hearth.

'Come on, Sixpence! The game's started. If you aren't hidden in two minutes flat I shan't be able to "seek" you, shall I? Thrill of the chase, and all that.'

He dragged her, protesting, away from Bessie and Edgar.

'The others have got a head start on you, Sixpence. You'll be lucky to find a good hiding-place. Perhaps you'll have to squeeze in tight somewhere with Richard or Hugh?' He laughed and chucked her under the chin. 'Run along, then—quick sharp!'

Obediently, Eloise set off down the nearest passageway. Behind her she heard Harry dismiss Bessie and Edgar, rather rudely, to Eloise's way of thinking. She felt uncomfortable that he had not treated her as a servant, too. Then she reflected that Prince Harry was even less polite with young female servants. It was as well just to humour him with his game of hide-and-seek for the moment.

Skipping up the first staircase she came to, Eloise met Hugh at the top. He looked preoccupied, and tried to delay her.

'You don't want to come up here, surely?'

Eloise laughed and dodged past him. 'The Prince is coming to seek. I must hide——'

'Not in there!' Hugh leapt forward to stop her entering the nearest bedchamber. 'Er—it's already occupied.'

Eloise stood back. There was no rule against more than one person to a room. Hugh's guilty expression left her in no doubt—his brother Richard was in that room, and up to no good. Poor Hugh thought he was protecting her. Eloise thought of the previous evening, when De Sable had trapped her in a similar corridor, caressing her with glances . . .

'Don't worry, my lord Hugh. You need not explain. I shall find a hiding-place that will cause you less embarrassment.'

Genuinely relieved, he patted her arm. With Harry's cry of 'Coming!' Hugh sprang away to the head of the stairs. Eloise dived into a room opposite where she suspected De Sable to be busying himself.

Giggles from beneath the bed and behind wall-hangings showed this chamber to have been a popular refuge. There would be no room. In desperation, Eloise looked back out into the corridor. Hugh had gone down past the curve of the staircase. Only his shadow was visible on the wall. Of the Prince there was no sound. He must have taken another corridor.

Suddenly, a little of De Sable's devilment infected Eloise. She would burst in on her wicked master, shaming him for the silk-mouthed rogue that he was. That would teach him to toy with her emotions!

She slipped across the corridor and into the forbidden room. To her astonishment, it was completely deserted. Strangely, too, for a chamber on an upper floor, it had no windows. In the darkness there was no rustling, or giggling. It was completely silent.

Why had Hugh stopped her entering? Perhaps it was the room of Lord and Lady Braceur. It smelt clean enough, and there seemed to have been no overnight guests. But why was it so dark?

Mailed footsteps began to ring along the corridor outside. This room was out of bounds, for whatever reason. If Hugh had warned her away, then she did not want to get him into trouble.

Eloise ran towards the far wall of the gloomy room. The footsteps were closer—almost outside the door now. Fumbling in her haste, she squeezed into the gap between the wall and the great tapestry that hung upon it. The space was choking with the smell of new limewash, but she was not a moment too soon. Hugh's voice was raised outside in the corridor, then joined by that of De Sable. It was lucky that she had found such a good hiding-place.

Her luck was changing. In the darkness, Eloise felt the smoothness of plaster beneath her fingers give way to the polished wood of a door. Her hand closed upon a latch.

Eloise lifted the latch and the door swung easily on well-oiled hinges. Immediately the smell of soap and sweet herbs wafted out to entice her. She slipped backwards through the door, sure that she had found an excellent hiding-place.

The mystery of the missing window was solved. Expecting to find herself in a dark cupboard piled with the family valuables, Eloise was astonished to see that she had entered a room. A false wall had made a secret chamber beyond the Braceurs' bedroom. Small, but light and airy, the scent of new money still hung on the richly coloured tapestries decorating the walls. The stone-flagged floor had been recently scrubbed, and luxurious, fluffy sheepskins laid down against any chill.

A large wooden bed dominated the room, the letters 'RR' intertwined along the top rails and down the wooden pillar at each corner. Eloise stopped gaping, closed the door behind her and stepped softly into the room.

It had not taken her long to realise what she had stumbled upon. As she drew near the sumptuous bed her suspicions were confirmed. Here the double 'R' initial was surmounted with a carved crown, and the words *'Dei Gratia'. Robertus Rex*—King, by the grace of God.

There was nothing that Eloise could do. King William would be overthrown, and Duke Robert of Normandy put in his place. This room had been prepared for the Duke's arrival. He must be expected at any time—that was the reason for the bunting about the castle.

Eloise tried to imagine the terrible panic that the Braceurs must have felt, having Prince Harry arrive on their doorstep. He would have no qualms about turning traitors over to his brother William Rufus—if the price was right. He had already had his ear to the ground. Even now, he would be using the game of hide-and-seek to probe, explore and possibly even discover, as she had done.

Eloise went to the bed, touching the rich red and gold hangings that would enclose it when in use. What a shame that such an elaborate thing was to be wasted on a character like Robert of Normandy. How beautiful the bed was. Its luxury was so desirable...

There was no one about. The voices outside had died away again. No one would know. Not if she was quick.

She lowered herself down gingerly to sit on the edge of the bed. Soft as thistledown, the bedding yielded to her with a soft rustling of fine silks and linens. So different from her thin sheepskin sleeping-mat! So like the bed that she had slept in back home, in Brionne.

Greatly daring, Eloise lay back against the heap of feather bolsters and cushions supplied for Duke Robert's use. Looking up, she saw that the wooden canopy over the bed was not only carved, it was painted, too. Birds and animals, fruit and flowers were arrayed in gaudy beauty overhead...

There was a noise in the outer room. Someone— several people—were coming. Eloise jumped up, frantically looking for a place to hide. To be found in a place like this with the Braceur household so nervous—she couldn't risk it. And what if it was Prince Harry?

None of the tapestries went right to the floor. She couldn't hide behind those. The bed itself? No. They would notice if the hangings were closed. There was only one place. The blanket-chest at the foot of the bed.

She would have to be very careful. Eloise remembered a terrible tale of a girl playing hide-and-seek who locked herself in a chest by accident. Her body wasn't found for years.

Burrowing under lavender-scented blankets, Eloise took care to stop the lid closing completely by wedging the lid open a crack with her fingers.

Not a moment too soon. The latch clicked again and two or three sets of footsteps entered. When Eloise heard who the first speaker was, her blood turned cold. It was one of Montgomery's men.

'Sit down there.'

'I prefer to stand, if it's——' De Sable's voice was interrupted by the sound of a blow. 'All the same to you.'

'Sit down!'

He sat down. On the blanket-box. A searing, agonising pain tore through Eloise's hand—unbearable torture, but she could neither escape nor cry out. That would mean certain death, or much worse, from Montgomery's men.

Eloise felt herself dragged towards the oblivion of unconsciousness, but the next words forced her to endure.

'You've been chosen, my lord Richard.' There was a sarcastic laugh in the voice. 'Things are getting a bit hot for us, what with Prince Harry arriving. You're the prettiest of the bunch. And with an air of the mysterious about you, too. Rufus will go for that. The county's all meeting up tomorrow, on account of the King's being in the area. There's to be a great hunt. You're going to put yourself up as the King's quarry. On the sly, if you know what I mean.'

Eloise knew all too well. The pain and sickness threatening her reared up with renewed force. The black knight went on:

'When you suggest a little diversion to the Hanging Man Glade, alone, like, King William Rufus will follow you like a lamb.'

'And you will be waiting there for him, I take it.'

'Oh, yes. Oh, yes, indeed.' The second ruffian spoke now, and drew closer. Eloise knew she would have to cry out if he sat down too. He didn't.

'One way and another, the two of you are going into that clearing at four o'clock tomorrow afternoon, but

that'll be an end to it. Either you finish Rufus then and
there, or we do for both of you. But succeed or fail,
your life won't be worth a light, son. You know too much
now.'

There was a pause, then De Sable spoke slowly. 'And
Duke Robert sent you these instructions himself?'

Montgomery's men guffawed with mirth. Eloise tried
not to scream and cry out loud.

'No, no. We don't take orders from no one but the
Chief. Chief's managing matters while old Gamberon's
fooling about building sandcastles on his honeymoon.'

When De Sable spoke again his voice was hollow and
dull. All the finer emotions had been squeezed from it.
'Then the Lord of Montgomery will be in charge of
England in Duke Robert's absence?'

'Chief will *be* England, mark my words, son. The new
order's coming, and it's starting tomorrow!'

'Pity you won't be around to share in it!'

The second voice chimed in happily as Montgomery's
men moved to the door.

'Come on, then, my lord Richard. You don't want to
miss a minute of your last day on earth, do you?'

His comrade was not so kind. 'Nah. And just remember, you tell anyone, any living soul what's going
on, and——'

'What? You'll kill me? You'll be doing that anyway,'
De Sable said with disdainful calm. There was a pause
and Eloise prayed that they would go, go and leave her
with her fear and agony.

'Oh, we'll kill you all right. And fast, if you're a good
lad. But if not...' Montgomery's men cackled throatily
'...we'll take a nice long time about it...'

Mercifully Eloise was spared further details. A dead
faint claimed her and she knew no more.

At first Eloise was puzzled. Then she remembered. It
was dark because she was hidden in the linen-chest and

the gnawing ache in her left hand gave a sudden reminder of the horror that she had overheard.

She listened intently. All was silent. After hearing only the pounding of her heart for half a dozen beats, Eloise raised the chest lid an inch or two with her good hand. Nothing happened, except a shooting pain through her trapped fingers as the pressure was released.

The room was empty once more. Eloise got out of the chest and rearranged the linen as best she could with one hand. The fingers of her left hand were purple-black and swollen where they had been cruelly crushed, but despite the insistent pain Eloise had hopes that they were not broken.

She hurried to the door and listened again. What if they were outside, waiting? For minutes on end she waited, listening. Thankfully there were no sounds of any sort from the Braceurs' bedroom. Opening the door, Eloise slipped into the gap behind the tapestry and so out into freedom.

De Sable was under sentence of death. Eloise tried to tell herself that only days ago she would have welcomed that news, even been glad to turn him over to King William's men herself. It was no use. She hadn't been able to do it then, and it hurt her to see it happen now. De Sable might be misguided, but he was a world away from the likes of Montgomery and his men. Although Eloise held such different views from her lord, she knew how deeply De Sable's respect for Duke Robert ran. His was a selfless admiration, not guided by the greed of Montgomery and his like. And now it was being used to bring about not only the King's destruction, but also the death of De Sable himself.

Eloise went quickly downstairs. The game had finished, or moved on. Everywhere seemed deserted, until she came to the great hall.

Tired of hide-and-seek, Prince Harry had draped himself over a chair in the great hall, a hound at his feet and a girl in his arms. Eloise looked away modestly and tried to creep past unnoticed. Harry, however, never missed a trick.

'Hello, Sixpence. What's up? What have you done to yourself?' He got up, although whether genuinely interested or merely bored with his companion it was difficult to say. The girl was deposited with little ceremony.

'A silly thing, my lord. I shut my hand in the door...'

It would do as an excuse. Harry took her wrist and looked at the damage thoughtfully.

'Richard doesn't look after you very well, does he? Poor little thing. Run along out to the kitchens. They'll put some butter on it for you.'

He ruffled her hair good-naturedly and turned back to his girl. As Eloise reached the door, Harry thought of something else, and freed himself with reluctance from an intimate embrace.

'Oh, and Sixpence? While you're out there...my chaps are doing a bit of work for me. Tell them they've got the rest of the day off when the business with Tyrell is settled. If it isn't—well, they'll know what to expect. Either way, I'm not to be disturbed for...oh...ever so long.'

The girl giggled as Harry laid hold once more, and Eloise scurried out. She thanked goodness that De Sable did not flaunt his amours so publicly, then remembered that he would have no further opportunities for dalliance. No opportunities for anything, ever again.

She scoured the yard for him as she crossed to the kitchen block, but he was nowhere to be seen. Eloise wondered what she could say when next they met. It might be for the last time. An uncomfortable pang racked her and she realised again that her unspoken feelings for her lord might run deeper than mere loyalty. And now it was too late.

The kitchen was unbearably hot. It took so long to get a decent blaze going that even in August the fire had to be maintained at all times. Harry's men sat at the coolest end of the great kitchen table, one either side of a man that Eloise hadn't seen before.

Nothing unusual about that. There were so many crowded into the castle she could not have remembered all the faces. Still, something made her notice him. Prince Harry's men were laughing, slapping him on the back and pouring him drink after drink. The man seemed reticent, shrugging and occasionally shaking his head as though in bewilderment.

The cook manipulated Eloise's fingers with detached humour. He confirmed her hopes that there were no bones broken, and slapped on a mixture of rancid butter and minced rocket leaves. As he bound up his handi-work, Eloise watched Harry's men, and wondered if they were about the business that Harry had talked about.

'He doesn't seem very impressed, although they're spoiling him,' Eloise observed to the cook, who spat liquidly into the fire.

'Then they 'ent reached the price 'ee d'want for the job, whatever that might be,' he said curtly, and spat again. 'There's no such thing as friendship in business, and I should know. Look at the trouble I got, trying to get someone to do a little job for us . . .'

The cook finished his bandaging, then bidding her stay where she was disappeared out into the yard. A few moments later he returned, carrying a grinning, gulping toad.

''Old yer 'and out.'

Eloise did so, half afraid of what might be coming next. The cook passed the toad over her hand three times, muttering an incantation as he did so.

'There. That'll see the pain off.' The cook glowered at the toad, which blinked slowly. 'Or it would do, if some was to do their duty.' He dropped the toad, which hopped off out across the greasy kitchen floor. The three men at the other end of the table did not notice. Business at last seemed to be progressing for them.

'It feels better already.' Eloise tried to wiggle her fingers, but they felt stiff beneath the bandaging.

'Not for long. It's the twentieth year since a prophecy was last brought about. Now here we are, Lammas-tide, and nothing been done about seeing the debts cleared. Unless someone brings about a miracle, all the little healing spells and weather charms will be as nothing. Suffering and bad harvests for the next twenty years.'

Eloise shrank back in horror. 'Witchcraft?'

The cook laughed. 'Ssh! We don't want 'em up the other end o' the table getting the wrong end of the stick, eh? It's only a few little words, to help folk along. Like yourself. But it'll all come to nothing unless the next prophecy's brought about soon:

> "Twenty years of ill made good,
> When Red Boar's blood spills on new wood."

But can I get anyone to help us out? Oh, no, not a soul. Make-believe for the old and feeble-minded, they all say. Or—not worth the expense to do a job for nothing. I don't know what this place is coming to, I really don't . . .'

The cook grumbled on, but Eloise made an excuse as soon as possible and went to deliver Harry's message. His two men were delighted to hear of their unexpected holiday, and jollied their associate along with even greater glee. They suggested that he should spend the afternoon drinking with them, and when he protested about lack of funds Eloise saw a small leather pouch change hands. After counting and recounting the coins it contained, the man was all smiles and left with his new friends.

Eloise went out behind them, even more eager to find De Sable. She had heard Edgar sneer about King William

Rufus, calling him 'The Red Boar'. It didn't take a genius to relate 'New Wood' to 'New Forest'. The place was devoted to Duke Robert's cause, and, worse, staffed by murderous heathens. If that weren't bad enough, Montgomery's men were poised in readiness for action. Whatever happened during the next few days was bound to have blood all over it.

She knocked at the door of the main hall, and found with relief that Prince Harry had disappeared to continue his courting in more private surroundings.

It was not long before she found De Sable. Two of Montgomery's less charming men lounged outside the doorway to the De Sables' chamber. As Eloise approached they barred her way, leering, but at sharp words from within the chamber edged back sullenly.

De Sable was alone in the room and seated at the table, writing. He looked up at her knock and smiled cheerfully until he saw her bandaged hand. At once his eyes became troubled, although not only with the genuine concern he voiced at her mishap.

'I was hoping you would play "Willow" for me alone tonight.'

For the last time. The thought twisted Eloise's heart cruelly. She saw how truly fair he was, in both body and mind. He would be loyal to his lord to the end.

She wanted to go to him, hold him and explain that she understood everything. But that was too dangerous. If the men outside should hear—the revenge of Montgomery's men would be too dreadful to contemplate. Instead, Eloise went to stand beside her lord.

'I can sing for you, if you like. Now?'

'Later.' He took his hand from the parchments that he had been writing upon. Although it had looked a casual movement, the parchment curled up, conveniently obscuring what he had been writing. 'Last thing tonight. I shall be going out very early tomorrow, Eloise.

Before you will be up and about ... Oh, no! What is it?
Don't cry. Here, come and sit down.'

He led her to the bed. Eloise tried to contain the overwhelming grief that she felt, but still silent tears coursed
down her cheeks. De Sable dragged out a corner of the
bed sheet and held it up for her. With her good hand
and linen she tried to stem the flow of tears, but it was
of no use.

'Shock, I expect,' he said simply. They sat together
for a while, then without any of the usual merriment or
force De Sable said simply, 'Eloise...I wonder...would
you mind very much if I were to put my arm around
you?'

This is how it will be, then, thought Eloise. He is going
to die tomorrow. How can I refuse my lord anything,
knowing that? She nodded, slow and silently.

Gentle as a whisper his arm slid around her waist. He
sighed, long and deeply, before leaning against her as
she sat beside him.

'I have done many things in my life of which I am
not proud, Eloise,' he said, at last. 'But recently I think
I may have learned the meaning of honour. I must have
made your life a misery over the past few weeks.'

He gave her a squeeze, but all Eloise could do was
shake her head. Speech was beyond her.

'If things had worked out differently, I would have
been honourable towards you. Knowing what I know
now. You are made for better things than a mere serving-
girl, Eloise. I would love you, if you would let me.'

He looked away as he said the last few words, and
Eloise realised what they had cost him in terms of pride.

'My lord?' Her voice trembled with suppressed tears,
but Eloise looked at De Sable steadily enough. 'I wish—
that you would not go—hunting—tomorrow.'

He laughed, but Eloise knew how forced that merriment must be.

'Oh, but I have to, my little nightingale. The King himself will be there!'

'The staff are to have a picnic in the forest. Could you not stay with us for the morning, and join his grace the King for the—events—of the afternoon?'

De Sable cupped her chin in his hand and gently turned her face to look into his. He was so beautiful, his hand so steady. No trace of the fear and horror that she felt on his behalf.

'Close your eyes, Eloise.' He looked deeply into her soul, his blue eyes soft as morning mist. 'Close your eyes, for I know that if I were to blow out the candles you would be alarmed, and that is not my intention.'

Eloise did as she was told, more in longing than fear now.

'Suddenly I find that, though pretty words have always come easily to me in the past, truth finds me ashamed in the light.' His words were spoken with a rueful smile, she could hear. There was a pause as he gathered his nerve. 'I love you, Eloise. You are the brightest star under heaven, the dearest . . . no, don't say anything. I don't deserve your love, nor even your respect. Go now, leave me. But let me take one last kiss . . . to remember . . .'

His lips touched hers, the last words a mere whisper. Gone was the pawing insistence, the frantic lust. Instead he was sincere and loving, holding her like a piece of rare glass, accepting love from her lips as she gave it freely. Only when Edgar arrived outside, provoking Montgomery's men to snarls, did their embrace end, and then unwillingly.

'Ah, Edgar.' De Sable's arms slid from her as the little serving-man barged in past the sentries. 'Little Eloise has had a bit of an accident. See she's well looked after, will you? I've got some documents that need signing. I'll go and find someone to witness them for me. Then I've some pressing business, and after that I have a request to beg of my lord of Montgomery's men.'

With that he was gone, not even giving Eloise a backward glance.

When De Sable returned, a long time later, he dismissed Bessie and Edgar for the afternoon. With a wry smile, De Sable suggested that Eloise keep him company while they were gone, much to Bessie's disgust.

When they were alone, De Sable took out the chessboard and Eloise helped him set out the pieces with her one good hand. When their hands touched accidentally, Eloise found that although her fingers were trembling De Sable was a picture of calm.

Eloise could not bear him to be so distant, but after pouring such raw emotions into his earlier speech he seemed to have little left to say.

All through the game Eloise waited for him to make a move towards her, but at all times he was politely distant, as though his mind was elsewhere. She could not bring herself to speak, to hope that the words he had spoken were true.

Whenever Eloise looked up, De Sable seemed to be gazing at her. Whether they were speaking of the game or preparations for the party that evening, there was no hint of either his earlier revelation to her or the terrible secret that he bore. As cheerful as ever, he tried to joke Eloise out of her melancholy until at last she had to make the effort. To please him.

CHAPTER THIRTEEN

THAT evening at the party, Eloise watched the Braceurs. They played their parts very well. Had she not known that anything was going on, Eloise would have been as carefree as Prince Harry. Seeming quite oblivious of any plots, he was enjoying himself with a rare vigour.

'Oh, Sixpence, what did you want to spoil my evening for?' Harry reached across De Sable and tweaked her ear. 'I was looking forward to hearing you play again tonight. I've been thinking about a song that Robert used to like. What was it called?' He rocked back in his chair, one hand on De Sable's shoulder to steady himself.

'No tide, wall or frontier the onslaught will stand,
When God leads dear Normandy on to new land...'

As Harry spoke the words, so the assembled diners faltered in their conversations, and looked. Knowing what was in the minds of all assembled, Eloise spoke quickly as he finished.

'I haven't heard that for a very long time, my lord. I thought that it was a Norman national song.'

'Or Breton.' He grinned slyly.

'And you have always been so proud of the fact that you were born in England, my lord.'

His eyes clouded and Eloise realised that he was listening to a conversation further down the table. She moved closer to De Sable.

'My lord——'

'Richard. That is my name, if only you would use it. Please. Though you would not do so before.' He moved

210

his thigh very close to hers beneath the table, warm and reassuring.

'Prince Harry. He knows...'

'When you and I share the same plate here at dinner, and sit so closely? I should hope that everyone knows, not merely Harry.' He put down his knife and reached for her hand. 'Everything is going to be all right. Trust me. No harm will ever come to you.'

His voice was calming, reassuring. Eloise looked into his eyes and knew that he spoke the truth. He released her hand and stroked thoughtfully at the small silver cross that hung about his neck.

'I am truly sorry that I cannot say the things in cold blood that I would like you to hear.' De Sable looked into the distance, uncomfortable with even these few words. He defused the situation with a nervous laugh. 'See, you did get to wear your new dress again.'

He stroked at the rose damascene of her skirts, but it was with regretful longing now and not lustful insistence. While noise and merriment swirled about them, he looked down, dark lashes sooty against his golden skin. With a low murmur he spoke so that only Eloise could hear.

'I—I have a surprise for you, Eloise. It was to wait until after supper, but as I confess that I have no appetite this evening...' He smiled at her self-consciously, then seemed to gain conviction all of a sudden. 'Neither have you, I see. Come, take my hand now.'

He stood up and, taking his leave of Prince Harry and the Braceurs, led her out of the hall. The cool twilight of the stone-flagged passageways was hushed. Only the crackle of torches lighting their way broke the silence.

Eloise suddenly realised that the ever-present shadows of Montgomery's men had followed them out of the hall. Forbidding dark shapes detached themselves from the gloom and caught up with them as they reached the steps of the Braceurs' private chapel. Eloise froze with terror and shrank before the men, but De Sable squeezed her hand. Raising himself to his full impressive height, he turned to them.

'The lady knows of you gentlemen only by reputation,' he said levelly, 'and is not aware, as I am, of your charming true natures.' With a mock bow he stood aside for them to enter the chapel. 'My dear brother has taken care to arrange everything, gentlemen, but I dare say the priest will not object to an extra couple of witnesses.'

Eloise had not dared to hope, but now her dearest wish was to come true. As she entered the chapel and saw candles lit and the well-scrubbed, relieved faces of Bessie and Edgar, realisation dawned. Hugh was there too, trying not to look too delighted on such a solemn occasion.

For a few brief hours of happiness, Eloise and De Sable would be man and wife. No one, not even Montgomery's men, would ever be able to deny them that. De Sable smiled down at her and Eloise was lost in wonder.

The ceremony drifted past Eloise in a haze of incense and sweet wine. There might have been two or two dozen others in the room. Eloise and her Richard had eyes for no one but each other.

The priest blessed De Sable's signet to serve as a wedding ring. It would be too large, once her ring finger was healed back to its normal size, but to Eloise it was perfect.

When all was over, De Sable took her in his arms for a long, lingering kiss. Eloise was hesitant, too aware of the lurking horror of Montgomery's men leering at them, but De Sable soon filled her thoughts. Holding her close he whispered, 'Wait for me in the Braceurs' room. We'll find somewhere without an audience.'

They thanked the priest and his assistants. Hugh could not contain his happy laughter, and Eloise realised that he could not know what was to happen the next day.

With an embarrassed goodnight to Bessie and Edgar, Richard and Eloise left to go to their guest room.

Our room, now, thought Eloise, then with a catch in her throat realised how quickly bride would be widow. Montgomery's men followed them relentlessly, right to the door of the room. Eloise felt her hand dampen as she clutched Richard nervously. He spoke to their audience with a laugh in his voice.

'Goodnight, gentlemen. I trust you do not wish to come further?'

Richard raised an eyebrow in a parody of good manners and the two men scowled, lips drawn back in evil snarls. Each ruffian carried a sword, but that was not their only weapon. They were each equipped with a short stabbing-knife tucked just inside their jackets. Nothing if not well prepared, Eloise thought, and shivered.

De Sable took Eloise into the room and removed his sword belt. 'Well, wife. Aren't you even going to ask what I've done to warrant such attentions from the lord of Montgomery's men?' He spoke loudly enough to be easily heard by the listeners outside. Eloise tried to hold the grief from her voice.

'No, my lord. I—I am afraid that you would tell of some new foolishness...'

'What? Call me foolish, would you?'

'No, my lord. But I would not double your strife by becoming an accessory to any wickedness you may have committed.'

He was laughing quietly, expression full of pride and admiration that she refused to be frightened into silence because mortal enemies stood outside. Only when the tears began afresh did he envelop her in another tender embrace.

'Shy, my little one? This room's not built for modesty!
I know. Take your things and get ready in the garde-
robe. But don't be long, mind. I shall be waiting!'

He released her, urging her on with his eyes where
words would have betrayed them. Eloise snatched up
her comb, perfume bottle and clean nightdress, while De
Sable found a bottle of wine and two goblets. Pouring
a drink for himself, he wrapped the bottle and second
cup in a towel and handed it to Eloise, who hid it in the
folds of the nightdress.

She had to push her way between Montgomery's men,
who were lounging outside the door. One put his foot
out to trip her, but at a sharp word from De Sable he
withdrew it and spat viciously instead.

Once around the corner and out of sight, Eloise ran
as fast as she could. Past a couple of Harry's dozing
guards, she went down the back staircase and on to the
Braceurs' room. It was empty, and would be for hours.
Eloise doubted that the Braceurs were any more relaxed
at that moment than she was. They wouldn't turn in
before Prince Harry, and he was always about until the
small hours.

She had bathed before supper, so quickly changed into
her nightdress and combed her hair into a river of dark
waves about her shoulders. There had been no time to
look out any cosmetics or exotic oils from her collection, so Eloise would have to rely upon her own fair
looks. A touch of lavender water at wrists and neck finished her toilet, and she sat nervously on the edge of the
bed to await her new husband.

There was nothing further to do, and Eloise had time
to think. This time tomorrow and she would be alone.
There would be only desolation where now there was
love and longing.

With the slightest rustle, De Sable entered the room
and was beside her. His quiet laughter at evading his two
shadows soon changed to a gentler sound.

'Never did I think to be in this position. Me—a married man. See what you've done, little nightingale!' He took her hand and led her towards the secret door, shouldering the tapestry aside. Eloise gasped at his nerve, which he took as amazement at seeing the room for the first time.

'I told you that there were better places for romance than the open road. There! What do you think?'

The royal bed stood waiting, shadows rippling about the rich hangings as De Sable lit candles that stood about the room.

'We can't possibly...someone will see the lights from outside! We'll be caught!'

'We're married, aren't we? Life's too short for worries, Eloise. And I'll dim the lights soon. Very soon.'

He bolted the door. Even if the hounds of hell themselves arrived outside, Eloise and her Richard were safe for the moment.

Eloise sat nervously on the blanket-box and at first declined the goblet of wine that De Sable poured her. Only when he coaxed her with kisses did Eloise accept the drink. Even then she doubted that it could bring her much relaxation that night.

De Sable went about the room snuffing the candles until only the one beside the bed remained. Eloise sat in the darkness, waiting for a sound outside. None came. At last De Sable came to her, placed her empty cup on the bedside table and extinguished the final candle. As he stood before her, Eloise sensed the warmth of his skin and the gentleness of his breath on her hair.

The wine had warmed her senses and she responded to his kisses tenderly. Only when he took her up and placed her gently between the sheets did the awful memories come flooding back.

'Richard...oh, Richard, I'm so afraid...'

He moved back a little, stroking her hair softly to reassure her.

'There is no need, sweetheart. I love you, and will look after you——'

'But I am afraid for you... Oh, Richard, how will I live without you now?'

He knelt on the bed beside her as she twined her arms around his neck. As he drew her into his arms she felt his heart racing and found herself weeping for the youth and vitality that were to be so cruelly cut down.

'How did I ever manage to entwine you in this? What foolishness of mine enticed you into the trap that holds me so fast?' He sighed, caressing her with infinite gentleness. 'Whatever you know, my love, however you may have learnt it, forget. Everything, for tonight. This is ours. Who knows, things might yet happen—I've prepared for the worst, but will hope for the best. Whatever happens you will be all right, my love.'

He pulled away from her, and she heard the soft sounds of his shirt being unlaced.

'And now, I'll pull the bed-hangings tight shut, and everything outside of our own little world can fly away.'

The curtains closed about them and at last they were alone together.

It was still dark, although Eloise guessed it to be the early hours of the morning. She lay in the bed still as stone. The regular breathing hesitated, altered, then the strong arms that had enfolded her began to ease away. Twisting in his arms, Eloise turned and was at once caught up in a rapturous embrace.

'I didn't mean to waken you...'

'I haven't slept.'

'Not at all?' He was concerned, and paused in his caresses.

'A little. I thought to move would disturb you.'

'Eloise...' He reached up and pulled aside the hangings about the bed. With a light kiss he laid her back upon the pillows and got up. At once she was alert.

'Don't go!'

'We must eat, my love! And what is the use of "shadows" if one cannot get them to do one's bidding?'

He threw a robe about his shoulders and went to the door. Unbolting it, he stepped outside and Eloise heard the murmur of sleepy voices. The voices rose in querulous argument, and Eloise sat up to listen.

Not only Montgomery's men were lying in wait in the outside room. The Braceurs were horrified that their secret room had been commandeered, but when De Sable returned he was laughing again.

'It won't hurt them to spoil us a little. Just this once.'

He threw aside the robe and slid back into bed beside Eloise. Love had long since transformed her shyness into pleasure and now, as he nestled against her, all her thoughts were of the brief time that might remain.

'Don't go with the hunting party, my love. Don't throw your life away...'

'Hush, my little one. Whatever fancies you may have, destiny cannot be changed.' His voice was as quiet as a sigh, and in warning he held his finger to her lips. She kissed it, then spoke as softly as he had.

'But couldn't you escape now, through the window, and go to the King? Warn him?'

'A warning would not come well from one who would have to confess a certain interest in events. I am Duke Robert's ally as much as Montgomery's men are.' He shuddered visibly. 'Although thankfully there the similarities end, I hope.'

He grinned and put his arm around her. As Eloise began to yield beneath the firm, cool insistence of his lips, one of Montgomery's men burst in unannounced and dumped a tray noisily beside the bed. With a few words of mock gratitude, De Sable dismissed him. The man left only grudgingly, and after he had closed the door De Sable sighed.

'It would be of no use. Matters have been taken over by the Lord of Montgomery and his henchmen. Even if their plan was foiled this time they would try again. King William Rufus cannot be saved. And neither can I.'

He handed Eloise a cup of buttermilk from the tray and cut bread and cold meat for them both. Eloise refused to eat, but De Sable was more realistic. As he ate he explained the plans that had been laid down in his will. Hugh was to take charge of everything. He would take Eloise home with him to Brittany. As good and trusted servants, Edgar and Bessie would go with her. In Brittany she would be taken in by the De Sable family and treated as one of their own.

'Oh, don't cry, my love! They won't eat you, or treat you like a poor relation! As I said last night, we must prepare for the worst but hope for the best. I managed to arrange a special dispensation to attend the staff picnic with you this morning, so who knows what may come of that? There might be something for us just around the corner!'

Some time later Eloise and De Sable entered the great hall. Although it was still early, Prince Harry and two of his men were already huddled in conversation around the fire. De Sable sighed, and Eloise looked up at him questioningly.

'Oh, nothing. I was merely thinking... No. It was a disloyal thought. Harry might have made a better King of England, but he is so brutal. If only dear Duke Robert could bring himself to be as vigorous in his treatment of the Montgomerys.'

'That he would never be,' Eloise said thoughtfully, as the ever-present shadows were heard behind them. 'Richard, my love, I wonder...I'm sure to regret missing breakfast. Could you ask the kitchen to put a little extra into our picnic? I'm sure they wouldn't mind.'

De Sable smiled at her, a life of longing trapped in his gaze. He went out happily enough, but only one of Montgomery's men followed him. Eloise cursed her luck silently. She must be judged a risk, too. There could be no direct appeal to Prince Harry now.

'Oh, Sixpence, what have you done to Richard? It's the talk of the castle! You've managed to trap the world's most eligible bachelor!'

'And I thought that was you, my lord!' Eloise felt the thug behind her close in.

'Not any more. I'm going to make an honest woman of somebody, very soon. Perhaps sooner than any of us imagine!'

Harry's friends laughed, but he silenced them abruptly. 'I recognise that man.' A bitter glare transformed his features as he spotted Eloise's shadow. 'He cost one of my men dear at the gaming table last night. If he's so keen, perhaps you two lads would like to give him a little more practice?'

Smirking, Harry's two friends stalked Montgomery's man across the hall. He was torn between staying with Eloise as instructed or being forced into a game of dice. The sheer size of Harry's men helped him come to a swift decision.

'And now, Sixpence, entertain me,' Harry said loudly. Montgomery's man glared at her with small, evil eyes, and Eloise found her resolve failing. What might they not do to her love if she were to tell? Harry took her roughly by the arm.

'Come along! For a blushing bride you seem remarkably troubled. What is it?'

'A bad dream disturbed my sleep last night, my lord. Nothing more.'

'Only a dream disturbed you? Not Richard?' He was laughing at her now, mirth concealing his hard features.

'I dreamt that your brother the King would be in great danger, my lord. While hunting.'

Harry's hand tightened painfully on her arm, but his voice remained light. 'Piffle! Dreams? Who needs them? I only acknowledge facts!'

'I was afraid, my lord.' She slid her good hand into Harry's as though for comfort, but squeezed it quickly, four times.

He looked puzzled for a moment, then said coolly, 'Numbers of men might take advantage.'

There was a question in the word 'numbers', and Eloise looked at him hopelessly. 'I have been awake since four o'clock this morning, my lord. By this afternoon I shall be fit for nothing.'

Harry grinned, the message understood. Four o'clock that afternoon. He looked thoughtful. 'Where was dear Richard to let that happen?'

How on earth could she hope to slip 'Hanging Man Glade' into the conversation? The man from Montgomery was already distinctly uneasy.

Eloise shook her head wordlessly. She had already said far too much. To her surprise Harry's grasp on her arm changed to a friendly squeeze, and he muttered a re-assurance under his breath.

'Oho. Now that is a serious matter,' he said in a low voice, yet loud enough to get Montgomery's man straining his ears while he lost money. 'Perhaps others ought to hear of this. Jack? Here.'

Torn away from his dice game, Jack was sullen and silent, slouching over to Harry with bad grace.

'Sixpence here reckons old Rufus is going to pull a fast one on us today. Seems talk among the staff is that he's penned up all the best game to keep for himself. He's only going to take us after a few puny runts that he wants got rid of. Typical! I vote we split up from the main party as soon as we can. Wherever Rufus leads, we'll shoot off in the opposite direction.'

A slow smile spread across Jack's face, helped on its way by Harry's wink. The ears of Montgomery's man were practically flapping.

'Perhaps your friend will want to join us,' Harry said loudly, looking down his nose at Montgomery's man. At once the thug added curiosity to his range of sneers and edged closer.

'What do you say to a little illegal sport, out of the King's way? We'll be assured of a few fat bucks, and the hunting party's so large we'll never be missed.'

Montgomery's man thought, the process so unusual and difficult for him that it furrowed his brow and squinted his eyes. 'No,' he said at last. 'I got to stay with the King.'

'Oh, come on.' Harry laughed and, rising, slung his arm around the man's shoulders. 'You don't look the sort to be afraid of a spot of poaching. And I am the King's brother. He's hardly likely to cripple one of my friends, is he? Ah, if only my old friend Belleme were here. What sport we'd show, the two of us.'

The name filtered through the thug's mind. 'Belleme? Then you know the Chief, guvnor?'

'Know him? My word, I can read him like a book. We'd be out there, after all the game that wicked old Rufus is trying to keep safe from us...'

Montgomery's man licked his lips, the thought of a plump buck all to himself proving almost too much. At the last moment he faltered, Montgomery's revenge proving too awful a prospect. 'Later. After,' he muttered rapidly. 'Meet you at the Stag's Stand Oak.'

Harry looked puzzled and stroked his chin thoughtfully.

'Sorry, old chap. Can't place it. Only a visitor here, you see. Where's it near?'

Montgomery's man grinned happily. 'You can't miss it, guvnor. About four mile from here, straight up the main ride and after you reach a fork in the track it's a few hundred yards through the trees on your left.'

Harry's glance flickered over Eloise, and she gave a tiny shrug.

'Sorry, not quite with you. Are there any other landmarks nearby?'

The thug looked at Harry warily and chewed a grime-blackened thumb. 'Not as I know of, offhand, guvnor.'

Eloise moved closer to Harry. 'I think I might know, my lord. Straight out of here, then after a few miles the ride starts to go uphill. When you get as far as being able to see the Hanging Man Glade on your right——'

'No, no, no!' the thug said in sudden exasperation. 'Your Hanging Man Glade, that's away down to your left. And well hid off the track. You'd never see it in passing. No, your best bet is to keep on towards the Winchester Road...'

At the mention of the glade Harry looked at Eloise and raised one eyebrow quizzically. She responded with a relieved smile, but Montgomery's man did not notice. He was too busy guiding Prince Harry's party away from the fateful glade.

Harry finally decided that he might be able to find the Stag's Stand, and together the men drew up a plan of action. Eloise feigned interest, but as soon as she could sidled away.

Montgomery's man was not to be given the slip. No sooner had Eloise caught sight of De Sable and his shadow coming out of the kitchen block than the hall door clattered open behind her.

She ran towards De Sable, expecting to be cut down at any minute for revealing the plans. She reached his loving arms without any incident. Indeed, Montgomery's man seemed highly delighted with what had gone on and could not wait to share his good fortune with his mate.

There was no way that Eloise could reveal what had happened, even though her excitement was obvious from the spring in her step. De Sable clasped her hand tightly and they went towards the stables.

Preparations were already well under way for the hunt. Hounds of varying shapes, sizes and colours lolloped and scratched and fought in the straw while a bellows roared in the smithy nearby. Horses were led back and forth across the courtyard to loosen their muscles and check their shoes. Noisy shouts of the children mingled with the warnings of their mothers as a festival atmosphere filled the air.

Eloise was quietly confident that Harry would put a stop to Duke Robert's attempt on the throne. He knew all the details. It would be a simple matter for him to pounce when the time was right, and put Montgomery's men to flight. Eloise was quite certain that Harry would know what to do when the time came.

Harry was not the only one with a sense of timing. Roger Belvas chose exactly that moment to slouch around the corner of the stable block towards them.

'Doesn't take long for news of easy money to attract vultures,' De Sable muttered.

Eloise felt her heart sink, but was relieved when Roger looked about to pass them without comment. De Sable stared at him pointedly, waiting for a clever remark.

Only when he was well out of range did Belvas turn and call back, laughing, 'Which is it—are you making an honest woman of her or is she making a dishonest man of you?'

De Sable stopped, Montgomery's men in close formation behind. 'Come here and say that, Belvas.'

Roger Belvas spread his hands wide and laughed, showing the remnants of his rotting teeth. 'A case of the truth hurting? Really, Richard, I'm amazed you proved such an easy catch. I never thought to see the day when you'd be trapped by some fancy little chit . . .'

With great care De Sable loosed himself from Eloise's grip and walked with slow menace towards Belvas. Roger

was not to know that Montgomery's men were stalking
De Sable rather than attending him and, at the sight of
three impressive figures bearing down upon him, not one,
he shrank visibly.

'What's the matter? Can't you take a joke?
Richard——'

De Sable caught Belvas by the jacket and lifted him
clear of the ground.

'I am not a violent man by nature, Belvas. But if I
hear one more remark from you, or catch you within
ten yards of my wife, you're a dead man.' He shook
Belvas like a puppy before dropping him and returning
to Eloise.

'Don't pay any heed to what he says, Eloise. He is
beneath contempt. He and his type sneer at honour. I
would ask you to remember that always.'

Eloise nodded wordlessly. She would remember, no
matter what was to happen that afternoon.

De Sable checked their horses and a groom hurried
to saddle the animals in readiness. Eloise felt more hope
now that Richard would be saved by Prince Harry. She
allowed herself to think of the future, just for a minute.
A future with her Richard, the two of them safe together.
It hardly seemed possible that she could be so lucky.

With a start Eloise rebuked herself for tempting fate.
Whatever happened that afternoon there was bound to
be fighting involved. He could be killed anyway, or, even
worse, wounded. Eloise couldn't face the thought of her
Richard lingering on in pain for days or weeks. She must
shut that thought out, and hope that Harry would come
to the rescue in time.

Montgomery's men were taking no chances. The ser-
vants' picnic was graced with two of the Lord of
Belleme's household as well as the new Lord and Lady
De Sable.

Three carts had been decorated with garlands of greenery and flowers. Even the oxen had necklaces of hopbines, starred with pink mallow and the blue of bell-flowers. Everyone was dressed in their Sunday best. This was distinguished from everyday wear by the fact that it was not so threadbare. It was just as grubby as their work clothes, soap and water being regarded with extreme suspicion.

Elosie and De Sable had finer feelings, and took care to keep upwind of their companions. Even so, they were grateful of the invitation and the kind wishes of the servants.

The carts crawled on towards the picnic site amid much chatter and laughing. Children spilled from their mothers' arms, racing and chasing about the grassland as the carts rumbled slowly on. The sun was already well risen in the sky before the party reached a large flat lea beside a stream.

Everyone ran in different directions, even Bessie and Edgar made lively at the thought of a whole day without work. The oxen were released from their carts and left to graze. Soon the only ones left in the meadow were Eloise, De Sable and a little way distant Montgomery's men. They threw themselves down on the grass, carelessly crushing the golden asphodel that shone in the sunlight.

'Pay no attention to them. Imagine that we are completely on our own.'

'We will be, soon.' Leaving her horse to nuzzle through the sweet grasses, Eloise sat down and started to idly collect daisies for a daisy-chain. 'I want to come with you to join the hunt this afternoon.'

De Sable crouched down beside her with a slow smile. Her heart swelled with love for him.

'No, my love. You must stay here with Bessie and Edgar, where it will be——'

'Safe?' The whispered word was almost too loud. Both De Sable and Eloise sensed that Montgomery's men were listening hard. 'Hunting is a dangerous activity, my lord, but one that I would gladly join you in.'

'I shall leave you with Bessie and Edgar.'

'I shall run away from them.'

De Sable raised an eyebrow, mocking her. 'Now who plays the child, my lady?'

'But I love you!' The blood burned brightly in her cheeks as she grasped at his hand.

'I know. That is why you must stay here with the others. I cannot put you to any risk. I want you safe.'

Eloise moved forward into his arms and nestled against his neck. 'Harry is going to help.'

She felt his muscles tense for a moment beneath her fingers, then subside.

'There can be nothing in it for him. And he never does anything without reward.'

'He was kind——'

'Do not pin your hopes upon him.' Gently, De Sable held her away from him and smiled. His eyes were as blue as the summer sky, the white and gold of his tunic glimmering in the sunshine. Eloise knew that she could not bear to leave him, now or ever.

'Take me with you——'

'No. We're going to have a lovely time together here, until the time comes for our goodbyes. We must live for the moment, Eloise, and put all other thoughts aside.'

CHAPTER FOURTEEN

DE SABLE sat down beside Eloise on the grass, and they watched the children being made to collect handfuls of corn mint 'for the good of the hay' before they were allowed to start their games.

The summer sunshine lent extra colour to everything warmed by its rays. Banners of bramble flowers bowed in the breeze, promising a rich harvest of berries for the autumn. Ripening fruits of lords and ladies at the woodland edge shone bright as yuletide holly berries. Autumn. Christmas. Would Eloise find herself alone, then and forever?

There seemed little to say. De Sable had no faith in Harry's ability to help, and that was the only thing that Eloise had to rely on. If Harry could not or would not help, then all was lost. The King would be killed and her Richard with him.

As Eloise and De Sable watched hand in hand, the shady woods began to rustle with returning villagers. Soon handfuls of wilting corn mint were laid, already drooping, into the carts. The children draggled behind, but, quickly realising that their tasks were finished for the day, the shouts and whoops of joy showed that they were soon recovered from their weariness.

While the adults set about unpacking food and ale, the children careered off to the waterside. Most were already barefoot and plunged into the shallows with glee. As they splashed and screamed, De Sable tugged at a grass stem and nipped at the end thoughtfully.

'I would have liked a son,' he said at length, scattering the dry husks of grass seed to the breeze.

'We cannot give up hope for you. Please say that there might still be a chance that Harry——'

De Sable half turned, and smiled at the two Montgomery men. He grinned at them wryly, but his jaw was set in a determined line. 'I got myself into this venture, although my motives were of the highest. Now those who are truly in control have changed the rules I can hardly complain. I must accept what is to happen, and can blame no one but myself for the misfortune that is to occur. My one and greatest regret is that I should have involved you.'

Eloise nestled against him, glad to feel the warm and vital life moving through his veins. 'There is no one that I would change places with,' she said lovingly, 'unless it were to spare you.'

He started to get up, pulling her up with him. 'Come. We shall miss our dinner. These country people have hearty appetites!'

They wandered towards the ox carts, conscious that Montgomery's men were close behind. Food was laid out, and a free-for-all was in progress. Everyone was pulling and grabbing at whatever food they could reach, with children squeezing through tiny gaps in the forest of adult legs about the carts.

As Eloise and De Sable drew near the excitement dimmed a little, and the crowd parted to let De Sable through. He returned to Eloise a moment later, holding a tray with mugs of ale and chunks of bread and cheese. He also carried a wicker basket, which he handed to Eloise gravely.

'A little something that I had put in for later. You said that you might be especially hungry.'

'I don't feel that I can eat at all,' Eloise said sadly, but he pressed the basket on her with a grin.

'You had better carry this, all the same. It won't do my reputation any good in the eyes of our friends to be seen carrying a basket!'

Eloise took the basket and carried it back to where they had been sitting on the grass. The crushed flowers and grasses gave off a heady perfume, and ever after Eloise was to think of that fateful hot summer day when she smelled it.

After dinner the games began. As a very great treat the Braceurs had donated a small slab of almond paste to the picnic. The villagers had agreed that it was too grand to be wolfed down by all and sundry, so the slab was cut carefully into tiny blocks. Each of these rare treats became a prize. The chldren ran egg-and-spoon and sack races. Everyone, including Montgomery's men, were dragged into the games and celebrations. The men competed in throwing horseshoes and wrestling, while for the ladies there were gentler competitions.

Bessie won a piece of almond paste for being the fattest woman, and even Eloise was pulled about despite her protestations. Her hair was let down and measured, but was not the longest. However, when the knotted measuring-string was drawn around her waist, she was found to have the smallest measurement there. She won the almond paste for that, but would not accept the prize, letting someone who had never tasted it benefit. Eloise had tasted enough fancy things in her life, and knew that today anything would taste as ashes in her mouth.

De Sable took little notice of her gesture. He had more important things on his mind. When the prize-giving committee had left them, he nudged her gently. 'Look.'

The larger, more pugnacious man from Montgomery had reached the finals of the wrestling. Unable to concentrate on more than one thing at a time, he was intent on the progress of his rivals in their bouts. He crouched in a crowd of men, thoughts only of the match to come.

Montgomery's second man was harder to spot. He lay on his back beneath one of the ox carts, an ale jug clutched protectively to his chest.

'I think we might be able to make an escape of sorts.'
De Sable summoned Edgar softly, and told him to take
the horses into the deep shade of the woods. It was a
hot day, and there would be nothing unusual about the
request.

They waited for a minute or two, but neither of the
Montgomery men had taken the slightest notice. Arms
linked like the loving couple that they were, Eloise and
De Sable began to stroll cautiously around the edge of
the meadow.

To reach the horses they would have to walk within
a few feet of the man beneath the cart. Eloise held her
breath and clenched her fists. If only he was too drunk
to notice them.

It took an age to reach the cart, and ten times that
length of time to pass it. Every second Eloise was
expecting a rough cry, a hand on the shoulder. Nothing
happened. Suddenly they were past the cart and into the
lush, herb-scented shadows of the wood.

The danger was not over yet. A fast gallop away was
sure to alert everyone. Eloise and De Sable walked their
horses quietly until well out of earshot before springing
into the saddles and hurtling away through the trees.

Within a mile or so they reached a stretch of the river
where the water rippled shallowly over pebbles. As the
horses stopped to drink, De Sable suggested that they
ride upstream in the water for a while, in case the
Montgomery men were to track them through the forest.
Eloise agreed, glad simply to have got him away from
them.

'How long will it take us to reach Southampton? It
shouldn't be difficult to get on a boat to Brittany. We
have plenty to sell to raise the fare, and when we reach
your home Bessie and Edgar can be sent for.'

'I knew I was doing the right thing in marrying you,
my love. You always have the best ideas.' De Sable's
voice was light and cheerful, but he did not look at her

as he spoke. Eloise noticed that the little lines of care had deepened around his eyes, even from that morning.

They rode for more than a hour, crossing and re-crossing the river several times to spoil their tracks. Where the ground allowed, they galloped the horses along the riverbank, eager to put distance between them and Montgomery's men.

Finally they crossed the river for the last time and struck out through the trackless greenwood. Eloise had perfect trust in De Sable, and would follow wherever he led. She only wished that Southampton was around the next bend, and they could be absorbed in the anonymous milling crowds of the big port.

At last the woodland thinned, sunshine dancing through the leaves brighter and brighter until they rode on to open downland. One solitary yellowhammer called for 'A little bit of bread and no cheese!' from a thicket of gorse, bees buzzing a chorus from straggles of purple heather.

There were no sounds of pursuit from the shadowy greenwood. Only the burbling of young cuckoos and the occasional carolling of a wren.

Eloise guessed the time to be somewhere between one and two o'clock. If only she could keep Richard to herself for another three or four hours, Prince Harry would have time to act. He knew that Montgomery's men were behind the plot. If only he could catch them in time!

A large building came into view, built into a rise in the ground. At its southern end double doors had been propped open, showing it to be unoccupied by man or beast.

'Oh, look,' De Sable said casually, waving away a lazy bee that buzzed up from the heather. 'A boar pit. We can shelter in there out of the sun, and be concealed from our two dear friends.'

The boar pit was a large wooden shed built into the side of the hill. The northern end, opposite the double doors, had a small wooden door reached by a flight of wooden steps. This led in to a viewing platform that ran around three sides of the shed, about five feet above the ground.

During the autumn, spoiled grain and vegetables were thrown into the shed and the wild boar would snuffle in for free food when the weather was hard. Sometimes the villagers would tether their sows in the open pen, hoping to breed a bit of extra hardiness into their piglets. At other times the villagers could be assured of plentiful pork by lying in wait for the wild pigs to arrive for their meal. Money could be made, too, by trapping boar in the pen for sale to the towns. Boar-baiting was always popular.

The boar pit had not been used yet that season. Sweet straw was still fresh underfoot, and the only foodstuffs about were a few bags of spoiled grain.

They entered the shed, securing their horses inside the large building. De Sable closed the door behind them and stood for a moment lit by sunbeams trickling through the roughly made plank door.

'I think that before we do anything else we should drink a toast.'

'Not to the new King?' Eloise burst out in surprise. 'Oh, you wouldn't be so insensitive!'

De Sable went towards her and gathered her into his arms. 'Of course not! We'll drink to us. You set out the food while I pour the wine.'

He knelt down beside the basket and as Eloise took out a skin of wine he caught at her hand.

'I'll do that. You see to the food.'

'It's all right, Richard, I can manage——'

'Aha! So I wasn't far off the mark when I told Gilbert that you showed a mettlesome streak!'

He kissed her playfully until she released her grip on the wine skin to return his caresses.

'There, now. I'll take charge of this, and you can busy yourself sorting out the food.'

Eloise turned away and did as she was told. There was plenty of food, but she had no appetite for any of it. To please Richard she ate one small meat patty, and he kept her goblet of wine well filled. De Sable drank nothing himself. Despite Eloise's urging he refused to find courage from the bottle.

The silence between them was friendly now, not awkward. They were happy in each other's company, and a smile was conversation enough.

Eloise felt herself slowing down. She only had to keep him here for another hour—two at most. That was still time enough for Montgomery's men to find him—for him to be taken back to die. If only Harry could get to Montgomery's men first, or at the very least warn the King.

It seemed to be getting very warm. Eloise was becoming sleepy with it, and muddled. If the King were to find out, what would become of her Richard then? Would he be thought of as guilty, tarred with the same brush as Montgomery's evil henchmen? She put a hand to her head, remembering too late what drink could do on an empty stomach.

'Come here.' De Sable moved to her side and drew her gently into his arms. 'There is nothing in the world that you would not do for me, nor I for you. Even so, I could not bear the thought that you might try and take a hand in matters this afternoon. It would be too dangerous for you, my love. I have told you that there are things that I have done in my life of which I am not proud. I'm afraid that this is one of them.'

He kissed her, softly at first, but then with a growing, powerful insistence. Eloise felt her head swimming with love and the effects of the wine and lay limp in his arms.

She was trying to remember something, something very important, but it flitted away before her. She wanted sleep—she needed sleep and felt herself pulled towards it.

Faint as a whisper, coming from the far distance, she heard a voice saying goodbye. It was too difficult, too tiring to reply. She sighed deeply, and slept.

Eloise struggled back to consciousness. Her head was a throbbing misery and her mouth dust-dry.

Richard was gone, as she knew that he would be.

Suddenly the events of the past few hours came back in a rush. The King—Richard had gone to murder the King, and to be killed in his turn! Eloise rolled off the pile of sacks where she had been laid and got unsteadily to her feet. With the blood pounding in her ears she leaned against the wall. Without her having moved a yard, the effort had exhausted her.

He had taken both horses with him. Eloise was quite alone. The wine and remains of their picnic stood in the corner, where she had moved them into the shadow. They were now in a patch of bright sunlight streaming through a missing plank in the door. For the sun to have moved so far around the sky she must have been asleep for hours.

How much time had she wasted? Could Richard still be saved—the King warned? Eloise tried to move towards the door, but her legs felt as though they belonged to someone else.

Perhaps wine would help. More food. She made her way unsteadily around two sides of the hut, leaning against the walls for support. Only when she had slumped down beside the food did the mists clear from her mind. That was how Richard had got away from her. The food had been drugged.

Or the wine. No sooner had Eloise looked at the wine skins but her mouth had become even drier. She would have done anything for a drink. But not that wine. There was only one thing for it. She would have to go out and try to find someone, risk stumbling upon a rebel with her story if the coup was not already over. Then who would be the rebel?

Fallen between two camps, her life would not be worth a light. Above all else, she had lost her Richard, forever. Eloise sat on the sweet straw and put her head in her hands.

Sparrows chirruped in the thatch above. Eloise could hear them fluttering in and out of ventilation slats high above, but could not look up. Her head ached, her throat was parched and her whole body felt weak and useless.

This is no good, Eloise told herself sharply. If she was to be of any use to her dear Richard, then she had to act and act quickly. She could be of no earthly use drooping about here in the boar pit. Taking a few deep breaths to steady herself, she scrambled up.

Her drowsiness was passing now, but it still took her some effort to get to the main doors. There were no handles on the inside. She rested for a moment then slipped her hands into the gap beneath one door. She pulled. Nothing happened.

The double doors were locked. From the outside. Eloise pulled and heaved at them, strength returning by the minute. It was no use. The doors rocked and complained a little on their hinges, a couple of boards creaked, but they stayed firmly shut.

Eloise pressed her forehead against the wood of the door and closed her eyes. This was not the way. There was the other door, leading from the viewing platform above. She would have to find some way to get to the upper level. What if that door was locked too? Richard would have been too thorough to have forgotten that.

Eloise mastered herself. This was no time for a faint heart. If the other door was locked too then she would—she must—find some other way to escape. The venti-

lation slats, or out through the thatch. There must be
plenty of ways.

Eloise stumbled back to the sacks in the corner. The
viewing platform was some five feet above the pit, level
with the bridge of Eloise's nose. She could put her hands
flat on the boarded walk, but from her low position did
not have the strength in her arms to lift herself up.
Somehow she was going to have to find something to
stand on.

At first it seemed that Richard might have mis-
calculated. There was plenty of straw, which Eloise
heaped beneath the platform. It would compact, but
could give an extra inch or two. Then she tugged one of
the sacks of spoiled wheat from the corner. Heaving it
on to the straw heap gained her another few inches. All
the empty sacks that had gone to make her bed were
folded and piled up. It was little enough, but it worked.

Eloise stood on the pile, and sprang. On the third attempt she managed to draw herself up as high as her
rib-cage and by leaning forward and wriggling scrambled
on to the viewing platform.

She was out of breath, and covered in dust. But she
had reached the upper door! Without pausing to congratulate herself, Eloise jumped up and tried them.
Locked.

All that time wasted. Richard had certainly intended
her to be kept securely. In desperation Eloise hurled
herself at the ventilation slats. It was no use. The wood
might be old, but it could easily withstand Eloise's
strength.

The only possible way of escape now was out through
the roof. Eloise sank down, shattered, wondering how
she could ever get up to burrow out through the thatch—
if such a thing was even possible. The sparrows chirruped on, but all at once there were different notes,
fainter, from outside. There was someone coming—they
were whistling!

Eloise ran around the viewing platform, looking out on every side. When at last a rider did wander into view her heart dropped like a stone. It was Roger Belvas.

She had a choice. Either wait for Richard to return, which seemed a faint hope, or run the risk of Roger's passion. Richard might never come back. He could be dead by now, for all she knew. But if he was alive there might still be a chance to help him. If only she could get out.

'My lord! My lord Roger!' Eloise burst out, before she could stop herself. Belvas rode on, unconcerned. He whistled and sang tunelessly as he rode his horse in a huge circle about the boar pit. He appeared to be about to return the way that he had come, despite Eloise's impassioned cries.

Quite suddenly, some hundred yards from the building, Roger stopped. He looked back. By this time Eloise had dropped all pretence at decorum and was snaking her belt out of the ventilation slats and calling, desperate to get his attention. Wearily he turned his horse and began to ride back.

'Oh, Lord Roger... Thank goodness you heard me!'

Roger leaned back in his saddle and stroked his stubbly chin thoughtfully. 'Well, well. If it isn't Richard's little prodigy. And what may I do for you, chicken?'

Eloise looked down upon the loathsome creature and quickly retrieved her belt. She had to get out, but without arousing either Belvas or his suspicions.

'I—I was a silly, wilful girl, my lord Belvas. It was a game—my lord is very fond of hide-and-seek—and I have accidentally shut myself in here——'

'And chained up the doors from the outside, I see. How very careless of you, my sweet.' He mused for a moment, but Eloise could see that his quick eyes darted from side to side. She would no sooner trust him than a ferret in a butcher's stall. He cleared his throat importantly. 'And where exactly is Richard now?'

'I do not know, my lord. But he cannot be far away.'

'In that case, I shall not disturb his game. Goodbye, my sweet.'

Belvas turned his horse and made to walk away, until Eloise pleaded with him again.

'Would you turn away from a lady in distress, Lord Roger?'

He paused, then rode back. 'That all depends.' He looked at her, then with a weary exclamation slid from the saddle of his horse. Eloise had always thought that Richard could put on an arrogant manner, but now faced with Belvas she knew what true arrogance was. She was completely and utterly at his mercy.

He strolled towards the boar pit, but did not immediately approach the door. Instead he leaned against the wooden wall and looked about him furtively. Eloise could smell his stale, musky odour even though her prison protected her from his immediate presence.

'I tell you what I'll do.' Belvas peered in at her through the ventilation slats. 'If you lean against the door and so brace it, I can work at the lock.' He peeled off his gloves and pushed them into his belt.

'But it is a delicate procedure, and I shall require complete silence in which to work.'

It was her only hope of escape. Obediently, Eloise went to the door and pushed her weight against it. A plan had come to her. When Belvas pushed the door open she would distract his attention—pretend she spotted Richard, for instance—and dash past him.

There was a long pause. Eloise could hear nothing, although she concentrated on listening for the click of padlock or rattle of chain. Only with a sudden burst of sunlight through the opening doors at the far end of the boar pit did she realise that she had been tricked.

Belvas entered. In his hands he held the long length of chain that had secured the main doors from the outside. With no hurry, merely a self-satisfied smile, he looped the chain through the door handles again. This time he led the securing chain beneath the doors and into the boar pit. Fastening it to the ring where the horses had been tied, he had ensured that he would not be disturbed.

Once Belvas had secured the doors he leaned back against them, and smirked.

Eloise turned to face him. She had only one chance left. The chance that Richard had taken with her. 'I am eternally grateful, my lord. Would you care to partake of the refreshments?'

'It depends upon what you are offering, my pet.' Belvas leered and Eloise felt sick to her stomach. She gestured in the direction of the abandoned picnic.

'The wine is particularly delicious. I can recommend it for its amazing properties, my lord.'

Eloise reasoned that whatever drug the wine contained must have been fast-acting. The quicker Belvas could be persuaded to take a draught the better.

He strolled nonchalantly towards the food, thumbs thrust into his belt. 'It always tastes better for being served by a lady, I think. Here.'

He summoned her with an imperious tip of his head. Eloise stood firm on the viewing platform.

'I fancy the air is a little clearer up here, my lord.'

Belvas laughed, and snatching up one of the wine skins swung himself up on to the boarded walk. Stealthy as a cat, he made barely a sound as he crept towards her. 'Strange. I detect no difference in the atmosphere.'

Then the fox cannot smell his own scent, thought Eloise, fighting against the stench of rising damp and mouldy cheese that hung about Belvas. He grinned, showing stumps of teeth in shades of green, brown and black.

'Don't look so surprised, my little pippin.'

He darted forward and grabbed her wrist. When she refused to be drawn towards him he dug dirty fingernails

cruelly into her flesh. With her free hand Eloise lashed
out at his head, but he merely laughed, dropping the
corked skin of wine and trapping her more securely.

'Now, now! That's not the way to treat a gentleman.
Especially one that's going to let you out of your little
cage. In time...' He laughed, drawing her close to him
firmly.

Eloise fought and squirmed and cried out, but it was
to no avail. Richard—her dear Richard was beyond help.
There would be no one to hear her, not for miles. Belvas
was upon her, pawing and slobbering over her like a
hound. The more she struggled, the more Belvas seemed
to enjoy it. Only when a sound like thunder rolled from
the great double doors did he freeze like a frightened
coney.

A second great roar echoed through the boar pit and
with a splintering crash the doors were torn free of the
chain that secured them.

Slowly the huge doors swung open. Silhouetted against
the bright daylight stood a figure. It spoke. 'What did
I tell you, Belvas?'

Richard De Sable waited for a reply, an apology, an
excuse. When none came he strode forward and leapt
easily on to the boarded walk. Grasping Belvas by the
shoulder, De Sable tore him from Eloise. As he did so,
Eloise seized her chance to dart away. De Sable stopped
her with a firm hand.

'Stay there.'

He was without sword, belt or cloak, but the dust and
splashes of blood staining the rest of his clothes spoke
volumes. *Blood*. Eloise stayed where she was.

De Sable lifted Belvas up bodily and shook him three
times, hard. 'That's how often I've had to tell you. Now
comes the time of reckoning.' He dropped Belvas from
the platform to the floor below and waited for the next
move.

'All right, my friend...all right...' Belvas whimpered, fumbling with his fancy clothes as he crawled away from De Sable.

De Sable leapt down from the viewing platform, prowling towards the grovelling Belvas. Shrinking before his inevitable come-uppance, Belvas edged away. His hand was working away at something within his jacket. De Sable stood above him, waiting for Belvas to get up and take his punishment. Richard De Sable was not one to strike a man when he was on the floor.

Belvas did not intend to play by any such rules. Suddenly, with the speed of a snake, he lashed out. Eloise saw the knife a split second after De Sable had sensed it was there.

CHAPTER FIFTEEN

BEFORE Eloise could shout a warning, Belvas struck. Fortunately De Sable was too much a veteran to have been caught out. He dodged sideways, at the same time unbalancing Belvas with a swift blow to the head.

'Of the two of us, I prefer to hold the knife.'

He placed a foot on his opponent's wrist and rolled the weight until, with a cry, Belvas let the knife slip from his fingers. Thanking him civilly, De Sable threw the knife to lodge in an overhead beam, safely out of reach.

'Now we're going to finish this properly.'

He dragged the terrified Belvas to his feet and propelled him towards the open door. Belvas cowered, refusing to face up to his opponent, but De Sable persisted.

'If you insist upon playing with fire, you must take the consequences. Come on, Roger. Aren't you willing to fight for what you seem to think your right?'

He pulled Belvas about with the rough ease of a mastiff with a toy, trying to goad him into attack. Belvas wasn't the sort to be goaded. He folded back down into a heap, all resistance gone.

'One of those that are brave only with the odds on their side? You know what happens to them, Roger.'

There was a burbling murmur from the wretched Belvas.

'That's right. They lose. In your case, everything. I'm taking your horse, its saddle and bridle and your fancy knife up there, and I'm going to hold them for ransom. I don't want to see your ugly, putrid face again until you've got the money to reclaim them. And then I don't want to see you around me and mine ever again. Do you understand?'

He shook Belvas once more to drive the message home, then frog-marched him outside. Eloise could not follow. Instead she sat down unsteadily, trying to stop relief shaking from her head to foot.

She heard Richard leap on to his horse to chase Belvas away once and for all. Waiting, too numb with relief to move, Eloise could hear the unhappy cries of Belvas fading into the distance. Galloping hoofbeats heralded the return of her dear Richard, but it was a minute or two before he reappeared in the doorway. He led both his own horse and that of Belvas, and tied them up in the corner.

It was a long time before De Sable spoke. It was a long time before Eloise could bear even to look at him. As he ducked about the horses, loosening their girths and settling them, Eloise noticed his cloak, slung over the saddle bow. A dark stain shadowed its folds.

De Sable went to the cloak and half-heartedly arranged it so that the worst of the gore was obscured. Then in an instant he had leapt up on to the platform and gathered her into his arms. They clung together, words unnecessary. Finally Richard spoke in a low, tired voice.

'King William Rufus is dead.'

Eloise cried, but it was not only for the loss of the rightful King. 'Then . . . we must get used to the sound of King Robert the First. And Montgomery's men . . . they will plague England now, as they have plagued Normandy. How did you get away?' She was coming to her senses properly now, but that was little comfort. 'My love—I never thought—they will be after you—Richard, we have to escape! We must get away while we still have the chance!'

'No. Not yet. For the moment at least we have plenty of time.'

With an air of utter weariness he passed one hand over his drawn features then helped her down to ground-level. They wandered in the direction of the picnic basket. All the while De Sable was shaking his head, as though he could hardly believe the events of the past few hours.

'Wine?'

Eloise stooped for a bottle that lay on the floor, hesitated, then at his laughter rounded on him. 'You tricked me. And not married a whole day yet!'

With a grin he picked up the bottle, took a long drink, then offered it to Eloise. 'It's quite safe. No more tricks.'

Still she held back, and Richard tousled her hair gently.

'I could not bear to see you distressed at our parting. The addition of a small sleeping-draught to your cup was to keep you safe. For your own protection—whether with Bessie and Edgar or here...'

His eyes were dark and sadly thoughtful now. Life would never be the same again. While their little refuge was quiet and still, that didn't change the facts. The King was dead. Barely a few miles from their haven the countryside must be in turmoil.

Eloise was caught up in turmoil enough of her own. She knew that, as her husband, from now on Richard would have to be followed and obeyed in whatever he did. Her heart spoke differently—she loved him now because she could not help herself. Even if he had murdered the King and was an outlaw.

Though it would make no difference, Eloise had to know. She had to hear the truth from Richard's own lips. 'Did you—did you kill the King?'

'No.' His tone was sharp at the memory, then softened. 'It was over before I even reached the hunting party. Some of us tried to revive him but it was no use. No use. All those months of planning, and in the end he's the victim of an accident...'

He took another long drink and laughed.

'The whole party were either Duke Robert's allies or Prince Harry's cronies. William Rufus didn't have a friend in sight. Murder would have been an easy matter. But an accident...a simple accident. Someone's stray arrow glancing off a tree. It could have happened to any of them...'

'But it happened to the King.'

Richard gave her an odd look at her tone, then continued. 'Poor Tyrell. He was beside himself.'

'Tyrell?' A seed of suspicion began to grow in Eloise's mind, blossomed, then bore fruit. 'Tyrell? Then there was something in it for Prince Harry, after all——'

De Sable shot her a look of grim amusement. 'That we have yet to see, my love, although I think you have more wit than the rest of Duke Robert's allies put together.'

They sat together in a pool of sunlight while dust motes spiralled around them. Richard took another drink, and this time Eloise accepted a draught too. He drew her even closer to him. Taking his left hand in hers, she noticed the reddish cast over the palm. He hurriedly rubbed his hand on a nearby sack, removing the dreadful evidence. Half afraid of what she knew, Eloise could bear to keep silent no longer. She had to tell.

'Prince Harry's men were offering Tyrell money yesterday. I thought it was a bit odd. Why him, especially? And why payment in advance? Now I know.'

De Sable whistled through his teeth, but looked no less careworn. There was a long pause in which even the sparrows in the thatch read solemnity. They fell silent.

'I have done a dreadful thing.' De Sable handed the wine skin to Eloise. 'I have betrayed my friends, and my lord.'

'You tricked me.' That was Eloise's immediate concern. 'You worked on my soft heart and better nature, even though I am now your wife! You used me—again.'

'I had to save you——' De Sable burst out, then remembered himself. 'From yourself. You were a danger to yourself, my love. That is over now. We are free.'

Eloise had had time to consider his earlier words, and hesitated. 'How can you have betrayed your lord? William Rufus is dead. That was the intention. To remove the King.'

'I——' Words came to him only with difficulty now. 'I delayed our allies. Held them up at the scene—made them look to William Rufus, make speeches of intent to the gaping proles, when all the time...Harry was getting clean away. I saw him go—while I held my lord Robert's men back...'

Eloise stared at her hands in silence. Her fury at being tricked was ebbing now, and in its place flooded back memory of her terror in the blanket-box. 'It must have been so painful for you to have been disillusioned by Montgomery's men when they cornered you with their plot.'

He turned to look at her directly. 'Eloise, how did you know? Not even Hugh was in on the sorry business...' His eyes narrowed quickly. 'Beforehand—Harry waylaid us in the corridor—some nonsense about a game of hide-and-seek. You were in there, weren't you? In that room. You and who else?'

Eloise looked at her bandaged fingers. 'Hugh did such a good job of keeping everyone away from the Braceurs' chamber that I thought you must be—er—occupied within...'

'Never! Not since we first met.' He looked uncomfortable, then added, 'well, perhaps once...'

Eloise remembered the flashy redhead, and quickly changed the subject. 'I hid behind the large tapestry and so found the secret chamber. When you arrived outside I hid in the blanket-box——'

He remembered at once, and realised. 'Your fingers! Caught in the lid!' Taking up her hand, he turned it about, studying the bandages with renewed horror.

'They are healing. It was either that or suffocate. I didn't intend being discovered by your "friends".'

De Sable kissed each bandaged finger tenderly. 'Oh, my love. If they had found you, it would have been the end. The Montgomery men take no prisoners. It was bad enough being party to their evil myself, without thinking that you knew so much. I thought that the secret was surely too awful for any normal person to bear.'

'Let that be a lesson to you. No councils of war during games of hide-and-seek.'

He smiled faintly, still beset with troubles. After a little while his thoughts returned to his friends. 'Duke Robert's allies think Harry was overwhelmed with grief at the death of his brother, and that was why he dashed away.'

Eloise had not missed the irony in his voice. 'What do you think has really happened?' She clung to him, still half afraid that she would wake from a dream and he would be gone again.

'Harry will seize the crown of England while he has a chance.'

'Richard! You sound as though you want that to happen!'

De Sable let his actions speak, covering her amazement with a tender kiss. Gradually the horrors of the day were slipping from him. 'Duke Robert is like me—unsuited to the rough and tumble of politics. I see it now. Let more ruthless types squabble over lands and possessions. As long as we have sufficient for our needs, let that be enough.'

Eloise looked up into his gentle, loving face, stroking away the last few lines of care. Suddenly he closed his eyes and moaned.

'We must go. Now.' The urgency of his speech belied his reluctance. He made no move, but remained in Eloise's loving embrace.

A moment more, then he leapt to his feet. 'It is no good. We must go, or stay here to be caught by Edgar. That would not be quite the done thing, would it?'

Laughing, he pulled her to her feet.

'Richard—where are we to go? What will happen to us?'

'Nothing but love ever after, I hope!'

With regret they left the solitude of the boar pen. This time Eloise was pleased to ride before De Sable on his horse while he held her with one hand and led Belvas's horse with the other.

'I left your horse and a message with Hugh. Edgar was to come and release you at five o'clock this afternoon. After——' He stopped. Neither wanted to dwell on what might have happened. Eloise lay back against him, hardly daring to believe that he was still safe.

'Promise never to leave me, or trick me like that again, Richard? Whatever sort of outlaws we must become?'

His honey-gold hair ruffled in the breeze, shining against the healthy glow of his skin. 'Outlaws? Deus, the lady turns rascal into husband, now tries to turn and turn about! We are in no danger for the moment, my love. Montgomery's men are more concerned with Prince Harry and his whereabouts. The struggle paused with us for a while, but now moves on! If Harry succeeds in gaining England—well.' He squeezed her tightly to him and she relished the warm smell of his nearness. 'We'll be on our way home to Brittany by then.'

On the long journey back to the castle, Eloise learnt all there was left to know about her dear husband. Destined for the Church, Richard had become heir to the family estates on the death of his elder brother. Thrust into a stern apprenticeship in the Holy Land, he had been completely at a loss until the Duke of Normandy had taken pity on his inexperience. De Sable had wanted to repay all his kindnesses. To help his mentor gain the crown had seemed ideal.

'Now the awful game is over. It was a foolish mistake to imagine that a few loyal friends could overwhelm the influence of Montgomery on poor Duke Robert. Meeting them recently, I can well believe your tales of private wars and public feuds in Normandy. They are evil men.'

'Then you will renounce the Duke?'

De Sable looked at her intently for a moment. A flash of noble pride made his eyes glitter azure as the summer sky. 'No, that I cannot do. Even though it may pain you. Duke Robert was so very good to me.'

'Good,' Eloise said softly. 'I know what it is to be indebted for a kindness. But you have told of the past, and the present. What of the future?'

'We shall return home to Brittany as soon as possible. Hugh, all the staff and my most precious——' He kissed the top of her head. 'I should like to help Duke Robert in Normandy, but—no. His is a hopeless cause.'

He stretched his legs out before him as he rode, studying the muddied splashes on his boots. A sudden thought struck him, and he caught his breath sharply. 'All the money and jewellery that has been collected...it will all have to be returned. Whatever else I am, I am not a thief.'

'You could give it all to Duke Robert, anyway,' Eloise said carefully, looking up and around at him. 'After all, it was donated to his cause. And it wasn't your fault that Harry seems to have beaten your side to the Crown. They cannot blame you directly.'

'No. They will call our misfortune an act of God.'

'There you are, then.' Eloise was bubbling with life and good ideas once more. 'Perhaps with your funds to help him, Duke Robert won't need to be so beholden to the Montgomerys. And if this new wife of his is half as good as you say——'

'The Lady Sibyl is better than I can convey. Indeed, there is only one young lady in the world that is her superior in all things...'

Eloise smiled up at her gentle rogue, and, when his hand slid tentatively over hers, she could barely keep the longing from her voice. 'Richard——'

'When I saw Roger's horse outside I realised what a fool I'd been in the past, forcing myself upon you. I have been little better than Belvas in that respect. Even in the matter of our marriage!' He squeezed her close to him again. 'Although I do not remember having to drag you to the altar, my love.'

They both laughed softly, lulled by the gentle motion of the horse beneath them.

'Strange,' De Sable said at last. 'When once introduced to a life of fun and excess by Duke Robert, I never thought to forsake it for the simple pleasure of marriage. But once I saw you, my love, I was lost. Completely and utterly. Every approach I made was crude and clumsy, with no experience of gentle young ladies. Oh, Eloise, can you ever have wanted me in the way that I longed for you?'

'I thought I was foolish to hope. To see you every day, flirting with each and every woman——'

'Pale substitutes because I thought that you did not care.'

A slow smile spread over Eloise's face at the honest ardour of his words. 'Even the flashy redhead?'

'Er—who?' He looked down at his boots intently.

'At Lefèvre's.'

'Can't remember.'

Gallantry plainly affected his memory, but Eloise was willing to forgive him that. As he drew the horses to a halt beneath a shady tree, his thoughts were all for her.

'From now on, I'll never look at another woman. Ever. As God is my witness.'

He got down from the horse, weariness creeping up on his movements and expression. Lifting Eloise from the saddle, he set her down to stand beside him on the grass.

'I never even asked you if you would marry me. I was so tangled up with foreboding, the thought of losing you forever... I needed your love, but could not bring myself to admit it until it was nearly too late. I was a fool, cursed by my stupid pride. But from now on, things are going to change. I shall court you properly—flowers, presents... Oh.' He looked horrified, and let go of her hand. 'What if you are only humouring me? You never expected me to come back from the hunt. Was that why you made no complaint at the marriage?'

Eloise could hardly stop herself from laughing out loud. Standing in front of her, Richard suddenly dropped down on to one knee.

'Forget that we are married already. Such things can be undone—just answer me truly, as though it were a genuine request. My lady—Eloise—will you marry me?'

Eloise could play a game as well as the philandering, reckless De Sable. With an enigmatic smile she turned away from his outstretched hands. He said nothing, and did not move. She looked across the sea of campions and marguerites that starred the rides with red, pink and white flowers.

'I'll think about it.'

There was silence about them for a long time. Eloise let a ladybird run from her skirt on to her hand, and blew it away home.

At last she could stand the suspense no longer. When she turned De Sable had risen to his feet, but stood motionless, staring unseeing at the turf.

'I do not know how long a divorce will take...' He shrugged hopelessly. 'The fault is mine. All mine, so now I must suffer for it. I coerced you...'

She had hurt him. He had been in deadly earnest, and she had made light of the matter and hurt him in the process.

'Richard——' Dashing to him, Eloise put her arms about his sorry figure.

'Don't feel you have to be kind. But Eloise—dearest—you will at least consider it?'

'Oh, Richard, do you even have to ask?'

'My love...' he whispered with relief, drawing her gently into his arms. Kissing and caressing her, he awoke the passion that yearned for his touch. For now there was neither politics nor misunderstanding to come between them. Differences melted with the warmth of their love, and happiness joined them in the safety of one another's embrace.

Edgar rushed out to meet them as they rode slowly back in the gathering dusk. He had learnt that De Sable was safe, yet was still all excited concern. Even so, the frantic enquiries died on his lips as he saw the look that Eloise and her Richard shared. When they reached the castle courtyard Bessie, too, needed no explanation.

De Sable stirred himself to ask what was happening in the castle. Edgar was pleased to report that Montgomery's men had left to pursue Harry. They had no illusions that Harry was off after the crown. The Prince had the advantage of a tenacious nature and several miles' start, so no one was in any doubt of the outcome.

'King Henry the First,' Bessie said, overjoyed with the Gamberon celebratory wine it had seemed such a pity to waste. 'Wonder if we'll have new money struck to go with 'im.'

'I'd settle for some of the old money, right this immediate moment,' Edgar grumbled, a little jealous of his master's only interest.

'You might like to set about earning some, then,' De Sable said with mock severity, thrusting the blood-stained cloak at Edgar. 'See to the horses while I have a bath, then you can help me get ready. Bessie can be similarly employed with the Lady Eloise.'

'Get ready? What for?' Bessie asked, bewildered.

'All this bunting and party conceits—I've a fancy that my bride and I will be the only ones that the Braceurs will have to grace their fancy guest room now. Before we leave for home our little wedding party might make the best of all this unending hospitality, don't you think?'

Bessie looked from her young master to Eloise, who laughed happily.

'I'm quite sure Lord and Lady Braceur will not mind. An offer of hard cash never comes amiss. I know that you will manage negotiations for us admirably, Bessie. And if you could also manage to ask the Lord Hugh to join us for supper in our room—— ?'

'Well, I never! Well, I never did. You're taking up with the airs and graces awful quick, child!'

'Not so much of the child now, Bessie.' De Sable slipped from his saddle and swept Eloise down from the horse. 'The Lady Eloise is your new mistress. No longer is she a poor pawn, manipulated by destiny. She is a knight's true lady. Madame Eloise De Sable.'

And he kissed Eloise until once more she grew dizzy for his love.

The other exciting

MASQUERADE
Historical

available this month is:

LADY
OF SPAIN

Sally Blake

Arriving in London in 1851 to arrange the Montalban
Wine display at the Great Exhibition created by
Prince Albert, Eduardo Garcia has been charged by
Dona Adriana Montalban to bring her
granddaughter to Spain.

Bereft by the death of her aunts, and confronted by
this autocratic stranger, Serena Montalban learned
for the first time about her mysterious background.
Should she go to Spain, meet the family who had
disowned her father – and stay close to Eduardo?
For a quietly reared Victorian lady, the decision was
difficult . . .